# Belle's heart was beating so fast she wasn't sure she could speak.

"I tried not to come," Mitch said. His voice was dull, like a man in a trance.

"Mitch." She moved in front of him, reached up and touched his cheek. "It's all right. I wanted you to come."

"It's not all right," he said. He shook his head slowly. His stubble was raspy, yet soft, against her fingertips. "It's all wrong."

*"Why?"*

"Because I'm here for one thing only." He looked at her with those glimmering eyes. "Do you get that? I'm here because I want to make love to you. I'm dying, Belle. I'm burning up with it."

Her breath suddenly went shallow, as if her lungs were too small.

"I want that, too."

Dear Reader,

Shakespeare once wrote that "what's past is prologue." William Wordsworth said, "The child is father of the man." They, and probably a thousand other great thinkers, obviously believed your childhood sets the stage for your adult life.

But what if your childhood wasn't all that great? What if you were horrified to be told old patterns must be repeated forever? That's how Belle Irving—the mystery woman you met in earlier Bell River Ranch books as Bonnie O'Mara—feels. She's haunted by memories, terrified she'll never be able to shake off their shadows.

She's been running from her past a long time. Now it's time to stop. Time to fight. And where better to make her stand than at beautiful Bell River Ranch, where the indomitable Wright sisters have carved out a victory over their own troubled history?

And where Mitch Garwood, the man she's loved and lied to for so long, has been waiting...*she hopes.*

From your emails and letters, I know that you (just like poor Mitch) have been impatient to learn the truth about Bonnie. It hasn't been easy for me, either! I've been dying to reward this brave, lonely woman with her happily ever after.

Probably, like me, you believe we all have the power to rewrite our own stories and make them end more happily than they began. So I hope you'll enjoy watching her find her courage and fight her way to the future she deserves.

Warmly,

Kathleen O'Brien

PS—I love to hear from readers! Come say hi at kathleenobrien.com, facebook.com/kathleenobrienauthor or twitter.com/kobrienromance.

# KATHLEEN O'BRIEN

—

## Reclaiming the Cowboy

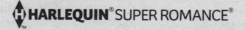

HARLEQUIN® SUPER ROMANCE®

Recycling programs
for this product may
not exist in your area.

ISBN-13: 978-0-373-60874-4

Reclaiming the Cowboy

Copyright © 2014 by Kathleen O'Brien

**Printed in U.S.A.**

# ABOUT THE AUTHOR

Kathleen O'Brien was a feature writer and TV critic before marrying a fellow journalist. Motherhood, which followed soon after, was so marvelous she turned to writing novels, which could be done at home. After decades of fun with her emotional counterpart—she's the mushmellow, he's the stoic—she's convinced that opposites really do attract, even heiresses and cowboys. The scuffles that inevitably follow? They're just part of the thrill!

**Books by Kathleen O'Brien**

**HARLEQUIN SUPERROMANCE**

*The Heroes of Heyday
#The Sisters of Bell River Ranch

Other titles by this author availabe in ebook format.

# *CHAPTER ONE*

IT WAS A MEAN March midnight, the road a sludgy river of asphalt oozing in slow loops under an icy moon. Mitch Garwood's mood was sour and his face frost-burned as he rumbled up to the back door of his cottage, one of the six they'd recently finished on the eastern edge of Bell River Ranch.

Tilting off his helmet with one hand, he twisted the key with the other, silencing the growling motorcycle before any of the adjoining guests woke up and complained. Although why they should sleep soundly when he knew darn well *he* wouldn't...

Still astride the bike, he stared at the dark windows of the cottage, envisioning the cold, half-empty spaces within. A bed. A sofa. A bookcase. A refrigerator full of bottled water and blackening guacamole dip. Six hours of tossing and turning...alone...till dawn, when he could finally get up and distract himself with work.

This was a life?

It was his choice, of course. He'd never been *forced* to be alone, not since he hit puberty and discovered that rusty-brown hair and a few freckles over a goofy grin actually appealed to some females.

He definitely hadn't needed to be alone tonight. At least fifty bored women from a cosmetics convention in Crawford had jammed into the Happy Horseshoe Saloon. Two-thirds of them were nice, half of them were hot and at least two of them were both.

But not one was interesting enough to take home.

He shoved his helmet into the storage bubble on the back of the bike, a little too roughly. He heard the fiberglass crack against the rim. He'd better watch out—he'd already fractured two helmets this way. He'd probably coil himself up so tight he'd break his own bones if he didn't find a woman soon.

Problem was, the only woman he wanted was the one he couldn't have.

*Bonnie.* His chest did a painful cramping thing, as if the two syllables were electric prods applied to his heart. *Bonnie,* he thought again, like the masochist he was, just to feel the reaction once more.

*Bonnie O'Mara.* If that was even her name.

For one amazing year, the beautiful mystery woman had seemed like his own personal miracle. Turned out she was a mirage instead. Nearly nine months on the road together, running from something only she could see, and then, one morning, Mitch woke up and she was gone.

That was six months ago. So yeah—he needed someone new.

He inhaled deeply, the Colorado frost stinging his lungs. Too bad he didn't drink. His friends assured him that getting lightly buzzed could put a sparkle into even the dullest diamond.

But he'd tried that once, a few months ago, on his twenty-seventh birthday. He'd found a bottle of Johnnie Walker and a smart, lively redhead visiting from Crested Butte, and he'd mixed them together to see what happened.

He told himself it was allowed, darn it. He wasn't ready to be a monk just because True Love had spit in his face. At the very least, he owed it to himself to make sure his machinery still worked, right?

But—get this—he'd been bored to death. Apologizing as politely as he could, he'd left the confused woman after about five minutes and five kisses, already feeling the hangover churning in his stomach. He'd spent the rest of the night chucking big ugly rocks to see if he could bust a hole in frozen Silverbottom Pond. He'd only succeeded in scaring the deer.

So no more nights like that. The machinery could shrivel up and fall off before he'd repeat that pathetic fiasco.

Mitch rocked the bike up onto its kickstand,

then took the steps to the cottage two at a time. If he had to go in, he might as well get it over with.

But the minute he opened the door, he froze. Something felt…different.

The house wasn't empty and still. Someone was here.

He left the lights off as he moved through the kitchen, using only the weak beams of the fingernail moon and the LED displays on the appliances to guide him. As he entered the living room, he picked up a poker from the fireplace, holding it over his shoulder like a baseball bat.

Then he heard a woman's voice, softly, from the darkness.

"Mitch?"

His grip went numb. The poker clattered from his hand. *"Bonnie?"*

A shadow near the sofa stirred. It formed into a human shape and then became a blur as she ran blindly toward him.

It *was*. It was Bonnie. He knew her silhouette. He knew her scent. He knew the way she ran and the way her boots lightly tapped across the hardwood floor.

He was only ten feet away. She crashed into him hard, wrapping her arms around him and burying her head in his chest. He had to take a step backward to balance against the collision.

For a split second, he was reminded of the desperate embraces he sometimes got from his nephew, Alec, when the boy was in pain. When the poor kid had run over a squirrel with his bike or found a dying baby bird, fallen from the nest.

But then, as Bonnie lifted her pale, moonlit face to his and smothered his cheeks, his chin… and finally his lips…with kisses, all thoughts of Alec evaporated.

All thoughts of *anything* evaporated.

His brain shut down entirely, his body taking over.

"Is it really you?" He dug his hands into her silken hair and pulled her as close as he could, close enough to smell her, taste her, own her. Close enough to make the six months of loneliness go away.

"Bonnie," he whispered against her mouth, and maybe she said his name again, or maybe she merely moaned. Her lips were wet where he'd moved over them and so warm. He dragged his kisses, hard and possessive, down the column of her throat and up again. His hands stroked her back, down to her hips, tracing the sweet curve he knew so well.

After so many dreams, so many ghost Bonnies that had come to tease him in the night, only to disappear just short of heaven, he had to convince himself she was real.

She was. He had no idea how this gift had come to him, but he was beyond questioning it now. He lifted her legs so that she nestled against the fire between his, and they both groaned, remembering.

He stumbled backward, not caring whether he was loud or clumsy. Not caring whether he broke everything in the cottage or whether he looked a fool. He kissed her as he walked. He bent his head to find her breasts, though he nearly killed them both as he keeled backward toward the wall.

He made his way, somehow, to the bedroom. He fell with her onto the bed. She was fumbling with his belt and with her own, and he was tearing buttons, hers and his, and shedding clothes and boots as fast as he could.

And there she was, open to him. The same— oh, heaven help him—exactly the same as his dreams. Her breasts were like snow in the moonlight, and he claimed them because they were his. They had always been his, whether she was in his bed or lost in some invisible nowhere.

He went lower, then lower still, as she wriggled under him, wrestling free of scraps of denim and lace. And then he couldn't take it anymore. He rose swiftly up on the heels of his hands, ready.

She fumbled with him, and he realized she was covering him with a condom. He groaned. Even that light touch was torture. And did they need this? She was on the pill…or had been…

Somehow she got it on, though her fingers trembled. When she finished, she lay back with a soft gasp and lifted her legs again, clasping them around his hips.

He had to have her. He didn't care why she felt they needed protection. Maybe she had been...or maybe she thought he had been...

He couldn't think. He couldn't slow himself down. He'd hungered for her so long. He'd been so unbearably alone.

He murmured her name once more. Then, though he knew it might be too soon, he drove into her, at once animal and poet. Master and slave.

Every inch of his body pulsed and burned. His rhythm was hard, fast, relentless, and he heard the tiny hitch in her breathing that meant she was ready. Her head tilted back, exposing her creamy throat. Her legs tightened. Her heels dug into him, asking for more.

He knew her. He knew what she wanted. A few deeper, more powerful thrusts, the wet nip of his lips against her hardening breasts—

Oh, yes, he knew her. She cried out, her back arching, her legs going limp. Seconds, minutes... no longer than that...and, with an agonized groan, he exploded, too. Liquid gold fire poured through his veins, dizzying him, weakening him, dislocating him from time and place.

It lasted forever, for both of them. Of course it did. The river of their passion had flooded behind the dam of separation. Six months of longing, pent up, roiling in powerful currents. Six months of heat and tension and pain.

Finally, he was empty, but amazingly she still shimmered around him, like a crystal bell that no longer rang but filled the air with an exquisite humming. She hadn't opened her eyes, and her breath was still shallow.

His Bonnie. He knew her. Tenderly, he touched two fingers between her legs, closing over the wet heat and coaxing the last invisible tremors free.

She shuddered helplessly, every sensation written on her beautiful face. He held on, poised above her, until finally, finally, her fierce internal pulses stilled. And then, unable to hold himself up an instant longer, he collapsed onto the bed beside her.

They lay together, with braided legs and tangled arms, palm against belly, cheek against breast, until the air grew cool around their sweaty bodies. She moved only once, stretching up to lift the glass he kept by his bed and taking a deep drink from it, as if she was parched.

Then, with a hum of satisfaction, as though the tepid liquid had been sweeter than simple water, she dropped back to his side and laid her head against his chest.

As he breathed in the daffodil, yellow-sky perfume of her hair, something inside him began to relax for the first time in six months. It wasn't just sex. Amazing as that had been, this was deeper than sex.

This was as deep as his soul. He smiled at himself, aware the poet lingered, even now that the animal was sated.

His soul had come back to him.

They dozed. Slept, even. Much later, he woke to a dark, frigid room. He closed his hand over her hip, just to be sure she was there. His fingers must have been icy, because she shivered. She must be freezing. They hadn't even pulled a blanket over them.

He cursed himself for a selfish fool.

"I'm sorry. I'll start a fire." He raised himself on one elbow, extending his other arm, hoping he could reach the bedside light.

"Don't." She stopped his arm with gentle fingers. "No fire. No lights." She rolled over, until her slim body was half on top of his. "We can make our own fire."

"But...I want to see you," he said. His voice sounded odd in the dark room. Why didn't she want him to turn on the lights? The cold had stabbed his chest, and he suddenly felt very afraid.

Or very angry.

"I don't think we should." She spoke softly, and he felt the motion of her head as she glanced toward the window, as if to check to see if any of the neighbors were awake yet.

That was all it took. Suddenly, he knew.

"You're not home to stay, are you?" Both the

anger and the fear dripped from the question like icicles. "You're going away again."

She rolled even closer, until her torso was completely on top of him. Her hands tucked beneath his armpits, as she used her arms to lift her face several inches above his. Her eyes were cool, shining with blue moonlight. Her hair, which he now saw was still dyed that ridiculous shade of auburn-black, dangled like dark silk over her breasts and curled around her nipples.

In spite of his anger, he felt himself growing rigid all over again.

"Tell me," he insisted.

Slowly, she nodded. "I am going away again. I have to leave at first light." She paused. "I should go sooner, but…"

She shifted her weight, and, with the sweep of one pale, graceful leg, she straddled his hips. His erection hardened, readying itself without his permission.

"But there's a little more time." She leaned down and kissed his jaw. "There's enough time, if you want it."

She moved, tilting her pelvis so that she came so close… If she scooted two inches higher, it would be enough. In the old days, he would have cupped her velvet ass with his hot palms and made it happen.

"Enough for what?" He sounded so cold. He

sounded like someone else, someone who didn't love her. "For one more goodbye tumble?"

"Time to make love," she whispered, and the sweet sensuality in that voice was meant for the real Mitch, the old Mitch—not for this scarred and angry man beneath her now.

"What about protection?" He stared up at her, his face immobile. "Did you bring extra condoms, just in case? I mean, obviously you can't be sure where I've been these six months...who I might have slept with."

"Mitch, don't." She put her fingers against his lips. "There's so little time. Don't spoil it by being angry."

"But I *am* angry."

He made a harsh motion under her, and she understood. Tilting to one side, she slid off him and sat on the edge of the bed. For the first time, she tugged at the hem of the sheet and pulled it up to cover her nakedness.

He stood, ignoring his own exposed body. Nothing there she hadn't seen a thousand times. She'd seen it, possessed it, maddened it...and then rejected it.

"I'm going to take a shower," he said. "If you're still here when I get out, it had better mean you're ready to tell me what's going on. It had better mean you're ready to stay."

She looked at him, her expression numb and slack with pain. "I can't stay. You know that."

The disappointment— He shook his head roughly. *Disappointment?* What a laughable word that was for the lava spill of hot fury and pain cascading through him now! Like any volcanic eruption, it left only a blasted devastation behind.

"But if you're *gone*," he continued in that same stranger's voice. "If you're gone, Bonnie, don't *ever* come back."

She whitened, whiter than the moonlight, whiter than the sheet. She stood, the bedclothes trailing behind her, and moved toward him. "You don't mean that, Mitch."

"The hell I don't."

She was close enough now he could see her eyes were filled with tears. Well, so was every single goddamn vein in his body. Tears were for children. They didn't solve anything. They didn't *change* anything.

"You can't play with my life this way. If you have to go, then go. But don't ever show up here like this again, looking for a midnight romp—or whatever it is you were after."

She flinched, and he had a sudden terrible thought. Had she run out of funds? Was she alone out there, on the run, without food or shelter, or—

"There's money," he said matter-of-factly. "It's in my dresser. Top drawer. You can take it all, if you—"

*"Money?"*

Without warning, she reared back and slapped

him. Hard. The crack of her hand across his cheek
rang through the room like a gunshot.

He stood there a second, feeling the stinging
ripple across his skin, abnormal waves of heat
against the frigid air.

Then, laughing blackly, he put his hand on the
bathroom door.

"Goodbye, Bonnie," he said.

"You okay, hon? Anything wrong with those
eggs?"

The snub-nosed, friendly waitress hovered over
Bonnie, metal coffeepot in hand, frowning down
at her uneaten breakfast with a maternal worry,
which was ironic, really. Even though the two were
probably about the same age—mid-twenties—
right now Bonnie felt about a hundred years older
than anyone in the restaurant.

"No, no, they're great." Instinctively, Bonnie flipped over the paper place mat she'd been
doodling on. Her Florentine morning-glory vines
weren't exactly great art, but they weren't your
everyday scribble, either. She knew it was paranoid, but she never wanted anyone to remember,
later, that the nervous young woman had seemed
talented, an art student, maybe?

She picked up her fork and smiled as brightly
as she could. The woman's name tag read "I'm
EDNA! How can I help you today?" and apparently Edna took her mission seriously.

If only she *could* help, Bonnie thought, spearing a forkful of eggs, then trying to swallow them around the rock in her throat. If only *anyone* could.

Apparently unconvinced by the bogus smile, Edna let her gaze flick expertly over Bonnie's face. Bonnie's cheeks grew warm. She'd spent so long trying to avoid attention that even this kindhearted scrutiny made her heart pound.

"You coming in from the back shift or heading out to the day watch?" Edna raised the coffeepot, as well as her eyebrows. "Maybe I should top you off, unless you're headed straight to bed. You look about done in."

That was probably an understatement. Bonnie had stopped here not because it looked appetizing, but because she simply couldn't make it another mile.

The old-fashioned diner squatted on the side of U.S. 24, just outside Colorado Springs. Judging by the crowd at 7:00 a.m., Bonnie figured one of the big defense employers must be located nearby. Or maybe one of the technology companies. She probably should be flattered that Edna considered her capable of holding down a real job like that.

She felt more like a piece of muddy flotsam tossed up by a river flood. She'd been driving almost all night, ever since she left Silverdell—and Mitch. The days before Mitch blurred, but for a week, at least, she'd known nothing but driving, driving, driving…and death.

Her mother's serene face rose in her mind's eye—Bonnie was so glad, so profoundly relieved, that, as her poor, troubled mother faced death, the woman had finally found peace. And Bonnie was so glad that she'd returned to Sacramento, that she'd sneaked into the nursing home that last night. She wasn't sure how she'd known the end was near…but she'd felt the urgency, as clearly as if she'd heard her mother's voice calling her.

She'd stayed only long enough to say goodbye. As she'd left, she'd taken—*stolen*—the silly quilted-calico mobile that hung in her mother's window. "Heather," the flowered cloth letters said. Her mother's hands had made it, though probably one of the aides had helped, since her mother had no longer been able to spell her own name.

The lumpy letters were in Bonnie's purse right now. She'd reached in and touched them, every hour or so, as she drove. Going back to California had been risky, but she was glad she'd done it. She couldn't have endured learning of her mother's death online…even though she'd been checking every day for two years.

Was she glad, too, that she'd driven to Silverdell afterward to see Mitch? Or had that been a terrible mistake? Had it been the final straw?

A month from now, she would have been able to come to him openly. She would have been able to tell him everything. She should have been strong enough to wait.

But she'd been so bereft, so desolate. Even though her mother had been as good as lost to her for years, there was something about the finality of death that hurt Bonnie in a way she couldn't have imagined. Now she was truly alone.

She'd needed his arms around her.

She touched her fingers to her inner brows, shoving down both images—her mother's empty face and Mitch's cold, hard eyes. She was too tired right now to think about any of that. When she found a hotel, when she got some sleep…then she'd allow herself to grieve.

"Actually, I've just arrived in town," she told Edna. "I was hoping to find a decent hotel, not too far off the highway. Reasonable, if possible."

Edna, bless her motherly heart, looked relieved that Bonnie wasn't trying to go to work in this condition. Or maybe simply thankful this be-draggled customer was only passing through and wouldn't be a regular.

"Marley's is just what you need," Edna said brightly. "About a mile down the highway, toward town. Respectable, if you know what I mean. No frills but clean as a whistle."

Bonnie nodded gratefully. "Sounds perfect," she said. Smiling again, she forked another small lump of eggs and made sure her posture was upright enough to help Edna feel free to tend other customers. "Thanks so much!"

Slowly, the waitress moved away. Bonnie fought the urge to let her shoulders slump back down. It wasn't enough to fool Edna into thinking Bonnie had adequate starch and courage to face this day. She needed to fool herself, too.

She turned her place mat over again. Inside the border of morning-glory doodles, she slashed quick crisscrossing lines, creating a grid of empty squares. Then she numbered the squares—one through thirty-one.

She leaned back, looking at the makeshift calendar. Thirty-one days. That wasn't so long, was it? And one of them was over already. She took her pen and drew a large *X* inside the first square. She traced over the mark, then traced it again and again, until the *X* was the darkest spot on the whole paper.

One down—thirty to go. She closed her eyes, then dragged them open, for fear she'd fall asleep and do a face-plant in the eggs. She blinked, squared her shoulders again and stared out the window, trying to get her bearings.

The sun had come up an hour ago—she'd been driving toward it, watching through the dusty car windshield as the golden ball had lifted itself sleepily over the horizon. The light had mesmerized her, then nearly blinded her, which was why she'd decided to pull over.

At first, she'd been too exhausted to notice much of anything. But now she saw that, right across the street, a huge nursery had blinked to life—electric lights illuminating the large metal-and-glass building. Behind the structure, sunlight sparked off sprawling rows of open-air plants and garden sculptures.

Crystal Eden, the nursery was called. She spotted several workers moving around, readying the place for opening. *Lucky people!* Her fingers closed over her palms, itching to hold a trowel or burrow into cold, reluctant earth.

They sold a lot of trees, she noticed. The effect was primarily green. But when she looked carefully, she spied the sprinkles of color.

Crocus, forsythia, daffodil…

Bulbs, already? Nervously, she glanced at the sky. March was a dangerous month. Spring was so close. You could smell the promise of warmth, floating behind the chill. The temptation to rush the planting was almost irresistible. But frost and snow remained a threat for at least another couple of months, and gardeners who forgot that often regretted it.

A little like her own situation, wasn't it? Her winter of exile had lasted almost two years. Now she was down to thirty days, and she could feel her impatience rising. She could feel herself wanting to rush, to let down her guard, to take risks and dream of spring.

She wondered whether Crystal Eden was hiring. Sometimes, in spring, nurseries added staff as customers poured in, hungry for rebirth. She'd worked at other nurseries along the way. Once, she and Mitch had both landed jobs at the same tree farm.... Virginia, she thought, or maybe it had been in Kentucky. Summer...June or July. Every day, they'd come back to their hotel hot, sweaty and half-mad from working alongside each other, forbidden to touch.

She shook away the thought. She didn't need a job, of course. When she first went on the run, she'd brought enough money to see her through five years, if she were careful. She'd had no way of knowing how long the ordeal would last.

But it had lasted only two. How was that possible? Just two short years, and already her mother was dead. Most of the money she'd started with was untouched.

Still, she wanted to work. What else would she do with her days, with her mind? How else would she feel a part of the living world? What else would keep her from going mad?

"Someone picking you up?" Edna was back, and her expression warned Bonnie she'd been letting her emotions show on her face. "You're not driving, are you?"

"Just as far as the hotel." Bonnie tried to sound reassuringly competent. "Then I think I'll sleep all day."

As Edna turned, Bonnie called out impulsively. "What's the weather report, do you know? Are they calling for any snow this week?"

Edna shrugged. "Don't think so. But you know March. At least if you're from around here, you do."

Her curious eyes invited Bonnie to share, but no amount of tired could ever make Bonnie be that foolish.

"Good," Bonnie said. She wondered how crazy Edna would think her if she knew she was worrying about those vulnerable forsythia and crocus across the street. "I hate driving in the snow."

Edna laughed and, giving up, moved on. Bonnie transferred her gaze back to the window. She'd hoped to get farther away before she hunkered down to serve her remaining days. Ohio, maybe. Or, even better, New England. Every mile was safety, another layer of protection.

But Colorado Springs was a decent-size town. Sacramento was already eighteen hours behind her, and even if Jacob was looking for her, he couldn't be sure which direction she'd headed.

She stopped herself. *If* he was looking for her? There was no "if" about it. Her mother's death had lit the fuse. The end would come, one way or another, in thirty days. Jacob knew that just as well as she did.

But maybe sprinting to the other edge of the

map was the chess move he expected her to make and paradoxically would be the least secure.

*Oh, God.* She rubbed her face hard with both hands, unable to bear the twisted, looping logic. For two years, she'd second-guessed every decision this way.

She couldn't think straight anymore. Her brain was dazed, as if the pain of the past few days were the equivalent of blunt force trauma.

She folded her place-mat calendar into a neat rectangle small enough to fit in her purse. Picking up her check, she slid her chair back and headed for the register. As she paid—cash, of course— she kept her eyes on the landscape boulders and evergreens in the Eden across the street.

Someone opened the door, and she heard a wind chime blow in the breeze, its notes wafting easily across the clean, crisp air. The sound reminded her piercingly of Bell River—though she couldn't quite say why.

But suddenly she had her answer. She was tired of running. Every mile took her farther from Mitch. Whether he wanted her or not, he would always be the fixed foot of her life's compass. Everywhere she went, forevermore, she would measure it in terms of how far it was from Mitch.

This was far enough. Any farther and she might not be able to breathe. If she could get a job, she'd stay.

# CHAPTER TWO

"YOU'RE JOKING." Mitch stared down at the dense paragraphs of legal mumbo jumbo, knowing he should be trying to read the document he held but unable to register anything except the ludicrously large number. It was such a big number it seemed to pulse and glow slightly on the page.

"You're trying to tell me somebody already wants to buy and make the stupid thing? And they want to pay…"

He couldn't even say the number out loud. This absolutely had to be a joke. He wasn't an inventor or an overnight success story. He was the younger Garwood boy. The party boy. The goof. The one who had resisted growing up so long his big brother, Dallas, secretly feared he never would.

Surely this was a prank. If he fell for it, Dallas would jump out from behind the door and die laughing.

But Indiana Dunchik, Mitch's well-respected patent lawyer—also known as Ana, though not to Mitch—hadn't cracked a smile. She was a gorgeous blonde he'd hired because she worked out of Grand Junction, not Silverdell. Therefore, she was less likely to think it was by definition preposterous that Mitch Garwood, screwup extraordinaire, might've invented something worthwhile.

Okay, that, and she was a gorgeous blonde.

Obviously, he hadn't hired her for her sense of humor. She seemed bewildered that he was chuckling.

"Of course it's not a jest, Mr. Garwood. Nor is it, in my opinion, a *stupid thing*." She laid her slim pink-tipped fingers flat on her desk. "We've spent months getting these patents because we believed your jacket was a marketable and useful product. I'm not surprised we have an offer. In fact, I'll be surprised if this is the only offer we receive."

Ordinarily, he disliked the royal "we," but the truth was, this patent-application process had been such a drawn-out bore, and Ms. Dunchik had wrestled with so many searches, claims, actions and appeals, that he knew full well it had been a joint effort. In fact, she'd had the more difficult half, because when he'd designed the Garwood Chore Jacket he'd mostly been—what else?—screwing around and having fun.

It had all started almost two years ago, when he'd said, "These coats should come with a cheat sheet for the feed formulas. And somewhere to put my phone that I can actually reach it."

Dallas had rolled his eyes—Mitch was always

trying to find a way to do less work. His last "invention" had been a gravity feeder to eliminate all those trips from the loft with buckets. Dallas had laughed at that, too, but it worked.

However, Alec, Mitch's nephew, had agreed about the jacket wholeheartedly. "We need somewhere to put Tootsie Rolls, too," he'd added with feeling.

That really got everyone laughing. Bell River Ranch was a family venture—and not even Mitch's family, except by marriage. Dallas had married Rowena Wright, the oldest of the Wright sisters, who had inherited the gorgeous spread and decided to turn it into a dude ranch.

So everyone assumed that Mitch was just hanging on, working with the horses, his first love, while he decided what to do when he grew up. But, later, Mitch kept thinking about the jacket. He had another idea, for a more comfortable back vent. And then some thoughts about a better, warmer lining.

Still, he'd just been fooling around—as evidenced by the fact that Alec, a ten-year-old, was his only cheerleader.

Well, Alec and Bonnie.

Reflexively, Mitch thought about how thrilled Bonnie would be to hear that he'd actually followed through and applied for the patent.

And now this offer. She'd squeal and leap into his arms and say "I told you so" a thousand times, between kisses. She'd always insisted his ideas were genius, and, though he knew she was blowing sunshine, it would be pretty nice to tell someone who wouldn't be insultingly shocked.

But then he remembered. He wouldn't be telling Bonnie anything anymore. Two weeks ago, he'd put paid to that possibility, once and for all. Even if she ever stopped running, she wouldn't come back to him.

He glanced down at the contract again, and the number no longer glowed. It didn't represent freedom or validation or kisses in the romantic places he'd promised to take her someday, places like Ireland or Spain. It was just money. And Mitch hadn't ever really cared much about money.

He glanced at the woman behind the desk. "So what do we do now?"

The lawyer tightened her lips, which Mitch had learned was her thinking face. "In my opinion, we should wait. Of course, if you would like to have the cash in hand sooner, we can have our contracts department look this over and make recommendations. But…unless you need capitalization now…I think waiting will be fruitful."

*Fruitful.* He almost smiled, thinking of his preacher father, a fire-and-brimstone bastard, and how often the old man had reminded Mitch and Dallas that the line about being fruitful and multiplying wasn't a mandate to go around making babies all over Silverdell. The brothers had wasted an absurd amount of time creating other comic interpretations of the quote.

*Suck lemons in math class, my son.* Stuff like that. Mitch had thought it was hilarious. No wonder his father had always warned him he'd never amount to anything.

For the first and only time in his life, Mitch momentarily thought it was too bad the old tyrant wasn't around anymore. It might be fun to shove this contract in his face and see what he thought of the number.

*How about them multiplying fruits, Dad?*

"I'm not in need of immediate capitalization," he echoed, unable to resist playing Ms. Dunchik's multisyllabic elocution game.

"Good." She nodded regally and began scooping papers into a neat stack. "We'll wait a few weeks, then. We have a department that can bring your design to the attention of some likely candidates, and we'll see what happens. But I'll be very surprised if we can't end up doubling this. At least."

More money than he needed, times two. He shook his head, trying to imagine what he'd do with that much "capitalization." He drew a blank. Every plan he'd made for a long, long time had revolved around Bonnie.

So no, waiting for the money wasn't a problem. Obviously, he could use an extra few weeks just to invent a new plan. A new reason to live.

"Smile, Mr. Garwood." The lawyer leaned forward, and her eyes twinkled, as if she really saw Mitch for the first time. "You're going to be a moderately wealthy man."

He tucked one corner of his mouth up. It was the best he could do.

"Well, then," he said. "Hurray."

A WEEK LATER, Mitch sat in the back booth of a shadowy restaurant on the far side of Silverdell, feeling a little like Al Capone. The small cardboard box on the bench seat beside him didn't have drugs or dirty money inside, but he couldn't have been more uncomfortable if it had.

A few minutes later, Dallas slid in opposite him and shrugged off his jacket. Though Dallas was Silverdell County's sheriff, he wasn't in uniform today. Mitch had deliberately chosen an off-duty moment to ask his brother to break the rules.

Dallas waved away the hovering waitress, then faced Mitch with a half smile. "I have to admit, your message intrigued me."

"Yeah. Well, thanks for coming." The perfunctory words felt stiff on Mitch's lips. They hadn't seen each other in a couple of days, but they were close and didn't usually waste time on pleasantries.

Dallas raised an eyebrow, noting the formality.

"I wanted to talk to you alone, away from the ranch." Mitch ran his hand through his hair. "And away from your office, too. What I want… It's personal. Not official, if you know what I mean."

"I get the general idea." Dallas's smile broadened. "You know, you're the only person I know who would actually leave the words *I want you to do something unethical for me* on an answering machine."

"Well, I do, so why lie?" Mitch shrugged. "If you weren't willing to consider it, there wasn't any point wasting your time. Besides, I'm not much for sugarcoating."

Dallas's other eyebrow went up. "Might be splitting hairs there. No lying, but you want to do something unethical?"

"No. I want *you* to do something unethical. A very important distinction."

Dallas laughed, as Mitch had known he would. The one thing he could always do was make his brother laugh. The one thing he could *rarely* do was make Dallas take him seriously.

He'd also never been able to make Dallas fudge the rules. Not in years, anyhow. Once, way back in their childhood, Dallas had been a little wild. Mitch remembered that clearly, if only because it had caused such violent rows with their dad. But in his midteens Dallas had gone straight. Superstraight. Even before he'd started wearing a star, he'd strutted around Silverdell with a halo.

Since he'd gone into law enforcement, even worse. He'd never so much as helped Mitch wriggle out of a parking ticket. So Mitch didn't really hold out a lot of hope that Saint Sheriff Garwood would help him with this far-more-unprincipled request.

"Go ahead, then." Dallas leaned back. "Out with it."

Mitch put the box on the table. It looked innocent enough. Three weeks ago, it had held a pair of binoculars Rowena's sister Penny had ordered for bird-watching classes at the ranch.

"I've got her fingerprints on a water glass. I thought maybe you'd be willing to get them ID'd for me. Discreetly."

Dallas didn't answer right away. At least he didn't ask anything as dumb as *whose fingerprints?* Everyone at Bell River knew there was only one female on the planet Mitch cared about—and certainly only one who needed to be identified through fingerprints.

Finally, Dallas sighed, as if his little brother, who had always been so annoying, was continuing the tradition. "Why now?"

It was a sensible question, and Mitch didn't mind answering.

"I saw her again. Three weeks ago. When I got home, she was in the cabin."

"Really." Dallas always kept his face and his tone under control, but Mitch knew him well enough to recognize true shock. "Did she explain where she'd been?"

"No. Nothing. She explained nothing. I didn't

ask at first, because—" Well, that part didn't need sharing. "Anyhow, it wasn't long before I realized she wasn't home to stay. I…I was pretty upset. I told her if she ran away again, I didn't ever want her to come back. But she left anyhow."

*"Wow."*

"Yeah." Mitch was glad, finally, to talk to someone about it. Especially someone like Dallas, who would really get it. He knew Mitch better than anyone, and he'd hear all the things Mitch couldn't bring himself to articulate, like how much it hurt.

Dallas's eyes were thoughtful. "Did you mean it?"

"Damn straight I did. Look, I'm trying not to be a jerk here. She has the right to make her own decisions, and if she feels she can't trust me, fine. But I can't do this anymore. I—"

He stopped himself as he reached the invisible stoic-guy boundary. He couldn't whine. But… he'd carried around his fury, mixed up in a big, boiling, nasty stew that included both heartbreak and terror, for three weeks now. He had to bring closure to this mess. He had to, or he'd lose his mind.

Not that he ever said words like *closure* out loud.

"Anyhow, I know it's technically against the rules to run prints for me. But who else can I ask? I thought about Jeff—"

Dallas smiled. Jeff Shafer and Dallas had been deputies together, under old Sheriff Granton, before Jeff left for wider pastures, explaining that he needed to solve more interesting crimes than cow tipping and jaywalking. Jeff had always been the rebel of the two young deputies. He was a good guy, but, unlike Dallas, he believed that sometimes the greater good required breaking a rule here and there.

"Okay. You thought about Jeff." Dallas cocked his head. "But?"

"But I can't bring anyone else into this." Mitch put his hands over the box, instinctively protective, then moved them again when he realized how transparent that body language might be. "I don't think Jeff's got loose lips, but who knows? She's really scared, Dallas. You saw that. She's running from something—or somebody—and I can't risk putting a spotlight on her."

"Then why ID her at all? Why not just let her go? She clearly believes we can't help her. Maybe she's right."

"Maybe. But…" Mitch's hands balled on the table, and his neck grew hot. "Damn it, Dallas. I would have thrown my body under an oncoming train for that woman."

Dallas's gaze softened slightly, though not enough to qualify as pity, which would have made things worse.

"I know you would have," he said. "And she

knows it, too. Problem is, how does that help her? You're dead, and the train's still coming."

Mitch heard the logic. He really did. But it didn't stop the helpless anger from radiating across his body in hot waves.

"Fine. I get that. But if I am going to move on, I have to know I did everything I could. I need to close this book, Dallas. I need to type *The End* on this stupid story. And I need you to help me."

Sitting as straight as a fireplace poker, he gave his brother a hard, unblinking glare. "So. Bottom line. Will you do it or not?"

"Sure."

Mitch dropped back against the cushioned booth, and the padding let out a whoosh of air that sounded just like the sigh of relief he felt in his chest.

"You *will?* Even though it's against the rules?"

Dallas shrugged. "I won't be advertising that I did it. But you'd be surprised how often it's done. I bet Sheriff Granton's daughter never dated a single guy who wasn't innocently offered a Coke while he waited, for this very reason. Drinking glasses are good for fingerprints. So are the hoods of patrol cars."

Mitch chuckled. Dallas never ceased to surprise him. He shoved the binocular box across the empty table. "Take it, then. I picked it up with a paper towel, so the prints are probably all still there."

But Dallas made no move to claim the box.

He simply smiled at Mitch, then lifted a hand to summon the waitress. "How about we get some coffee?"

Mitch nodded roughly, though he didn't want coffee or anything a waitress could bring. All he wanted was for Dallas to grab that box, hustle it back to the sheriff's department and force some miracle machine somewhere to spit out an identity.

"Take it," he said again, glancing down at the box.

"Don't need it." Dallas waited, not speaking, while the waitress poured their coffee, then gave her a warm "thanks." Waitresses always loved Dallas. They even flirted with him until they noticed the ring. Sometimes even *after* they noticed it.

When she left, Dallas shook his mug in small circles, letting some heat escape, then took a sip.

The display of serenity drove Mitch nuts. "Dallas. What the devil do you mean, you don't need it?"

"Exactly that. I don't need it. I've already got a set of her prints on a glass. Ro gave me one a year ago, and it's been locked in my bottom desk drawer ever since."

"Ro gave you one *what?*" Mitch frowned hard. "A glass with Bonnie's fingerprints on it?"

"Yeah. Apparently, she'd saved one, right from the start, thinking she might need to probe further someday. She gave it to me while you and Bonnie were on the road. She thought I might want to try to track you down, to be sure you were okay. She thought it might help the search if we could find out who Bonnie really was."

*"Is."* Mitch said the word hotly, like a threat. "Who Bonnie really *is*."

"Of course."

Mitch could tell Dallas was clearly making a conscious effort to keep his tone calm, to prevent Mitch's frustration and fear from escalating.

*Too late.* Mitch felt his lungs tighten, as if they didn't want to send him air. "You've had it a year? And you haven't run the prints? What on earth have you been waiting for?"

"Hey. I don't break the rules for fun. Or to satisfy my curiosity." Dallas shrugged. "You sent postcards, so I knew you were alive. You knew how to get in touch with me if you needed help, so I didn't have any good reason to invade Bonnie's privacy. Then, since you got home, I've been waiting for a sign from you."

"From me?"

"Of course." Dallas met his gaze steadily. "Bonnie O'Mara, or whoever she is, is your mystery, Mitch. Only you can say when you're ready to solve her."

BONNIE'S HOMECOMING, after two years on the run, could have been a splashy, trashy, conspicuous celebration. If she'd wanted to, she could have chosen to appear in sequins, sparkles and feather boas, holding a neon sign that said "Surprise, sicko! You lose!"

Instead, as she slipped into the large elegant hotel ballroom where her mother's charity auction was being held, Bonnie wore head-to-toe black. It seemed fitting, somehow, since she hadn't been able to attend the funeral.

Missing that service had been very painful. She'd even dreamed, briefly, of sneaking back here to Sacramento, just for an hour. She'd imagined herself standing unobtrusively in the rear of the church, with glasses, maybe, or a veiled hat.

But that would have been suicide. No disguise would have been adequate. Jacob undoubtedly had anticipated her showing up, and he would have been ready.

So instead she'd marked the day, privately, at her nursery job at Crystal Eden back in Colorado Springs. When the church bells down the block had rung the noon hour, she'd stopped right in the middle of hauling potting soil, dropped the handles of her wheelbarrow and shut her eyes.

She'd said a prayer. And when she'd glanced up, a tangerine cloud shaped like a ballerina had been executing a grand jeté across the sky. She liked to believe it was a message from her mother, letting Bonnie know she'd found freedom and peace at last.

After that, her wait had been easier. She loved the nursery job, and the days flew. All thirty-one of them.

A month and a day. That was how long had passed, between the night her mother had died and this clear April afternoon when Bonnie had finally come home.

If she could even call Sacramento home anymore. She'd lost so much over the past two years. But somehow she had survived. That was all that really mattered now.

She had outwitted Jacob. She couldn't really absorb that fact, even now that she saw him, up there, so sanctimonious and self-important in the first row. It was the first time she'd laid eyes on him since she had left, nearly two years ago.

It was the first time she'd seen any of these people since then. The auction house was filled with friends of her grandmother, collectors, critics, other artists and other Sacramento bigwigs—people she'd known all her life.

They didn't recognize her yet, of course. They weren't expecting her. Most of them probably thought she was dead and assumed her body would never be located, or that if she ever were discovered, she'd be pathetic and half-mad in some art colony somewhere, as her mother so often had been found.

The stylish black hat she'd bought yesterday covered her hair, which she'd had stripped back to its natural color, but pinned tightly to her head, so that it wouldn't give her away too soon.

She took a seat quietly at the back of the auction room, attracting little attention from anyone except her attorney, who had technically known she'd be coming but had still looked relieved when she'd appeared.

Everyone else was focused on the oil painting that had just been brought out. A low rumble of appreciation moved through the audience as they caught their first glimpse of the portrait, the girl with the legendary cascade of red-gold hair.

It was, indisputably, one of the most beautiful of the Annabelle Oils, a series of paintings done by the California portraitist Ava Andersen Irving. Sixteen complete oils, all with only one subject—Ava's Titian-haired, blue-eyed, fairylike granddaughter, Annabelle Irving.

The series had begun when Annabelle had been just a year old and had continued until Ava died, when Annabelle was fifteen. The paintings and adjunct sketches had made Ava rich... well, richer, given that she'd already married into money.

And they had made little Annabelle famous. It had made a million people think they knew her, made them romanticize and misunderstand her, as if she were Ophelia or Alice in Wonderland. Somewhere along the way, Annabelle Irving had stopped being a normal child and had started being a myth. Strange, ethereal, other-worldly, elfin, odd...just a few of the adjectives art critics loved to apply to her.

The portraits were officially known by numbers only. This was Fourteen, which didn't correspond with the subject's age, because Annabelle had been only twelve the year this one was painted. Twelve, and so tired of sitting still. Her grand-mother had positioned Annabelle next to a window, where the light hit her hair just right. Out of the corner of her eye, Annabelle caught a tanta-lizing hint of buttercups dancing in the wind, but she wasn't allowed to look. She was barely al-lowed to breathe.

That particular year, Annabelle had rebelled, briefly, the way preteens sometimes did. The slight puffiness beneath the famous blue eyes was proof of the storm of tears, the refusal to cooperate, the desperation to be set free.

Ava had been furious, at first, but eventually she had announced that the hint of sadness added pathos to the painting, which was ultimately price-less.

With a start, Bonnie came back to the pres-ent, realizing the bidding had begun. She didn't move a muscle. She didn't want this painting. She hated it. But she was glad to see the price rise higher and higher. Her mother had owned Four-teen outright, and she had left instructions in her will that it, along with a small pencil sketch of

Annabelle, the only two pieces from the series that legally belonged to her, should be auctioned after her death. The proceeds were to be donated to the women's shelter that had taken in Heather Irving so many times during her troubled life.

Jacob was bidding, too. Bonnie smiled grimly behind her black-dotted Swiss veil, watching him lift one elegant finger, then let it drop, then lift it again. Was he using his own money, she wondered, or hers?

He didn't win. When the figure sailed too high, he shook his head discreetly at the auctioneer, then turned around to see who had beaten him. Recognizing an elderly California art collector whose goodwill he obviously needed to keep, he threw a smile of graceful surrender.

As his smarmy gaze raked the crowd, Bonnie froze, wondering if he'd see her. It no longer mattered, not as it once had. She wasn't in danger anymore. He didn't have anything to gain by hurting her now.

But she wanted to do this her way.

The drawing was up next. Only nine-by-twelve, and unframed, it looked like the unloved stepsister of the larger oil. But Bonnie adored this picture, a practice sketch for Nine. In it, a seven-year-old Annabelle was in profile, one arm thrown over the back of a straight wooden chair, and she gazed longingly out the window. It was an odd little thing, drawn mostly to help Ava get the flowers right. Annabelle herself was rendered in simple charcoal, while the blooming gardens outside the window were bursting with vibrant color.

Bonnie remembered that summer so well. It had been one of the few times she'd been posed looking through the window. Being able to watch the bees buzzing around the roses and the butterflies dipping into the penta plant… It had made the hours so much easier to bear.

It had been almost as good as being free.

She raised her hand. The auctioneer glanced at her, too professional to show surprise at a new bidder this late in the game. Her attorney remained utterly still and impassive, giving nothing away prematurely.

She had many competitors. She wasn't the only one who could see the special joy in this sketch— one of the few pictures in which the infamous Annabelle looked like a normal child.

But she didn't care if everyone in the room bid against her. She would have this sketch, whatever the price. She was a rich woman now, and if she ended up donating every dollar of her inheritance to the women's shelter, that was fine with her.

She raised her hand again and again. Quickly, people began to stare at her. Jacob himself had turned half a dozen times.

He was merely curious at first. Then she saw him squinting, confused. And then a slowly dawning alarm.

His posture tightened, all the easy insouciance evaporating. Eventually, when the bidding had come down to Bonnie and one other, Jacob didn't even bother to pretend he wasn't staring. He sat permanently swiveled toward her, his neck uncomfortably twisted. He gripped the seat of his chair with both hands, as if he had to hold himself down.

Finally, her last competitor dropped out. The price was absurd, even for an Annabelle sketch. As the bid assistant bent over her, Jacob obviously couldn't endure the suspense another minute. He stood and started moving toward her, dark and malevolent, like the California mudslides that coursed down hillsides blindly, burying everything in their paths.

The bid assistant hesitated, confused and slightly startled by the frigid waves of fury suddenly pulsing through the air around them.

Jacob's face said it all. He knew. He had to know. He had to understand, at that terrible moment, that he'd lost. That all his attempts to outwit her, to ruin her... No, no euphemisms. Just state it baldly, like the hideous truth it was.

All his attempts to *kill* her had failed.

As Jacob approached, Bonnie stood, too. She lifted the veil from her face and smiled. Only five feet away, he froze, as if she were a gorgon, a Medusa—as if one look from her blue eyes had turned him to stone.

A murmur spread through the room. *Good.* She wanted everyone, from the millionaires to the janitors, from the journalists to the guards, to know her. She removed her hat with one motion, then pulled the clip that had held her hair in its tight twist. A cascade of red-gold hair fell around her shoulders, and the murmur rose to an excited buzz.

"Annabelle!" Jacob lunged forward.

Abruptly, her lawyer jerked to a standing position, as if to block whatever the crazed man might have in mind. But Jacob pushed past him, rearranging his face as he came toward her. By the time he touched her, he was affection incarnate, the epitome of cousinly love.

He reached out and enveloped Bonnie...Annabelle...in his arms.

"Belle, Belle!" He was so smooth, so good, that if she didn't know better, she'd believe he was overjoyed. "Oh, Belle, thank God you're alive!"

# CHAPTER THREE

IT SHOULD HAVE been a peaceful Monday afternoon at the ranch. Instead, having counted every single second in the week since his meeting with Dallas, Mitch was going crazy.

On TV it took about thirty seconds to get a fingerprint match. Even factoring in reality, and the need to do this through back channels, what could possibly be taking eight whole days?

And then, just as Mitch was winding up the training session with Rusty, one of Bell River's newest ponies destined to take the littlest guests on trail rides, he saw his brother coming toward him.

*Hell.* Dallas had news. And it wasn't good news.

Mitch could sense that much from a hundred yards, just watching the way Dallas walked, framed in silhouette through the doorway of the indoor paddock. The first clue was the tight, squared-off position of his shoulders. And when Dallas cleared the door and the overhead lights hit him, Mitch could read the grim evidence on his face.

"Scat, Alec," Mitch said to his nephew, not roughly but flatly, without sugarcoating. "Go help Rowena with the baby. Your dad and I are going to need some privacy."

Alec made an irritated snicking sound between his teeth. He'd been having fun helping Mitch, and he didn't want to quit. "Privacy for what?"

Mitch rolled his eyes. *Seriously?*

"We're making plans to sell your scrawny body for spare parts. We can't have you listening, so scram."

Alec started to protest again, but then he glanced over at his dad, and apparently the kid could read body language, too. When Dallas had a face like that, Alec wanted to be somewhere else.

So did Mitch, who was suddenly as terrified as if he, too, were a kid. He tried to stop his heart from thumping so fast. He tried to stop his mind from imagining all kinds of horrors. Okay, the news was bad. *How bad?*

Bonnie was married. Bonnie was a criminal, a nutter...

Or even worse, she was still a mystery. If her fingerprints hadn't turned up a match, then they were no closer than before to finding out who she really was.

Or... The thumping inside his chest stilled viciously.

Or Bonnie was dead. Whatever she'd been running from had caught her.

"Hey, there." Dallas reached Mitch just as Alec disappeared through the side doors, leaving a trail of kicked sand behind him. Dallas patted the new pony's neck. "How's Rusty doing?"

"He's fine." Mitch stroked the pony's flank approvingly. "But don't make small talk. You know something. Tell me."

Dallas continued to rub the pony's glossy coat. He hadn't yet met Mitch's eyes, which was truly unnerving. Dallas was rarely daunted by uncomfortable truths. It was one of the traits that made him a good sheriff. He could deliver bad news with as much composure as he delivered the good.

"Dallas." The drumming against Mitch's ribs sped up. "You're killing me here."

Dallas finally looked straight at him. "We should probably sit down."

Mitch didn't argue. He waved a finger to one of the stable hands who was in the corner viewing room, talking on a cell phone. He pointed to Rusty, and the young man scurried out to take the pony away.

"Okay. Let's go over here." With the horse disposed of, Mitch led the way to the far side of the paddock. He opened one of the latches on the kickboards and took the first of the spectator seats on the first row of bleachers.

Dallas left an empty seat between them when he sat. He laid his hat down there with a sigh.

"We found her," he said. "She's alive and well. She lives in Sacramento. But…her name's not Bonnie."

At first, all Mitch could feel was the relief. *Alive. Well.* Damn, those were beautiful words.

But then the rest of Dallas's sentence sank in. *Her name's not Bonnie.* It shouldn't have shocked him. He'd known she must've been using a fake name—nothing else made sense. But, as he heard it confirmed, he was glad he was sitting, as if the solid floor might have turned to swamp.

He thought of all the times he'd said her name. Laughing. Whispering. Crying into the night air.

*Damn it, Bonnie, where are you?*

*Bonnie, Bonnie, please…*

"No, of course not." He sat up straight. "What *is* her name, then?"

Dallas eyed him for a minute before speaking. Mitch felt as if he were being measured, like a horse being fitted for a bit, to see how much of the truth he could take between his teeth at once.

"Annabelle Irving."

The name was oddly anticlimactic. It meant nothing to Mitch. It was the name of a stranger.

"Okay," he said slowly. "But who is Annabelle Irving?"

Dallas smiled. "I didn't know, either. Apparently we're just a couple of dumb cowboys. But with the cultured crowd she's *somebody*. Her grandmother was a well-known artist, and Annabelle was her favorite subject. There's a whole set of paintings of her called the Annabelle Oils, and collectors go nuts for them."

*Okay...* Mitch rubbed the knee of his jeans. That was okay, right? An artist's model. He could live with that. And instinctively, he could believe it. He remembered how unnaturally still and self-contained Bonnie could be. She didn't even change her expression, sometimes for many minutes at a time. He'd once wondered whether she'd been a nun, because she seemed so accustomed to sitting in silent immobility.

But why would an artist's model need to go on the run under an assumed name? It wasn't as if your average person had ever heard of her. She could have shouted, "I am Annabelle Irving" from the rooftops of Silverdell, and no one would have so much as blinked.

He narrowed his eyes. "Wait a minute. To match her fingerprints, you have to have a set on file, right? I mean…her prints as Annabelle Irving had to be in the system. How does an artist's model get her prints into the database?"

One of the trainers had just brought a palomino into the paddock on a lead line. Mitch wished he could yell at her to get out and come back later. But Bell River was a working dude ranch, humming with staff, guests and wall-to-wall activities. He wasn't going to find complete privacy anywhere.

Dallas flicked a glance toward the young woman, then bent forward, his elbows on his knees, and lowered his voice.

"She was in the system because about seven years ago, when she was eighteen, she stabbed a man with a pair of pruning shears."

Mitch drew back. *"Bullshit."* He said it too loudly, and the trainer glanced their way for one split second before studiously returning her attention to the horse. Mitch wasn't technically anyone's boss, but the family tie was close enough to make employees reluctant to cross him.

Dallas frowned, and Mitch shook his head roughly. "Sorry, but...stabbed a man? Like hell she did."

"I'm afraid that part isn't even disputed. There's a police report. She admitted stabbing her cousin, a lawyer named Jacob Burns. She says it was self-defense, because he tried to molest her. He says they were arguing over management of the estate, which, upon her grandmother's death, had been left to an executor."

Mitch felt a touch of nausea roll through him. "Her cousin tried to... What the devil do they really mean by 'molest'? He tried to *rape* her?"

Then he realized that, instinctively, he'd already decided Bonnie was telling the truth, not this disgusting Jacob whatever. "I mean...come on. The guy's her *cousin?* That's just sick."

"If it happened that way." Dallas sounded patient. "But clearly the cops didn't buy her story. Apparently, she had a history of erratic behavior, though this is the only episode that occurred after she turned eighteen. Earlier records are sealed, because she was a juvenile. And, no, I'm not going to try to get someone to pry them open."

"I wasn't going to ask you to." Mitch glared at his brother, his mind going a mile a minute. "So... what? What's the bottom line here? You think she was running from her cousin?"

Dallas lifted his shoulders. "Don't know. I didn't dig any deeper. You asked for a name, and I got one. At the time, no charges were brought, so even if she thought she was running from her cousin, there's no evidence that..."

"That what?" Mitch's lips felt stiff.

"That Jacob Burns is dangerous. He was never arrested. He was about twenty-five at the time, just out of law school. He practices in Sacramento now, and apparently he's a big deal. Annabelle, on the other hand..." He hesitated. "The authorities sent her for psychiatric evaluation, and she spent some time in a mental-health clinic. Just a few weeks, but—"

"But you think she's nuts. What the hell, Dallas? You knew Bonnie. We all did. You think she's insane?"

"No." Dallas spoke slowly, and pity dripped from the word. He pitied Mitch, because Mitch had fallen in love with a kook. "Not insane. But maybe…troubled. You know? Maybe she's trouble."

Mitch thought his blood pressure must be about a thousand—he could feel his heart beating behind his eyes. He wanted to punch someone or something. He'd punch Dallas, except that he'd learned better about twenty years ago. Dallas might be a saint, but he had a right hook like a demon.

"Yeah, well, I remember what Dad said about Rowena, back in the day," he countered acidly. "That she was *trouble* was the least of it."

The minute the words came out, Mitch felt himself flushing. That was a low blow. It wasn't fair. Mitch liked his brother's wife, always had. And Rowena had had her reasons for acting wild. But why couldn't Dallas see that Bonnie must have had her reasons, too?

"I'm on your side here, Mitch," Dallas said mildly. "I thought you were through with her, anyhow."

"I am." Mitch stood. "I *am*. But just because she broke my heart…that doesn't mean I have to pretend she's a monster. She's not. And she's not a liar."

Dallas raised his eyebrows.

"She's not," Mitch repeated. "A hundred times, when I was trying to make her tell me what was going on, it would have been easier for her to invent any old story, just to shut me up. But she didn't. She didn't want to tell me the truth, but she was too good to tell me a lie."

"Okay." Dallas nodded slowly, though he clearly wasn't convinced. "But there's one other thing you ought to know. If you look her up, you'll see. She's rich."

"I don't give a damn about that."

"I know. I just want you to be prepared. When I say rich, I don't mean comfortable. I mean *really* rich. Dripping, Rockefeller rich."

Mitch hesitated, looking down at his brother's somber face. "I see. What you're trying to say is that she's *out-of-my-league* rich."

"More or less, yeah." Dallas didn't mince words. "I'm saying she's trouble, and she's out-of-our-league rich. Look, she left you. You had a grand adventure, but it's over. She's gone back to her real life. You need to let it go, Mitch. You need to let *her* go."

MAYBE JACOB AND the rest of them were right, Annabelle thought as she knelt, here at this fork in the bricked path of Greenwood's butterfly garden, oddly paralyzed and unsure where to plant the final daffodils. Maybe she *was* crazy. Divorced from reality, dysfunctional, paranoid—just as her mother had been.

Because the way she felt, now that she was back home at Greenwood…

She felt like her own ghost.

So maybe they were right. Maybe it was loony to feel that her invented alter ego, Bonnie O'Mara, was more real than Annabelle Irving could ever be.

Maybe it was bonkers to insist on living in the Greenwood gardener's cottage and refuse to spend a single night in the elegant, twenty-two-room Italianate mansion where she was born and raised.

Maybe it was daft to dream of taking the Irving fortune, every hellish dollar of it, and burning it in a bonfire down by the creek.

But the truth was...being back here, being the heiress to *all this* had paradoxically stolen any hope of being happy. It had reduced her once again to an object, a thing, a possession, instead of a woman.

All her life, Annabelle had understood she wasn't a person. She was an idea. An arrangement of colors on canvas. A mythical, imaginary creature who came to life only in the minds of the people who romanticized her pictures. When the lights were off, when the museums were closed, she was supposed to sink back into the ornate frame, frozen in place, until another art lover came to imagine her into existence all over again.

"The irises will be coming out any day now."

Annabelle looked up as Fitz, the elderly gardener who had tended Greenwood since Annabelle was a little girl, came limping toward her, his wheelbarrow rumbling before him. She forced herself to smile. Fitz had been the one person she could honestly call a friend. Drawn together by their mutual love of growing things, he'd come to be like a father to her through the years.

And yet, in the end, even he had betrayed her.

"Yes, the irises will be gorgeous. And I'm so glad you put in day lilies." Shading her eyes with the knife blade she held in one palm, she peered up at him. Only about five-three, with a face turned to tree bark by the California sun, he looked even browner with the light behind him, casting him in shadow. "They're a wonderful addition."

He reached into his wheelbarrow and lifted out a straw hat. "Here," he said. "You don't want to end up a grizzled old piece of shoe leather like me."

"Don't I?" She took the hat, but she didn't put it on. She raised her face toward the sun. No one cared anymore—no one would punish her for getting dirty fingernails or letting the sun freckle her pale skin. And yet it still felt like the most luxurious act of defiance, to be out here at noon, with her hands in the earth and the heat on her face.

"No. You don't." Fitz plucked the hat from her hands and stuffed it on her head. "I bet you didn't even use sunscreen. You know, Bonny-Belle, you don't always have to do the opposite of what your grandmother would have wanted you to do. Sometimes she was right."

She looked down at her grimy fingernails, realizing the truth of his words. She could have put on sunscreen first, and she could have enjoyed her gardening without courting skin cancer. As it was, she'd be red as a watermelon by nightfall.

"You're right, Fitz—I'm acting silly, and—" But she couldn't complete her sentence. One of the maids was scurrying down the brick path toward them, her hand held up, waving urgently.

"Ms. Annabelle," she said as she reached them. "I'm sorry. There's a man, and he won't go away. I told him you weren't at home, and so did Mr. Agron, but the man says he isn't leaving till he talks to you. He's been here half an hour, and Mr. Agron said we should call the police, but—"

Annabelle's heart hitched. Could it be Jacob?

The maid stopped to catch her breath and maybe to find the right words. "I don't know if we should. He's not doing anything, and he's obviously not a reporter. He's kind of like…a cowboy or something."

Annabelle dropped her trowel and, without thinking it through, rose from her knees. She wiped her earthy palms on her jeans, then raised a hand to her hair, which was flyaway and tangled and probably littered with leaf debris and vermiculite.

"A cowboy?"

"Well, sort of. I don't know exactly. He doesn't have a horse or a hat or anything, but—" She shook her head. "Anyhow, he says you know him. He says if we'll just tell you his name—"

"What is his name?" Annabelle's voice came out tight, threaded with tension. She already knew the answer, of course. She knew because the maid was flushed with a pretty confusion, a heightened female awareness caused by a gorgeous young cowboy.

"Mitch," the maid said, her lips curving into a small, puckering smile as she formed the word. "Mitch Garwood."

MITCH HAD DECIDED he'd give her an hour. He'd wait out here, on one of the benches around the front fountain, till the sun disappeared behind the mansion's fancy white colonnades.

If Bonnie hadn't come out by then, he swore to himself, he'd go back to Silverdell and to hell with her.

But as the minutes dragged on, and it seemed likely he'd have to make good on the threat, he wondered whether he could really do it. Could he just hop on his motorcycle and head east, flipping the bird to Greenwood—and Bonnie—in his rearview mirror?

Because…if he did, what then?

He tried to imagine going the rest of his life without an explanation, without hearing from her lips what the whole crazy running thing had been for. He hadn't been able to unearth anything that made sense, though he'd combed the internet and studied every single photo of the Annabelle Oils till he could probably paint one himself.

The prim, lace-draped Annabelle Irving was Bonnie, all right. But not *his* Bonnie. The Annabelle Oils girl was straight out of a fairy tale, with floating clouds of red curls so pale they were almost gold and huge blue eyes that looked haunting and strange, as if you'd never be able to see what she saw, not if you stared at the same spot forever.

*His* Bonnie wasn't one bit strange. His Bonnie's eyes were smart, clear and friendly. She didn't wear lace, and she was too sexy to be allowed in a fairy tale. She was a normal, red-blooded woman. She hummed off tune and didn't care who heard her. She ditched her shoes the minute she got inside, and sometimes her fuzzy socks didn't match. She cooked a steak so tender it melted between your teeth. She bit her fingernails and looked killer in blue jeans.

So if he never found out what had happened— if he never found out how Annabelle became Bonnie, and then, like an evil magician's cabinet trick, turned back into Annabelle again...

Well, if he never found out, he'd be so angry and bitter inside he'd rot like a wormy apple.

On the other hand, he wasn't sure getting an explanation would make much difference. He might be doomed to sour from the inside out, no matter what.

He kicked the oyster-shell driveway beneath the bench and glared at the mansion, as if it were to blame. As if it had swallowed his Bonnie whole and was refusing to spit her out again.

But then he saw the big carved front door opening. He was on his feet in a flash. Even if it was just the stuffy butler coming out to warn him the police were on their way, anything was better than sitting here stewing.

A woman emerged. At first, in the shadows of the portico, she was barely visible. White shirt, long pants… Not the maid, then…

When the sunset caught her hair, he knew. *Bonnie.* His heart did that reflexive thing it always did, and his thighs flooded hot, thrumming with the urge to run toward her.

But he shoved his hands into his pockets and forced himself to wait. Not Bonnie, really. Not anymore. *Annabelle.*

She walked slowly. Carefully, as if she balanced an egg on her head. Her pace was measured, ceremonial, like a princess pacing down the wedding aisle. Or a queen walking to the guillotine.

Maybe she was buying time so that she could get her story straight.

Or maybe she was waiting for him to close the distance first.

He dug his heels a little deeper into the powdery shells of the driveway. *Not going to happen.*

"Hi," she said as she reached him. Her voice sounded rusty, as if she didn't use it anymore. Her eyes raked his face, clearly searching for clues to his mood.

He didn't respond. "Hi" seemed laughable, and everything else he could think of felt as if it came from some entirely inappropriate script. From a melodrama where people yelled things like "How *could* you?" or some slapstick comedy where the dumb cowboy went all "Shucks, ma'am" around the elegant lady.

Or, even worse, from that pathetic script where someone gushed, "You had me at *hi.*"

He set his jaw and refused to let any of that spill out. Let her do the talking. She was the one who had the explaining to do. She was the one with the secrets.

She cleared her throat and tried again. "How did you find me?"

He raised his shoulder. "Fingerprints."

*"Fingerprints?"* Her eyes widened, and he realized they did look a bit strange, now that they were set against the fantasy rose-gold of her real hair. The size of them, and the color... Nothing in the natural world should be that mesmerizing mix of blues, as if robins' eggs and sapphires and summer skies had magically melted together.

"Fingerprints," she repeated, her voice dropping slightly, as if she were disappointed in him. "Of course. The water glass."

He could have defended himself. He could have explained that Rowena had been the one to supply the fingerprints, not him. Technically, that was true. But it would have been a lie in its heart, if not in its facts.

He hadn't come all this way just to have another useless conversation laced with lies. So he simply stared at her, calmly defiant.

"I see." She clearly had taken the measure of his anger, and she now knew he hadn't come in peace. "All right, then maybe the more pertinent question is...*why* did you find me?"

He laughed harshly. *"Come on."*

"I mean it." She raised her chin. "You said you never wanted to see me again."

"No, I didn't. I said I was tired of thumping my head on the sidewalk while you used me like a yo-yo. I said I wasn't interested in being your quickie next time you snuck into town."

Her pale cheeks flamed red. To tell the truth, he felt a little flushed, too. He hadn't intended to sound quite so nasty.

"But I never said I didn't want *answers,* Bonnie. Because I damn sure do. And what's more, I deserve them. I think you owe me that much, after—"

After what? After she'd broken his heart? He

swallowed those words and gave her another hard, unblinking stare instead.

She was breathing fast. Her lips were parted a fraction of an inch, and he noticed suddenly she had a smudge of dirt right where a movie star might put a beauty mark. He glanced down, realizing she held a trowel in her left hand, its gleaming silver tip speckled with mud, too.

So at least that part hadn't been a sham—she really did love gardening. Back at Bell River, she'd always wanted to be outdoors, always wanted to be rooting around in the dirt. Once, before they'd fled from Silverdell, they'd planted a white fir sapling on the abandoned Putman property, partway up Sterling Peak. They didn't have the right—the property was in some kind of divorce dispute and couldn't be sold or occupied—but they'd liked to hike out there and dream of owning it someday.

He'd talked about the house they'd build, complete with his ridiculous inventions. She'd laid out the fantasy gardens, describing them so clearly he might as well have been looking at a painting.

He'd swallowed the dream whole, fool that he was. He was surprised he hadn't choked to death on it. She'd just been playing a game, playing house, as if she'd love to be the queen of the simple log lodge he was happily designing. *Ha.* All the while, she'd been keeping the secret of—he glanced at Greenwood, its marble arches slightly pink-gold in the sunset—the secret of *this*.

"I guess we should sit down," she said. "If you really want to hear the whole story, it's going to take a while."

She didn't seem to have any intention of inviting him into the mansion, so he dropped onto the garden bench where he'd been waiting the past half hour. He leaned against the scrolled iron back and waited some more.

She sat, too, and stared down at the trowel, which she'd rested in her lap, for several seconds. Then she looked up, met his gaze and shook her head slightly.

"I've thought about telling you all this so many times you'd think I'd have a speech ready. But it's complicated. The whole thing is so weird, so convoluted…"

"And I'm just a simple cowboy who couldn't possibly understand?"

Her eyes narrowed, and he saw her fingers close tightly around the trowel. "That's cheap, Mitch. You're not simple, and you're not even really a cowboy. And I'm not a snob. You can be angry, but you can't pretend we're strangers. I won't let you act as if all those months we spent together weren't real. I won't let you pretend *we* weren't real."

*"We?"* He shrugged, tapping his hand against the bench's cool wrought iron armrest. "Who exactly is *we?* Do you mean me and Bonnie O'Mara? Problem is, I don't see Bonnie here—

not a shred of her. So you'll have to excuse me if I don't quite know what's real and what isn't."

She flushed again—and he, who knew every nuance of her face, knew that shade of mottled red meant anger. Her flush of embarrassment was seashell-pink, and the flush of sexual desire was...

He tightened his jaw, trying to force those memories away. Forget all that—this look was pure anger. Well, fine. He might not be turning red, but he was mad, too. They were both mad as hell. Desire was a thing of the past.

She took a long breath, as if to steady her voice before she spoke. "Look, Mitch, if you want to tell me off, you should go ahead and do it. You have every right, and I won't stop you. But if you want to know the truth, you need to let me talk."

He nodded tightly. "Go ahead. I won't interrupt again."

She looked skeptical, but after a cautious second she started again. "As you can see, my grandmother, Ava, had a lot of money—some from her painting and some from her family. She left everything tied up in a life estate for my mother's use."

"Why? Why tie it up?"

"My mother had...problems." Bonnie looked away briefly. "She wasn't terribly responsible, and my grandmother obviously didn't trust her to inherit outright. But she did want to provide for her, so the lawyers suggested the life estate.

I was the first remainderman. That meant if I outlived my mother, I would inherit everything."

Mitch shook his head without really meaning to. How complicated could you get? Rich people were nuts.

Or maybe it was the lawyers who were nuts. He thought of his patent applications and the documents Indiana Dunchik had drawn up so he could sell his chore jacket to the highest bidder. The papers provided for every imaginable contingency and some that Mitch could never have imagined, not in a million years.

So of course the lawyers for the rich Ava Andersen would provide for the remote possibility that a perfectly healthy young woman might get hit by a bus or a meteor and die before her mother did. If Bonnie was the first "remainderman," there probably were ten other remaindermen behind her, just in case...

And then, finally, the lightbulb went on.

He got it. He felt like an idiot that he'd been so dense.

"Ahh," he said slowly. "So who was the *second* remainderman?"

"My cousin Jacob." She leaned back, as if she were suddenly tired. "I assume you know who Jacob is, since you found me through my fingerprints. He's my first cousin. His mother, my mother's sister, died giving birth to him, and his father, a lawyer in San Francisco, worked himself into a heart attack when Jacob was only twelve. That's when Jacob came to live at Greenwood and began to make my life hell on a regular basis, instead of just in the summers."

Mitch took a breath, but he didn't say anything.

"And—this is the part I assume you found when you looked up my prints—when I was eighteen, I was arrested for stabbing him with the pruning shears."

She didn't even glance at the trowel she held, so Mitch tried hard not to do so, either. But it wasn't easy. It was weird, almost freaky, to be sitting here with this woman who was half stranger, half lover and to be talking about wealth and violence.

Wealth and violence. He supposed those two things fit together in some sick way. People did crazy, terrible things over money. But neither word fit with Bonnie.

She paused, as if she expected him to interrupt again, probably to demand an explanation of the arrest, but he didn't. He was itching to know the truth about that, but right now he wanted her to finish telling him why she'd been on the run.

"Anyhow," she continued after a minute, "the will stipulated that if I died before my mother did, Jacob would inherit everything. No one expected that to happen, of course. My mother wasn't old, but she was very, very sick. Everyone knew she didn't have long to live. So it was almost impossible to imagine any way I would go first. Not naturally, anyhow."

*Not naturally, anyhow.* How calmly she said such a thing.

"And if you didn't die first, Jacob got nothing." Mitch took a breath, still sorting it out. His mind balked at the implications. "Are you saying your cousin wanted to kill you so he'd inherit your grandmother's fortune?"

She didn't answer for a long second. Finally, she looked him directly in the eyes. "Yes."

"Bonnie." He raised a hand, correcting himself. "*Annabelle.* Look, how much money are we talking about here? For a man to *kill*..."

"Enough. More than enough." Her voice dropped low and took on a harsh edge. "For pity's sake, Mitch, people kill each other every day. Over a bar tab, over a pair of sneakers, over a purse, a cash register, a car. Why is it so difficult to imagine that a man would kill to inherit thirty million dollars?"

"Thirty..." His jaw dropped, and he had to tell himself to shut it. "Okay. It's a lot of money. Still. Your cousin isn't exactly a pauper. And he's not a thug. I looked him up. He's a big-time lawyer, doing just fine for himself. Why would he risk all that—"

"So you don't believe me, either." The angry flush had drained entirely from her cheeks, leaving a chilled porcelain ivory behind. She sat so still she might have been a wax figure, not a woman.

"I didn't say that."

Her lips curved slightly. "You didn't have to. I know that look. I know that tone."

Of course she did. He mustn't forget that she was as familiar with every square inch of his skin as he was with hers. "Well, it does sound kind of…" He tried to think of a nonjudgmental word. "Kind of extreme."

"Crazy, you mean?" She lifted her chin. "Don't worry. You aren't the first to hint at the possibility. He is, as you say, a big-time lawyer. I'm just this spoiled, troubled heiress, the daughter of a suicidal drug addict. And I've already tried to stab him once, so it's obvious I have some paranoia issues."

"No, I don't mean crazy. But maybe…maybe just exaggerating the danger? I'm sure he was envious you got everything, and he probably gave off some fairly hostile vibes."

She laughed darkly. "Yeah. He tried to overdose me with barbiturates, so I'd say *hostile* is a fairly accurate description of his feelings for me."

"He did? How?"

"New Year's Eve. Jacob always gives a big party, and of course he had to invite me—otherwise people would talk. He must have slipped the drugs into my drink somehow. I woke up the next day in the hospital. On a ventilator."

Mitch's body temperature had dropped about ten degrees in ten seconds. The balmy California air moved over his skin like ice. "Are you sure? I mean…how do you know he was the one who did it?"

"Well, I knew *I* didn't do it. And, contrary to popular opinion, I'm not paranoid enough to think I have two different people looking to get rid of me."

Mitch frowned. "But how did he expect to get away with it?"

"Oh, that would have been easy. No one would have doubted it was suicide. It was public knowledge that my mother had tried to kill herself. Twice."

He made a low shocked sound, but she ignored it.

"And it wasn't as if he expected me to be able to deny it. He gave me a huge dose. If I really had been drinking alcohol, as everyone assumed I was, I would have died that night."

Mitch stared at her, speechless. Her own cousin didn't even realize she wasn't a drinker? He remembered all the times she'd carried a glass of soda water around at the Bell River events. She never made a thing of it, never got sanctimonious in front of people who did drink. He'd always figured it was simply a healthy-living kind of decision. Now he knew better.

The child of an addict would obviously avoid

taking any risks. And her caution had saved her life, though not in the way she'd expected.

"What about when you did wake up? Did you tell anyone? Did you tell the police?"

"No."

"For God's sake, Bonnie. Why not?"

"Because I'd been down that path before. Accusing Jacob. And I ended up in a mental-health clinic. No one was going to believe me this time, either, and while I was trying to convince them, he would have tried again. Eventually, he would have succeeded. So I ran."

"But..." He couldn't wrap his mind around any of this. "Surely the police...your friends...other family members. Hell, even a lawyer—"

"No." She shook her head implacably. "No one. There was no one I could trust."

He felt himself stiffen. "Not even me, apparently."

The sun had almost touched the western horizon, and he suddenly realized her face was almost entirely in shadows. Now, when he wanted desperately to be able to read her expression, he could hardly see a thing.

"No," she repeated. "Not even you."

It shocked him, the hot knife blade of pain that sank into him when she spoke the words. It shouldn't have been a surprise—*couldn't* have been a surprise. He wasn't a fool. He knew that if she'd trusted him, she would have confided in him months ago.

And yet, hearing her dull monotone confirm it…

"Well, that's direct." He leaned back, trying to project a detachment he didn't come close to feeling. "Guess there's no point in sugarcoating anything, not now."

"Mitch, be fair. How could I trust you? How could I trust *anyone?* My life was at stake. Even more importantly, my mother's life was at stake. Once he'd gotten rid of me, how long would he have let her stand between him and the inheritance? How long would he have let her live?"

"Did it ever occur to you," he asked slowly, "that I might have been able to help?"

She hesitated, then swallowed and shook her head. "No."

Heat radiated across his shoulders and down his arms. He couldn't decide whether it was anger or shame coursing through his buzzing veins. No? *No?* Damn it…he would have died for her. Literally. He would have *killed* for her.

But she hadn't believed him capable of providing any security. She hadn't seen him as up to the task of protecting her.

"Jacob is ruthless," she said, bending forward as if she could close the emotional distance between them by shrinking the physical gap. "He's vicious and such an expert liar. You have no idea—you can't imagine. And I'm glad you can't. You've lived with love all your life, surrounded by a family that adores you. You're sunny, and you're kind, and you think the world is good. You aren't consumed by ambition and greed. Those were the things about you I most…"

She stopped, swallowing the next word oddly. "I mean…that's what drew me to you in the first place. You were light, when all I'd known before was darkness. You understand laughter and joy. You don't understand cruelty and greed."

He made a harsh scoffing noise. "You make me sound like the village idiot."

She straightened up, as if scalded by his sardonic tone. "I'm sorry you take it that way. That isn't even remotely what I meant."

*"Sure it is."* He was so angry he could hardly keep his voice steady. He was doomed, wasn't he? He would eternally be the dopey younger brother. The likable goof. The good-time Charlie. He was used to being written off as a gadfly by Dallas, but he'd imagined that Bonnie was the one person who saw him differently.

*Wrong again, moron.* Maybe that just proved how naive and gullible he really was.

"Mitch, that isn't what I meant at all—"

"It's *exactly* what you meant. You meant that I'm good for a few laughs. I can provide a little comic relief on a boring road trip. And I'm not bad in the sack, of course, so that part was fun, too. But I'm not the kind of guy you take seriously. I'm not the person you'd trust with your secrets, your problems." He narrowed his eyes. "I'm not the man you'd trust with your life."

She was shaking her head. "No. You're twisting my words. This struggle with Jacob doesn't have anything to do with my real life or my real feelings. I just had to get through this one dangerous moment, and then—"

"And then *what?* Don't be so naive. Do you really think this is the last terrible thing you'll face?"

He stood. Coming here had been a mistake. There wasn't any such thing as "closure." There was only loss and more loss. If he'd never seen her here, with her Titian-red hair and her backdrop of opulence, he could at least have kept the memories of his Bonnie intact.

Now Bonnie and Annabelle would be forever tangled in his mind. And he would always know that neither of them had really respected him. Neither one of them had loved him. Not the way he'd dreamed.

"Mitch." She didn't move, but she looked up at him with those complicated, beautiful, haunted blue eyes, overflowing now with unshed tears. "Mitch, please."

"Troubles come to everybody, Bonnie," he said roughly. "If you live long enough. People, even careful people, occasionally end up in dark places—

in a courtroom, in a wheelchair, in chemotherapy, in disgrace. In tears, in therapy, in pain—all that's part of life. And it should be part of love, too."

"Yes. And it is." She held out one slim lily-pale hand. It trembled. "It will be."

"No, it won't. You don't think of me as a partner. You think of me as a plaything. And I have no interest in settling for that role in any woman's life."

She made a choking sound. He shrugged, thankful that, finally, numbness had set in and the pain had eased off, allowing him to come up with one final smile.

"Goodbye, Bonnie." He cast one last glance at the purpling sky, lowering itself over her mansion like a shroud. "Have a good life."

# CHAPTER FOUR

TEN DAYS LATER, when Annabelle arrived at Bell River Ranch with three suitcases in the trunk of her cheap rental car, she was carefully dressed—costumed, really—in worn jeans, faded flannel and scuffed boots. It was the way she used to look when she'd lived here before.

Except for one thing. Her hair had been dyed dark back then, and she'd quit coloring it long ago. Today, the red flame was tucked away in a coiled knot.

And her heart was in her throat.

She parked as far from the house as she could, giving herself time to adjust. She hadn't set foot on Bell River land in almost a year and a half, if you didn't count that night…the night her mother had died.

That night had been different. It was one thing to steal back in darkness as Bonnie O'Mara, to be seen by only Mitch, to spend a few secret hours in the comfort of his arms and then run away again.

It was quite another to show up in broad daylight, to announce herself to the whole family as

Annabelle Irving and to face their questions…
and, quite possibly, their hostility and rejection.

She'd decided not to approach by the front
door, but to look around outside, hoping she'd
find Rowena at work. Maybe she'd even find her
alone.

Luck was on her side. There Rowena was, standing by a fancy structure that must be the new stables. Her black hair flew in the spring breeze as she
talked animatedly to a crowd of people…guests,
judging from their too-expensive brand-new Western wear.

Ro must be matching the riders to the horses
they'd use during their stay at the ranch. Annabelle had left before the dude ranch opened, so
she'd never actually seen her friend do this. But
they'd talked about it so often. Annabelle would
be cooking or ironing, and Rowena would be
dreaming out loud, building the ranch in the air.
She'd made it real enough to touch.

Annabelle put her fingertips against the rough
splintered side of the old barn, unable to move for
a minute, overcome by a rush of emotion. She'd
been gone so long. Maybe too long.

She could already see how much the ranch had
changed. When she was last here, Bell River had
been a scrappy start-up business, struggling to
lay its ghosts to rest and build a future as a dude
ranch. Now it was sleek and polished under the
bright spring sun, beautiful against its jagged

mountain backdrop. They'd expanded the main house and put up at least a dozen new outbuildings.

And everywhere she looked, so many people. Guests and staff and…

So much change. What if it wasn't just the physical space that was different? What if it was the people, too? They'd been kind to her once, especially Rowena. They'd taken her in as unguardedly as they'd shelter a stray kitten. But she'd repaid them by breaking Mitch's heart. Mitch, the family darling, who could charm the rogue out of any horse or any woman. Any man, for that matter. His smile made the room sparkle. His veins seemed to be filled with laughter instead of blood.

Were they likely to forgive an interloper like Annabelle for lying to him, leaving him and, by doing those things, turning off all that sunlight?

She swallowed hard and tilted her face toward the sun, trying to breathe in courage. Maybe Bell River no longer had a place for her, but she *must* try. She needed to explain, partly because they deserved an explanation and partly because she intended to set things right. No matter how hard it was, no matter how long it took, she was going to get Mitch Garwood back.

Brave words, considering she had frozen in place, half-hidden behind the old barn and paralyzed with fear. Darn it, this wasn't how she'd in-

tended to start her new life. She tightened her jaw
and moved her leaden legs forward, crunching the
last patches of spring snow under her boots and
arranging a confident smile on her lips.

Rowena was so engrossed in sorting the guests
and horses she didn't notice Annabelle until she
was at the edge of the crowd. Ro glanced over,
started to glance away, then did a subtle double
take. Her green eyes grew very wide, but she
maintained her professional composure.

That made Annabelle's lips curve in a genuine smile. *Composed* and *Rowena* weren't words
used together very often. Or at least they hadn't
been, back then. Ro was all fire and energy, and
she never had seemed to pull any punches.

Now, though, she finished pairing up the current guest with a lovely young paint, then smoothly
excused herself and strode calmly to where Annabelle stood, waiting.

When she got close enough, she fisted her
hands in her riding jacket's pockets and planted
her feet several inches apart. She looked Annabelle over slowly, studying every inch of her face.

Annabelle had to fight to keep from lifting her
chin defensively. Whatever Rowena was going
to say, she probably deserved it, and she'd take it
without complaint.

Several awkward seconds passed, and then Rowena finally spoke, with that wry, throaty voice

Annabelle remembered. *"Well,"* she said cryptically.

Annabelle took a breath. She met Rowena's eyes. *"Well?"*

Rowena chuckled. "Well…well, nothing, really. I'm just surprised, that's all. Mitch said you looked like a completely different person, but then, he's in a major snit, so obviously he was overstating."

*A snit?* Was that what Ro called Mitch's intractable anger? That was definitely understating it a bit.

Annabelle wanted to break the awkward silence, but she hardly knew where to start. She had so much to say, so many apologies to make. She wanted to explain why she'd come, how she hoped she might be able to make Mitch understand and forgive, but how to begin?

"The red hair is a bit startling," Rowena said, tilting her head to continue her appraisal. "But otherwise you look exactly the same. Well, not *exactly,* but almost. You look a little sadder, but then…why shouldn't you? Mitch says your mother just died and your cousin is a homicidal, moneygrubbing sociopath."

Annabelle laughed in spite of her nerves. Rowena never had been a fan of sugarcoating.

"A sociopath who tried to *kill* you, for God's sake. Nearly getting murdered is enough to make anyone sad, and—" As Rowena's words broke off, she wrinkled her nose sheepishly. "And…

*Oops!* I'm suddenly realizing we should have this conversation somewhere more private. Come on. I'll ditch work, and we'll talk. I'll make you some tea."

She moved toward the house, but then stopped so fast that Annabelle, following closely, almost ran into her. Her feet tangled and Annabelle reached out to steady herself on Ro's elbow. Again, she had to laugh. How could she have forgotten how mercurial, how tempestuous Rowena's emotions were?

"Hey." Ro smiled. "It just occurred to me. Didn't we skip an important step?" And then, with a graceful simplicity, she held out her arms.

A hug. Such an easy thing, but everything Annabelle had hoped for was written in Rowena's dazzling smile. Ro was offering her the embrace of friendship, of forgiveness, of understanding.

Her chest muscles relaxing in a flood of relief, and her eyes welling with tears, Annabelle simply nodded, unable to form words.

"Well, okay, then!" Rowena enveloped her in an enthusiastic bear hug that left no doubt. Whether she arrived as Annabelle or Bonnie, brunette or redhead, enigma or heiress, she was still welcome in this corner of Bell River Ranch.

When they finally pulled apart, Annabelle felt a hundred years lighter.

"Come on. Tea and talk. It'll be like old times."

Still smiling, Rowena took her hand and headed for the house.

The big stone-and-wood two-story structure had been so thoroughly renovated Annabelle was a little disoriented at first. But Ro plowed on, up the back porch and then through the charming, busy rooms, giving Annabelle hardly enough time to take it all in.

Ro stopped for nothing. She smiled at guests but didn't pause to chat. She waved away a dozen staffers with questions until finally they reached a newly built wing, separated from the public areas by a small hall and a door.

"Our quiet, private Garwood haven," Ro said, putting her hand on the doorknob. "Although I'm not sure you can call a place 'quiet' when both Alec and a newborn live in it."

Annabelle pulled up, shocked. "A newborn? Is it…?" She began to smile. "Oh, Ro! You and Dallas had a baby?"

Rowena laughed as she flung the door open. "Well, frankly, I think *I* did all the work, but yeah. We named her Moira, after my mother. Moira Rose. Rosie for short. She's gorgeous, but she's a pistol. She's almost two months old now, and she's got us all wrapped around her fussy little fingers." She paused. "Didn't Mitch tell you?"

Annabelle shook her head. "We didn't talk about anything but—well, we argued, mostly."

Rowena groaned. "Oh, Mitch. You idiot."

"He's so angry, Ro." Annabelle could hear the fear in her voice. Fear that, this time, his anger might never go away. "He's angry because I never told him the truth. Because I left him."

"Oh, heaven spare me from Garwoods," Rowena growled. "They are the most stubborn men on the planet. Anyone with half a brain could figure out you only left Mitch to *protect* him."

Annabelle inhaled sharply, as if she could truly breathe for the first time in months. Rowena understood. Rowena loved Dallas, probably just as much as Annabelle loved Mitch. So she knew how impossible it would be to think you'd put the man you loved in danger. She knew you'd give up anything, even your chance at happiness, just to keep him safe.

"He doesn't see it that way," Annabelle said. "He thinks— I don't know. He's taking it personally, as if I underrated him. As if I didn't see him as man enough to trust in a crisis."

Rowena's green eyes flashed as she thought that through. "Yeah, that sounds like Mitch. *Idiot.*" But her tone was affectionate. "And you've come back to see if you can change his mind?"

"Yes." Annabelle was grateful Rowena made it all so easy to explain. "I've come to Silverdell to stay, and...if you'll have me back, I'd like to work here, at the ranch. I'll do anything, and I wouldn't want any pay. I just want to be here. I'll need chances to talk to him. To show him. And maybe I can…maybe he'll see…"

She let the words dwindle off, realizing how naive they sounded. How half-baked this plan truly was. It wasn't even a plan. It was the flailing of a drowning person, trying to splash her way back to shore.

But apparently the idea didn't sound dumb to Rowena. She narrowed her sparkling eyes and nodded. "Excellent. Okay, I'll have to think. We'll have to see what kind of work we can find. Can you start today?"

"Today?"

"Of course. In fact, yesterday would have been better." Rowena tugged Annabelle into the room and closed the door firmly behind them. Annabelle got a general impression of warm elegance, blues and creams and flowers everywhere. But she couldn't focus on anything except the female pillar of determination and grit in front of her.

Rowena was a force to be reckoned with— and, Annabelle realized with sudden gratitude, she would be a terrific ally. Ro put her hands on her hips, a sure sign she was ready to go to battle, and studied Annabelle, her eyes focused fiercely.

"Look, Bonnie. Or Annabelle. What do you want to be called?"

"Annabelle, I suppose," she said slowly. She'd thought about this a lot. She didn't want Mitch to think she was still playing games. "Or Belle.

Our gardener, one of my closest friends growing up, always called me BonnyBelle. I guess that's where I came up with Bonnie in the first place."

Rowena absorbed that a moment, then, with her usual pragmatism, moved on. "Fine. Belle works. So anyhow, Belle, I suspect you're not going to want to hear this, but there's a lawyer lady over in Grand Junction who's been hanging around Mitch for the past couple of months."

Annabelle steadied her nerves. "Well, I knew he would date. I didn't expect him to be—"

"This isn't just dating. Indiana Dunchik is her name. She's gorgeous, and she's ambitious, and she helped him patent one of his goofy inventions. A jacket that has magical properties or something."

Annabelle's mouth opened. "The chore jacket? Oh, that's wonderful, Rowena! I knew that one was a winner!"

"No, it is *not* wonderful." Rowena shook her head, as if she were talking to a child. "Focus, Belle. Believe me, I know Ms. Dunchik's type. She's trying to corral him, pure and simple. She wants to saddle him up and ride him all the way to the altar."

*The altar?* Annabelle's heart took slow dragging paces, as if it had hit an unexpected patch of molasses. She felt momentarily light-headed. *The altar.*

Had she waited too long?

"But surely Mitch isn't… He won't…"

"He might." Rowena shook her head again, but Annabelle glimpsed a soft gleam of understanding behind her eyes. "He doesn't love her, but she's clever. She knows he's wounded. And like any predator, she recognizes when it's time to close in for the kill."

Rowena sighed, as if the thought hurt her, too—or maybe she just knew how much it would hurt Belle.

"Anyhow," she said, rallying. "What I'm saying is…if you really want that idiot man back, there isn't a minute to lose."

MITCH KNEW THE dinner date was in trouble when he found himself playing the anti-Bonnie game. The game's rules were simple: every time he noticed something that was the opposite of Bonnie O'Mara, he took a swig of iced tea.

He'd played the game on every date for months right after Bonnie left, but he'd given it up a while back, finally recognizing that even the anti-Bonnie game was just one more way of obsessing about her.

Here he was, though, doing it again. By the time the bill came, he was on his fourth glass, and the waiter was looking at him funny. But Indiana made it so easy. The differences were endless. She was the epitome of the anti-Bonnie.

She wore three-inch heels, where Bonnie refused to be uncomfortable and always went for flats. *Drink*. She wore all kinds of expensive jewelry, including those ridiculous dangly earrings, where Bonnie had one pair of pearl studs she never took off, even to shower. *Drink*. She ordered the most expensive thing on offer, where Bonnie always shopped from the right side of the menu. *Drink*.

Indiana laughed at his dumb jokes, but she made refined chuckle noises through pursed lips, where Bonnie had found him so funny she sometimes had to cover her mouth to keep from spitting her tea everywhere. *Drink*.

The waiter smothered a sigh and strode over to refill his glass again.

Indiana waved the man away. With a smile, she reached her hand across the snowy tablecloth and touched Mitch's knuckles lightly. "How about we go to my place for coffee?"

Mitch summoned an answering smile, surprised at how un-thrilled he felt. Supposedly, the more points a woman scored in the anti-Bonnie game, the better. By that measure, Indiana was an A-plus. Her body was darn near perfect, too. And look at that face! The earrings kept swinging against her elegant jawline, sending out sparks of light that accented her blue eyes. Normal blue, nothing otherworldly, cryptic and mystical like Bonnie's.

*Drink*.

"Coffee sounds great," he said. Though he couldn't possibly swallow coffee, or anything else, as he was swimming in tea already, he knew she had no intention of brewing anything. *Coffee,* said in that particular tone, with that dimpling curve of the lips, was just another word for sex.

In fact, sex had been the foregone conclusion of this evening from the get-go. This was probably their fifth dinner, and they liked each other. A lot. Tonight, as he was leaving her office, she'd suggested a restaurant only two blocks from her condo here in Grand Junction. Their eyes met, and she had smiled with an honest, confident candor that said it all. She might as well have slapped a condom on the desk.

And so what? He really did like her, and not just because she was helping him make a lot of money. She was smart, beautiful, worldly, divorced and straightforward. He was tired of being alone.

If he said no to a woman like Indiana, he might as well go get fitted for a hair shirt…or a shroud.

The starry night was cool, so he gave her his jacket. Her hand was warm in his, but her long, immaculate nails grazed his skin, so unlike…

*For crying out loud! No more of that.* He was finished playing that game. If they were going to have sex, he owed it to her to be making love to Indiana Dunchik, not just the anti-Bonnie.

But he couldn't help thinking how different

her fingers would be on his skin. Some men had fantasies about long, predatory red nails tickling across intimate parts. But he'd developed a preference for scruffy, hardworking hands…. In fact, some of the best sex he'd ever had was the minute they got in the door from work, before either of them even showered to wash the mud off.

Suddenly, Indiana swiveled into his arms, and her face was so close it would have been rude not to kiss it. So he did. He dimly realized, by the warm temperature around them, that they must have entered the condo while he'd been distracted. He peeked between his lashes and noticed a lot of red and beige. Okay, not bad. A little impersonal, maybe, but a lot of elegance and a lot of clean.

Her eyes were firmly shut, so he risked looking more thoroughly. Yeah, her living room was superneat and tidy. Not a speck of dust anywhere, not a cushion out of alignment. If she had hobbies or quirks, she kept them out of sight.

He made a mental note *never* to take her to his place. Then he shut his eyes again and applied himself to the task at hand.

She knew what she was doing, and she had stamina; he'd give her that. After what seemed like several minutes, she pulled away, smiling. "Mmm," she said. "Nice."

*Yep. True.* It had been nice; he couldn't deny that. Nice like vanilla ice cream or a balmy day. Nice like this living room.

Not at all like a boiling in the blood or a storm in the senses. Not at all like—

"Come on," she said. "Let's get comfortable."

Well, that was direct, but then, he'd expected no less. He let her tug him through the sterile living room and into a large, equally sterile bedroom. As he took it in, he frowned inwardly. Had she bought the complex's display model or something? Maybe she didn't really live here full-time. Surely there should be a dumb photo or a coffee cup or a kicked-off shoe...

But nope. Nothing but an immaculately made bed and a dresser with a very large mirror that was strategically placed directly opposite. Accidental? Or was Indiana the type who liked to watch herself in action?

"I'll just be a second," she said, disappearing into the bathroom. At the last minute, she poked her head out again, still smiling. "Maybe you could get the bed ready. Turn the comforter down, okay? Four folds works best—and then you can just drape it across the armchair. Horizontally, please, or else the ends will touch the floor."

He stared at the red bedspread. Four folds? *Exactly?* Who gave a darn how many times the bedspread got folded? Who even counted?

He frowned toward the closed bathroom door, wondering what she'd do if he folded it three times, or five. And he felt his mood, which had already been lukewarm at best, go colder.

On a hunch, he stepped to the dresser and opened the top drawer. *Aw, man.* Her panties were color coded and folded better than at a store. Then, without shame—he had a right to know precisely what depth of weird he was wading into here—he walked across the room and inched the nightstand drawer open.

*Ho, boy.* A tray of condoms arranged by expiration date, with cardboard tabs separating May from June and June from July. A giant bottle of rubbing alcohol. Cotton swabs and hand sanitizer. And something that looked like an oral-sex mouth guard.

He backed away, his hands up as if to ward off evil spirits, even as he tried not to laugh out loud. *No. No.* Oh, *hell* no.

It was time he stopped being such a fool. Way past time.

He shut the drawer. "I'm sorry, Indiana," he called through the closed bathroom door. "Something's come up. I'm afraid I have to go."

BELLE HAD PARKED her rental car at the first overlook, about a hundred yards from the Putman property. She walked the rest of the way up the crooked stairway the Putmans had built first, believing the house would follow.

She loved climbing those hopeful steps, running her palm along the rough wooden rails and allowing the encroaching aspen to brush her cheeks. The night was clear, moon-washed and just cool enough to make a hike pleasant.

She loved everything about the Putman property, especially the fact that it was at least a quarter mile above any other dwelling on Sterling Peak. At the top of the stairs, you opened up on a large, meadowlike table carved by nature into the side of the hill. Dense stands of quaking aspens protected the land on three sides, but on the fourth side, the plain overlooked a view of Silverdell so magical you felt as if you were flying.

This was where she and Mitch had planned their imaginary home, ignoring the little detail that the property belonged to someone else, a John and Maggie Putman, who apparently had once imagined building a house here, too, but now held the land hostage in an ugly divorce battle.

There was a moral in that somewhere, though Belle wasn't sure what it was. *Don't dream?* She couldn't believe that. *Love never lasts?* In spite of everything, she couldn't believe that, either.

Her thighs grew warm as she climbed, though the incline wasn't steep. She was out of shape from living in a flatter landscape. But she kept going, eager to reach their spot.

In some ways, the Putman land, which didn't belong to her and never would, felt like the only real home she'd ever known. Ironic, wasn't it?

Beside her, gleaming white aspen trunks led

the way, and their leafy green tops whispered in the breeze. She'd never been here alone, even in the daytime—and yet, somehow, she wasn't a bit afraid. The moonlight was almost as bright as dawn. And besides, the memories were so powerful it seemed as if some echo of Mitch's presence walked with her.

Finally, she reached the small meadow. The closer she got to the cleared center, where an abandoned foundation slab marked the unrealized Putman dreams, the more aware she became of that lingering ghost. In fact, as she rounded the last of the aspens, her sense of Mitch was suddenly so strong that if Rowena hadn't assured her he was in Grand Junction tonight, she might have turned around and fled.

She should have.

Suddenly, there he was. Just five yards in front of her, Mitch sat on the bare ground, leaning against a spruce, with his hands locked behind his head and one knee cocked up for comfort.

He didn't see her. He was staring down at the lights of the little city below. She stared, too, as if transfixed—but she stared at the man.

The moonlight poured on him like some kind of iridescent milk, picking out every detail. His hair, shaggy and tumbled, moved in windswept waves over his forehead. The sleeves of his soft white shirt were rolled above the elbow, and the front was held together by only one button, as if he'd been swimming in the little creek that ran along the western edge of the property. Or as if he found being dressed claustrophobic.

She could have painted this picture entirely from memory—she'd seen him sit like that so many times. Most times, she'd sat with him, nestled between his legs while his hands roamed over her body and his lips burrowed into her hair... until, groaning, she had turned, and they'd made love beneath the tree.

The breeze picked up, opening his shirttails, tugging at that one button, revealing most of his muscular chest and a shockingly sexy ripple of abdomen beneath. She inhaled sharply as a spike of desire almost drove her to her knees.

At the noise, he looked over his shoulder, frowning but not alarmed. He probably assumed the sound had been made by one of the deer or cottontail rabbits they'd seen here so often in the past.

When he saw her, his leg jerked, as if it was trying to tell him to stand...or maybe to run. His thick arched brows drove together. "What the hell?"

No turning back now. She faced him with as much poise as she could muster, but, oh, this was not how she'd wanted to announce her arrival. She was hopelessly wrong-footed, off balance, unprepared.

"I'm sorry," she said. "I didn't mean to intrude.

I thought you… That is, Rowena said you were out of town."

"No." He had pulled himself quickly to his feet and stood with such casual nonchalance that you'd never know he was surprised to see her—though of course he must be. Or had Rowena told him?

"I was in Grand Junction earlier tonight, but I came back." He raised one eyebrow. "As, apparently, did you."

She flushed at the sardonic tone, too tongue-tied to answer. So much to say…but how to begin?

The breeze still tugged at his hair, his shirt—triggering old sensations, old emotions. And yet, he seemed cruelly different. Older. Harder. Harder, even, than when he'd driven out to California almost two weeks ago, overflowing with fury.

He tilted his head, waiting for a response.

"Yes, I did. I came back," she said awkwardly.

For a minute, he continued to watch her silently, the moonlight glistening against his eyes, giving him a slightly wild, undomesticated look. Then he spoke. "Want to tell me why?"

"Why? Because…because I had to."

"*Had* to? Again. Why?"

She lifted her chin, frustrated with the circular conversation. "You know why."

He laughed, and the sound sent something skittering through the tree branches above his head. "I'm afraid I haven't got a clue. Did you forget something last time you breezed through? You left in a rush, as I recall."

That wasn't fair. He knew why she'd had to run. She could have lashed back, but in this edgy, animal mood he seemed so strange, and she sensed he might subconsciously be spoiling for a fight big enough to end this once and for all.

She couldn't risk that. To make peace, she would have to be humble. She would have to be patient and honest.

"I came back for you," she said simply, but her voice was too loud, as if she had to project it across a vast distance. Funny how the few feet of rocky grass between them could feel like an unbridgeable gulf.

"For *me?*" He shook his head. "Then you've wasted the trip, Annabelle." He hesitated. "Is that the name you're using this time?"

"Yes. I mean, I've seen only Rowena so far, but I asked her to call me Belle. When I was little, I had a friend.... He called me BonnyBelle."

One side of Mitch's mouth turned up wryly. "I get it. Bonnie. Belle. *Cute.* Where did you get the O'Mara?"

She shook her head. "I don't know. I made it up. I couldn't risk using any name that was even remotely connected to my real life."

"Your *real* life." He smiled, but it was bitter. "Yeah, which means that Silverdell, Bell River, this place…" He swept one hand to indicate the Putman land. "And *me*. We're your *fake* life."

"You know that's not what I meant." She took a step forward but stopped, paralyzed by the cold glitter of his moonlit eyes. How could she make him understand, without sounding hysterical or pathetic—or crazy?

How could she explain that here, beside him, was the only place she'd ever felt entirely real? This was the only place she had been alive, awake and aware and *present,* every single second of every single day.

Back at Greenwood, she'd always felt like a thing, not a person. Even worse, sometimes, out of nowhere, she'd felt obscurely lost, a stranger to herself. And then there were the dark forgotten places…. At Greenwood, her subconscious was ragged with empty patches, zoned-out blanks, trances that might have been self-induced, designed to help her endure the unendurable.

She'd never mentioned those ragged, empty places to anyone, for fear they'd think her as unbalanced as her mother.

Even now, to her own ears, the words sounded slightly mad. She couldn't speak them, even to him. All she could do was ask him to forgive her.

She gathered herself and kept her voice as composed as possible.

"Mitch, I—"

"No. Wait. I want to ask you something."

The question was curt. It was the tone he might take if an acquaintance had borrowed money long, long ago, and Mitch was forced to demand an overdue payment.

"All right." She nodded. "What is it?"

"Why did we leave Bell River in the first place? You'd been here, and everything seemed okay, for months. Then, out of nowhere, you say you've got to run again. What brought that on? Were you just bored here?"

She frowned at him. "I'll answer any real question, Mitch, but not insults posing as questions."

"Okay. *Real question.* Why did we have to leave here in the first place?"

She tried to think of a succinct way to sum up the dreadful pain of that day. The day she'd realized she'd been betrayed by her only friend.

"The friend I just mentioned. The one who called me BonnyBelle? He was our gardener, an older man named Fitz, and he was my only real friend back at Greenwood. He was a genius with growing things, and he nurtured me as if I were one of his most precious flowers. So when I ran away, he was the only one I kept in touch with, the only person who knew anything about why I left or where I went."

Mitch's eyes were unreadable. She would have liked to tell him about Fitz, about the way he'd taught her gardening, starting when she was so young she'd believed each flower had a name and a personality.

Fitz had talked to her—and about her—in flower metaphors. "You're a shrinking violet today, Bonny-Belle, but someday you'll be as bold and bright as a sunflower, just you wait."

And he'd been right. Traveling with Mitch, she'd briefly been that sunflower, her protective petals unfurled, leaving her heart open and exposed. She'd felt sturdy-stalked and tall, able to grow free by streams and roadsides, as long as Mitch was with her.

What a joy it had been. At Greenwood, she'd always seemed like one of those fragile, strange, pale flowers taken out of their natural element and kept in a pot in a temperature-controlled greenhouse.

But she was taking too long. Mitch's cold gaze was waiting for the rest of the answer.

"Anyhow, Fitz has a wife, a wonderful woman. Marlene. And Marlene got sick…."

She shook her head, realizing she was still getting stuck in details, and he was getting impatient. "The bottom line is that Jacob got to him. He gave up everything he knew about where I'd settled, which wasn't much, thank goodness. I'd given him only a post-office box in Montrose. But that was close enough."

He didn't react to the information. He just nodded, then asked another clipped question.

"And that day in Maine, when you walked out on me. Why did you do it? Why that day, instead of any other?"

This was easier to explain…or at least a little less emotional, as it hadn't involved being betrayed by anyone. It had simply been one of those impossible bits of horrible luck. No one's fault, but fatal nonetheless.

"Someone had recognized me. Someone from Sacramento, who knew Jacob. She was vacationing there. She'd seen you, which meant Jacob would learn that you were traveling with me. It would be so much easier for him to track down two people than just one. So I had to go on alone."

His face remained expressionless. "And it wasn't even safe to tell me that much? I had to think you simply got sick of traveling with six feet of excess baggage?"

"No, it wasn't. Can't you see? I didn't know whether he might try to use you to find me. If you were genuinely angry, if he was convinced you knew nothing and no longer cared, then he had no leverage."

She searched his face for any sign he understood, that he recognized the truth of her logic. She found none.

A low-level thrum of nerves began humming in her midsection. "Mitch, I know I've hurt you. I know you think you can never forgive me. But

I've come back because I want to try to make things right. I've come back because I lov—"

"No." He held the word up like a shield to prevent her voice from reaching him. "Don't say it. I'm sorry, but it's too late for that, Bonnie. *Belle*. I know you mean well, but it's just too late."

Her heart thumped hard. "Why? Have you…?" She swallowed. "This woman you were with tonight. Ro said she was afraid you might be getting serious. Is it too late because you…because she…"

"It doesn't have anything to do with other women," he said. He ran his hand through his tousled hair and took a deep breath, which stretched his shirt open across his chest. As he exhaled, his hostility seemed to drain away, leaving a heavy weariness behind that was somehow more frightening than anger.

"It's about me, Belle. About what I feel. Or, more accurately, what I *don't* feel."

What he didn't feel? The sentence made her heart race.

"Mitch, please. Don't give up on us. I know you were upset I didn't tell you the truth. I understand why you're angry—"

"I'm not, not anymore." His tone was terrifyingly calm, and suddenly the wind moved on her skin like frigid, hostile fingers. "I'm just… over it. I don't want to be stuck in this emotional quicksand anymore. I'm ready to move on, and you should, too."

"I can't." She put her fist up to her chest.

"Of course you can."

Desperate, she closed the distance between them with a few paces, and she put her hand against his cheek. His face felt cool, but her skin flamed at the touch.

She gazed into his eyes and found them so empty it shocked her. Never, from the first moment they'd met, had they been able to touch without an instant and uncontrollable fire.

Those flat eyes said his fire had been snuffed out.

She tried to speak, but she had difficulty dragging air into her lungs, which suddenly seemed frozen.

"Look, I understand why you wanted to try. I really do." He smiled sadly. "A month ago—hell, maybe even yesterday—I might have done the same thing. But tonight… Tonight I finally realized I've been acting like a fool. For a long time now, I've been clinging to something that doesn't exist."

He took her hand and lowered it from his face. "I don't want to hurt you. But you should go home. There's nothing left for you here."

# CHAPTER FIVE

THE MINUTE MITCH opened the door to Dallas's part of the house the next afternoon, Alec barreled into him like a love-starved rottweiler.

"Uncle Mitch! Thank God you're here! This party is the pits!"

Mitch didn't bother feeling flattered. Alec always wanted attention, and since today was Rosie's two-month birthday celebration, he was unlikely to get it from anyone but his uncle.

Any infant was stiff competition, but Rosie was an adorable princess, complete with candy-heart mouth and pink chipmunk cheeks. Now, that might sound boring, but Rosie rocked it with her own flavor, adding a shock of black hair that stood straight up and a temper like a drunken sailor. When she started screaming, you just knew she was cussing a blue streak in Baby.

So an annoying ten-year-old boy didn't have much of a chance. Which was why Mitch always made a special effort to fuss over Alec when he was around.

"Yeah? Boring?" Mitch grinned. "Does that

mean Rosie hasn't pitched a fit yet? Why? Is she sick or something?"

"No, she's not sick," Dallas broke in, ruffling Alec's head affectionately as he sauntered up with a tray of sandwiches. "She's just waiting for the worst possible moment. She has impeccable timing."

Rowena, who was right behind him with a pitcher of iced tea, swatted Dallas with her free hand. "Watch it, buster," she said. "That's my daughter you're talking about."

Dodging the blow, Dallas winked at Mitch. "I meant…Rosie is being her usual angelic self, like her mommy. The part about waiting for the worst possible moment—did I say that out loud?"

"Where is the little angel, anyhow?" Mitch snatched a sandwich, took a bite and glanced around the crowded room. All the sisters were here: Ro, Bree and Penny and Tess, and that many Wright women in one place could cramp any quarters. Once you added their husbands and offspring, you didn't need extra guests to make a party. Though of course they always had at least half a dozen others, too. Their ranch manager, Barton James, had adopted them as family, and Fanny Bronson, who owned the local bookstore, was already building a library for Rosie, one mini-birthday at a time.

"Rowan is holding her," Alec said dismissively.

"You'd think she was the only baby on earth, the way they carry on."

Mitch smiled. Alec would probably never understand the delicate dynamic between Rowena and her biological father, Rowan Atherton-Reese, though he went by Atherton.

Rowena had discovered Atherton's existence only recently and had struggled with her natural fear of rejection for a long time before she could bring herself to contact the man. But the birth of the baby that would be Dr. Atherton's grandchild had finally broken down the barriers.

Rowan Atherton, who had been in a wheelchair most of his life, ever since a skiing accident he'd suffered before he'd learned that Moira was pregnant with his child, had burst into their lives the very night little Rosie was born. Literally. He'd rolled right up to the hospital door and announced he wanted to see his daughter.

And he had hardly been able to tear himself away since. Supposedly, he was a bigwig at a hospital over in Crested Butte, but Mitch would be darned if he could see how the man did any work. For two months, he'd pretty much always been here, bringing Rowena presents and cooing over the kid.

Even Mitch, who couldn't be accused of being sentimental, could get a little teary thinking about that miraculous happy ending for Rowena—and Rowan, too. She'd finally found a father. Atherton had found a daughter and a granddaughter, all in one night. A love reborn from the ashes of his old love. It was pretty good stuff.

But Alec saw only an old guy who wasn't interested in horses and clearly thought little girl babies were more important than preteen boys.

A young voice called from across the room. "Alec, come here!"

Alec glanced over, spotting Ellen, Penny's ten-year-old stepdaughter and Alec's best buddy. Instantly Alec's face brightened, and he lost interest in the uncle he'd been so delighted to see.

"Gotta go," he called over his shoulder, and he took off across the room. "Ellen, wanna go see a toad somebody ran over with the tractor? It's so disgusting you won't believe it!"

Yep. That was Alec, all right. For a split second, Mitch wished he could go outside with the kids. Toad roadkill did sound like more fun than trying to figure out whether little Rosie's smile was happiness or indigestion, which seemed to be dominating the conversation over there right now.

Rowena had moved away, too, which left Dallas and Mitch alone for the moment. Dallas was ominously quiet, and Mitch searched for a meaty topic to bring up before his protective big brother could start in on—

"So. You okay? About Belle?"

*Too late.* Mitch stifled a groan. He did not want

to talk about this. "Of course I'm okay. She came. She left. Life goes on."

Dallas frowned. "What do you mean, she left?"

Mitch rotated a shoulder, trying to make his jacket more comfortable. Why in tarnation did they have to dress up for a baby's two-month birthday party? Why all the pink balloons, just because she happened to be born on Valentine's Day? Why a cake and presents and all this fuss?

A minute ago, he'd found the fairy tale charming. Now, with one mention of Belle, it irritated him.

"I mean she left. We saw each other last night, and I told her she'd made a mistake coming here. I'm over it—the drama, the lies, the manipulation. I told her to go home."

"Yeah? Well, that's interesting. Because she didn't."

"Didn't what?"

"Didn't go home." Dallas smiled. He tilted his head subtly toward the kitchen, where, suddenly, Mitch could clearly see Belle, Tess and Penny laughing over the candles they were trying to light on the little pink birthday cake.

Belle scratched a match against its box, and the small light glowed across her face, turning her cascade of hair into a peach-colored fire.

"See? There she is. Still here, and obviously firmly ensconced in the bosom of the family."

Dallas sounded as if he might start laughing. "Turns out you're not the boss of her after all."

Mitch could hardly hear his brother's teasing words.

*Oh, Lord, she is beautiful.*

His chest and shoulders tightened instinctively, as if bracing for someone to punch him in the chest. *Damn it. Now what?* He'd been so proud of himself last night. He should have won a bloody award for that performance. He'd been so sure he'd convinced her his feelings for her were dead.

Heck, he'd been so good he'd almost convinced himself.

*Now what?* He could keep the pretense up a few minutes, maybe even a few hours. But if she was planning to stay...

*Hang on, there,* he told himself. He wasn't that weak, was he? She was probably just staying for the party so that she could meet Atherton.

But if it wasn't a temporary thing...

Well, if she stayed, he'd just have to try harder. And if he kept his indifferent facade up long enough, eventually it wouldn't be a pretense anymore. Sooner or later, if he didn't feed the flames, the pointless passion would die a natural death.

He shrugged, smiling at Dallas blandly. "Well, it's her decision, I guess. No big deal to me, either way."

Dallas did laugh, finally. "Suuure," he drawled. Then he shifted the platter of sandwiches, patted

Mitch on the shoulder and moved on, the echo of his chuckle floating back on the chatter-filled air.

For a minute, Mitch simply stood, feeling oddly disembodied, as if he were separated from the party and from his own body by some invisible barrier. A weird, embarrassing tension that felt like panic built inside his veins. He had to root himself in place in order to keep from bolting out the back door.

But how obvious would that be? Everyone who had eyes would see what it meant. Heck, even little Rosie would probably know her uncle Mitch was a coward, afraid of a showdown with an old girlfriend.

No, the smart thing to do was to walk right into that kitchen and say, "Hey, Annabelle," then yawn, or kiss his pretty friend Marianne Donovan, or stick his finger into the cake and lick the icing off while Tess scolded him.

The smart thing was to show, right off the bat, that Belle was no more significant than an ant at his picnic.

But before he could move, the ladies came sailing out of the kitchen, the sparkling cake held before them.

"Happy birthday to you!" The room picked up the tune, which made little Rosie's eyes widen in shock. "Happy birthday to you!"

Penny and Tess sang pretty well, but all Mitch could hear was Belle's sweet, slightly off-key alto.

His gut churned, and he cursed himself for being such an easy target.

When the singing finally ended, and everyone headed for the table to grab a piece of cake, he made his way over to Belle. He wasn't going to be able to avoid her forever. Might as well get it over with.

Before he could reach her, though, Rowan Atherton put out a hand and caught hers. She bent down with a smile to talk to the older man, and by the time Mitch arrived, the two of them were deep in conversation.

Obviously, Rowan was flattering her. Mitch knew that splotchy pink on her cheeks—it always came when she was getting more compliments than she knew how to handle.

"Why didn't anyone tell me Bell River was playing host to such a famous guest, Mitch?" Atherton looked up at Mitch, his intense green gaze so like Rowena's. "When she walked into the room this morning, I couldn't believe my eyes! The exquisite Annabelle Irving, in the flesh. I thought I must be dreaming."

Belle blushed even more furiously and shook her head, trying to dismiss the effusive praise. "Dr. Atherton, really, I—"

"Please. Call me Rowan. Like so many people, I feel as if I've known you for years, merely from the paintings. But now I see that even your grandmother's talent couldn't possibly do you justice."

*Oh, brother.* The damn man was so suave and courtly. Mitch had an overwhelming urge to punch him in the nose. Naturally an educated, renowned surgeon would be an art enthusiast and would know who Annabelle was.

But Atherton clearly didn't know how ambivalent she was about her identity. Belle's discomfort radiated out like heat waves. As if Rowena's sixth sense caught an SOS, suddenly Belle's name rang out from the kitchen.

With an apologetic smile, Belle excused herself, murmuring something about ice cream.

As she slipped away, Mitch saw Rowan's gaze following her intently.

"My God. *Annabelle Irving,*" the older man murmured softly, tapping long fingers against the arms of his wheelchair. He blinked, then glanced up at Mitch. "I bid on Number Three once. I lost, of course. Out of my league. So to actually meet her…" He sighed.

"Do you really think she looks like those paintings? I don't." Mitch smiled coolly, giving the man a challenging stare. On some level, he realized how silly it was to feel competitive with Rowena's father. The guy obviously wasn't flirting with Belle, who could have been his daughter. And yet…

Rowan looked curious. "No? How so? She was still a child in most of them, of course. But by Number Twelve, or at least by the teen years…"

His inward glance seemed to be scanning the pictures, which he obviously knew well. "I think her essence was captured brilliantly."

Mitch made a scoffing sound under his breath. "*Captured* is the perfect word. The girl in the oils is a chauvinistic fantasy, part child, part domesticated pet. No brain. No reality. No spark."

"Hmm. Interesting analysis."

Mitch waited, knowing he hadn't been exactly diplomatic, given how much Atherton apparently loved the paintings. And yet, his open mind was Atherton's most likable trait. He held strong opinions and clearly was accustomed to carrying any argument, and yet he always listened. And he heard.

"I take your point," the older man said finally. "She is even more compelling as a living, breathing woman. And yet a million art fans, who have been in love with the fantasy Annabelle for decades, would violently disagree with you."

"Whatever." Mitch shrugged. "Their call. I won't lose any sleep over it."

Rowan's eyes narrowed thoughtfully. "No, you wouldn't, would you? You're far more likely to lose sleep over the living, breathing woman." He smiled at Mitch's instinctive frown. "Too blunt? I'm sorry. I'm accustomed to speaking my mind. That's why people hate doctors."

Mitch forced himself to relax, even managing a smile.

"Well, that and colonoscopies," he said and chuckled softly. He put his hand on Atherton's shoulder, signaling a truce. "Excuse me a minute. There's something I should do."

Without any further dithering, he went straight into the kitchen. Luckily, Belle was alone now. It wasn't a large area—carving out any private quarters in the main house hadn't been easy for Rowena and Dallas. Providing gracious public rooms ate up most of the space.

Belle looked up, as if she had sensed his approach even before she saw him. With a composed face, she smiled politely, but her hands continued their work digging out ice cream from containers.

"Hi," she said. She surveyed the half-dozen pints arranged on the countertop in front of her. "I'm assuming it's still chocolate chip for you?"

"Yeah." Since the first cone he'd ever licked, at about three. "But I didn't come in for ice cream."

"I know." She glanced up at him calmly. "You came in to find out why I'm still here."

"Not exactly. You were friends with Rowena before I ever met you. So I get that you might want to spend time with her and meet the baby and her dad and all that. Heck, you'd probably like to see everyone at Bell River. It's been a while."

"Yes. It has. I've missed Bell River a lot. I was happy here."

"I understand that." He shifted from one foot to the other. "But I just hope you aren't thinking… I mean, I want to be sure I made things clear last night."

She put down the metal scooper, which glistened with creamy beige, quickly melting vanilla. Her fingertips were coated in the thick, pale goo, but she didn't seem to notice. She took a deep breath.

"Yes. You made it very clear. You're not interested in trying to patch things up between us, and you'd prefer that I go back to California."

"So…" This wasn't easy, especially if he wanted to be polite. He didn't have the right to order her to leave. Bell River wasn't his, not even close. He was just the little brother of the guy who had married one of the sisters who owned it.

But how would he endure it if she stayed? How could he cope with the fire that started to burn him up from the inside every time he looked at her? Even now, he wanted to lick the ice cream from her fingers and then take the rest and spread it all over her body and lick that off, too.

He gripped the countertop and tried to pull himself together. He forced himself not to look at her hands. "So what have you decided?"

For a long minute, she didn't answer. Her body had gone very still, in that way she had, where she seemed to separate her soul from her body in times of stress. It was eerie, unnatural—and it had been a long time since he'd seen her do it. The months they'd been together, on the run, she'd seemed happy, just a normal gal enjoying life with the guy she loved.

The last time she'd gone into that remote, trancelike stillness had been the night before she left him. Looking at her, sitting more like a statue than a woman on the bed in that cheap hotel room in Castle Hill, Maine, he'd known that something bad was about to happen.

He just didn't know how bad.

When he woke, she was gone, leaving a short note behind. "I'll be safe as long as you don't look for me." He wondered how long she'd worked on that line, creating the perfect eleven-word road-block to stop him in his tracks.

So what was driving her back into her shell now, making her stand like a mannequin while ice cream melted all around her? Was it being back here? Was it knowing Mitch wanted her to leave?

"Bonnie." He reverted to the old name without being sure why. "What have you decided?"

"I'm staying," she said, blinking as if awakening again after a long sleep. "At least for a while."

"I see." He tried to think of anything else he could say. But there wasn't anything clever in his brain.

She wiped her fingers on a kitchen towel absently. "You're right about Rowena—I do want to spend some time with her. We have so much to catch up on."

She glanced toward the main room, where the party was in full swing. Someone had started a game of four square with balloons, and the air rippled with bouncing, floating pink Mylar.

"But it's more than that. I need some quiet time right now. I have a lot of decisions to make. A lot of things to sort out before I can decide what I want to do with my life."

*Quiet time? Here? What a crock.*

"I'm sure you do," he said, an edge to his voice. "It can't be easy, being a famous heiress with a mansion and millions and all that stressful stuff."

She didn't seem to notice the sardonic tone. She merely nodded, as if what he'd said was true. "Yes, deciding what to do with Greenwood is probably the most difficult..." She knit up the space between her brows, her blue eyes clouding. "And I can't think there. Too many memories. Too many questions. Too many—"

"Too many what? Servants? Sycophants? Suitors?" He bit his lower lip as soon as the words were out. What was wrong with him? He sounded as petulant as Alec.

She lifted her eyes. Her expression was softly accusing, as if he'd disappointed her. "Ghosts. I was going to say too many *ghosts*. But you're right. There's too much of all those things, as well."

He felt himself flushing. He really was kind of a jerk.

"Anyhow," she went on briskly. "I decided to stay here for a while, to think things over and settle my mind. Rowena has said I can do odd jobs around the ranch, just to keep busy. And apparently one of the new cottages on the eastern edge is still unoccupied. She'll let me rent that one. Of course, I'll pay full price, and if she needs it for a guest I'll be happy to—"

"The eastern edge?" Belatedly, her words sank in. "That's over by mine."

"I know." She lifted her chin, but it didn't hide the emerging splotch of pink on her cheeks. Of course she knew. She'd found him there, the night she'd come home, and they'd knocked all his pictures off the wall in their clumsy stumble back to the bed. "Is that a problem for you?"

"It's ridiculous. If Ro thinks she can play matchmaker...if she thinks that proximity is enough—"

"It's the only cabin open right now." Belle widened her eyes. "I told her it wasn't a problem. You've made it clear you feel nothing for me anymore. I was under the impression I could belly dance naked on your breakfast table and you wouldn't glance up from your coffee."

She paused, which gave him plenty of time to visualize that. "Was I wrong?"

Though anger was building in his veins, he had to laugh. They really did think he was a child, didn't they? They thought they could move him across the emotional chessboard at will. Dangle sweet, beautiful Bonnie in front of him long enough, and he'd leap right onto the hook, dumb as a big-mouth bass.

He wondered if she and Rowena had cooked this up by themselves or if Dallas and the rest of them had been in on it. Heck, this plan was juvenile enough it could have been Alec's idea. Everyone at Bell River, right down to the housekeepers, felt sure they could handle Mitch's life better than he could.

Well, he'd show them. Bring on the belly dancing. He could handle that and so much more. He cocked his head, grabbed a spoon and the pint of chocolate-chip ice cream and dug in with a smile.

"Nope," he said as he shoveled a heaping mound of drippy chocolate toward his mouth. "You're not a bit wrong. You have my blessing, Annabelle Irving. Welcome to the neighborhood."

*"SERIOUSLY?"* MITCH LOOKED at the woman who had just come up and bet him ten bucks on the next game of pool. Better looking than any female in the Happy Horseshoe tonight, she was a stranger to him. If he'd met her before, he'd remember it.

She wore the skinniest jeans he'd ever seen, a head full of spiky red hair and a motorcycle jacket. And she was giving him the once-over, every bit as openly as he was studying her.

"I mean...*seriously*." He chalked his cue tip slowly, aware that over the past three hours Jude Calhoun, his best friend, had been plying him with more beer than he'd drunk in the past three years.

Memory-stomping beer, Jude called it. Four hours ago, after a long weekend trying to get his head straight, Mitch had decided that the best way to deal with Bonnie's return was to get plastered and play pool. Jude had come along as babysitter.

Mitch focused on the woman again. "Your name is seriously Crimson Slash?"

"This year it is," she said with a crooked smile. "And you're Mitch Garwood, right?"

"Right." He smiled back. She had a lot of humor in that grin and a lot of curves in those skinny jeans. And he had a lot of Dos Equis on his bar bill. "Do I know you?"

"Not yet." She shrugged, moving past him to analyze the lay of the table. "I work over at Needles 'N Pins."

He looked blank.

"Needles 'N—you know. The tattoo parlor?"

"Oh." His mind felt embarrassingly fuzzy. "Oh, yeah."

"Anyhow, I've been expecting you to come in and ask for a big red heart on your biceps with the name Bonnie in it. But now the word on the street is you're not likely to do that."

"I'm not?"

"Nope." She winked at him as she bent over. "*Stripes.* So anyhow, I decided I'd have to make the first move."

Was this for real? Mitch glanced over at Jude, who had dragged himself away from his fiancée, Tess Spencer, just this once because Mitch needed company. Jude gave him a wide-eyed, innocent stare that said he knew nothing about Crimson Slash. Nothing at all.

Mitch wasn't sure he believed that. Jude was quite capable of trying to set Mitch up with someone, anyone, just so he could get back home. He and Tess were in those first few irritating months of new love, where the air around them positively sparkled with sugary hearts and stars.

"Well, Crimson," Mitch said as he lined up for his shot. "I've gotta tell you. I'm not a fan of fake names."

She ran her fingers through her spiky hair. "Okay. And I've gotta tell *you*—" big smile and then a chuckle as he missed "—I couldn't care less."

For some reason, that seemed like the ideal answer. They played in silence the rest of the game, and she beat him easily. He had a feeling she could have beaten him with one hand tied behind her back. He hadn't been to the Horseshoe in months, not since his birthday. He was as rusty at pool as he was at drinking beer. Or flirting with redheads.

When they were done, he reached in his pocket and pulled out a ten. She took it politely.

"How about I buy you a drink with this?" She glanced toward Jude. "Your friend, too, if he's staying."

"I'm not," Jude said, holding up a hand. "Tess needs me." He patted Mitch on the back. "And you obviously don't."

Mitch nodded, setting the poor guy free. Then he scooted up onto the bar stool next to Crimson.

"I should probably explain," he said, glad that, though his head felt wooly, his tongue still could form a firm $X$ sound. "I didn't come here tonight looking for a female. Truth is, I came because I'm finished with females forever."

Crimson slid a beer toward him expertly enough that he wondered whether she might have been a bartender before she was a tattoo artist.

"Good," she said. "Because I'm not going to have sex with you tonight."

He nodded sagely. "No, ma'am, you are not." He drank half the beer in one swig. Then he wondered whether that statement had sounded ungallant.

"Look. You seem like a very nice lady, but I'm sorry to say I don't have sex anymore." He stared down into the rest of the beer. "I'm very, very, *very* sorry to say it, but it's true."

"Is that so?" Crimson seemed to be able to drink even faster than he did, because she was already calling for a refill. Maybe, he thought, that was why her hair stood up straight. Then he realized that didn't make a whole lot of sense.

*Aw, hell.* He'd gone and let himself get drunk.

"And this eternal celibacy." She handed him a fresh bottle. "It's because of Bonnie?"

"Yep." He started to drink, then put the bottle down, frowning at Crimson. "How do you know about Bonnie?"

She laughed. "Are you kidding? You two are like the Romeo and Juliet of Silverdell."

He widened his eyes, and she laughed again.

"Yeah, I know who Romeo and Juliet are. You have some fairly clichéd stereotypes about body modification artists, you know that, Mitch? I was an English major before I apprenticed as a tattooist. And an art major before that. Needles 'N Pins pays better than any of them."

"I wasn't surprised that you knew— I mean…" He tried to remember why he'd made a shocked face, but it seemed like a long time ago. "I guess I was just surprised that everyone knows about Bonnie. And me."

"Well, she's famous, isn't she? So naturally we're interested."

"She wasn't famous to me. She was just Bonnie. I'd never heard of Annabelle Irving."

Crimson chuckled. She had a very nice laugh. She sounded like...kind of soothing. "Yeah, well, you weren't an art major."

"Nope. I wasn't an anything major. I took some business classes while we were running around the country, but we never settled anywhere long enough to call it going to college. I did invent a chore jacket, though." He wondered why he felt the need to defend himself. "You'd be surprised how much money people will pay for a chore jacket."

"Probably wouldn't," she said. "Not much surprises me anymore."

"Ah," he said sadly. He knew what that meant. Crimson Slash had a story, too. Everyone had a story. Difference was, most people's stories had happy endings. His, on the other hand...

"Look, Mitch Garwood. I like you."

He glanced up, glad he hadn't actually worked himself into enough self-pity that his eyes were watering. "I like you, too, Crimson," he said sincerely. "But I'm still not going to have sex with you. I'm really, really not. I tried that, with Indiana, and it was a disaster. A frigging fiasco."

She laughed out loud. "You tried to have sex with the entire state of Indiana?"

"No. Just one woman. But wow. She was loony tunes." He held up a hand quickly. "I'm not implying you're loony tunes. I'm just saying I've got issues, you know? And I'm pretty sure sex is not the answer."

Still smiling, Crimson opened her little silver purse, a surprisingly girlie thing, considering the motorcycle jacket, and extracted a small white card.

"I think you're right," she said. "Here's my card. I'd like to see you again, when you're sober. I'd like to have dinner or something. And don't worry about the sex. I never sleep with a guy until at least the seventh date. Tenth, if he's on the rebound." She tilted her head. "With you, I'm thinking an even dozen, at least. Or more."

He liked the way she left the number open. Indiana would have had an Excel spreadsheet charting the exact number of dates it would take.

So he accepted the card. "Crimson Slash," it read. "Body modification artist." And a red heart with a jagged black lightning bolt right through it.

An electrocuted heart. Yep, she had a story, all right. He knew that story.

"Sound good?" She seemed to be waiting for an answer.

"Sounds good," he said, surprised to realize he was telling the truth. Twelve dates without pressure to get serious. Twelve dates to see if he could possibly care about anyone but...

Suddenly he was sobering up, just a little.

Crimson slid from her bar stool, then hesitated

and turned around with a quizzical glance. "You're not driving tonight, right?"

"Of course not." He didn't have his motorcycle with him. Jude had driven them both, and he'd probably gone home believing that Mitch would hitch a ride with Crimson Slash. "My brother has a place down the street. I'll crash there."

She seemed comfortable with that and, with a final smile, sauntered out of the bar, every man in the place following her confident hip action.

After a decent interval, Mitch paid his bill and strolled out into the crisp, silver-starred evening. Technically, he could walk home. Bell River was only a two-mile trek from the center of town, but no way he was showing up at his cabin alone, pathetic and addled with alcohol. Everyone—and by *everyone* he meant Bonnie—would be able to see him stagger in.

His brother did indeed have a place nearby. The Silverdell County Sheriff Department had a drunk tank that was almost never used. He could sleep it off in privacy, on the taxpayer's dime. He and Chad, Dallas's deputy, could play cards.

But what if Chad told even one person? What if Chad's mom stopped in with cookies, which she often did when Chad drew the overnight shift? Mrs. Bartlett was sweet and dotty and couldn't keep her mouth shut. It would be all over Silverdell before breakfast.

No, he needed a safer landing spot. He glanced

down Elk Avenue, mostly shut tight on a Sunday night, and saw a light on in the windows above Donovan's Dream. Marianne Donovan lived above her café, and, even better, the two of them had already toyed with the idea of becoming lovers and decided against it.

*Feh.* What had happened to him that he was actually relieved to have "friends" instead of "dates"?

As he climbed the outdoor staircase up to Marianne's apartment, his mind began to clear. Maybe it was the exercise, maybe the cold night air. Or maybe the depressing thought of working his way through the entire town, turning every hot woman who wanted to sleep with him into a buddy. Buddies *without* benefits.

Whatever it was, by the time he reached the top of the stairs, he was practically sober. And he knew what he should do.

He was twenty-seven, financially independent, emotionally liberated and sick of being a hanger-on at his brother's wife's dude ranch, especially now that Rowena had clearly launched her little "Fix Mitch" project.

The simple beauty of the plan temporarily paralyzed him, leaving his hand raised, frozen in the moment before knocking.

But it was obviously the answer. Why on earth hadn't he thought of this before?

It was time to get the devil out of Silverdell.

# CHAPTER SIX

MONDAY MORNING. AS she reported for work at Bell River Ranch, Belle felt as light as one of little Rosie's balloons, as if she carried her heart on a string. Silly, really, to be so excited. She had no idea what tasks Rowena would assign her. And obviously her plan to reconcile with Mitch had hit a serious roadblock, if not a dead end.

But still…just being back here, where the air smelled of melting snow and budding wildflowers, where the horizon was ringed with mountains and the pastures were alive with horses…

She was happier here than she'd ever been anywhere. Even when she and Mitch had been traveling together, she'd always felt Jacob's shadow at her back. She'd always known that someday, someone would recognize her, and she'd have to run again, leaving Mitch behind, perhaps forever.

It had been like living with a terminal disease, pretending to be well but knowing, in your heart, that any day could be your last.

Now, at least, the fear of physical danger was gone. The worst had already happened, and she could start climbing toward her future—however uncertain that might be.

For a week or so after Belle's very public appearance at the auction, Jacob had been on his very best behavior, sending flowers and cards, calling, asking to be allowed to come see her. She'd refused, and eventually the calls had stopped.

And that had been followed by total silence.

Unnerving silence. In her gut, she couldn't believe he'd simply fold his cards and go away. He was undoubtedly consulting attorneys, tearing Ava's will apart, word by word, looking for a weak spot. But what else would he do? What else might be brewing in that weird, unnatural silence?

She'd nearly driven herself mad wondering, but then she realized that, by obsessing about his plans, she was still letting Jacob control her life. So she packed a bag and drove to Bell River.

But was Mitch still interested in being a part of her future? Saturday night, on the Putman property, she might have said no. Those dead eyes, like a hearth filled with nothing but cold ashes.

But the other day, when she'd seen him at Rosie's birthday party, there had been something in his gaze…

Something that hinted there might be hope after all. It might have been no more than wishful thinking, but she wasn't ready to give up yet. Maybe all she needed was time.

"Hey, there!" Rowena, who had been kneeling in the dirt, digging in a small vegetable garden at the back of the main house, stood with a smile. She wiped her hands on a small towel. "Perfect timing. I've gotta go feed Rosie, anyhow. Ready to get started?"

Belle nodded. "I can't wait. I've imagined Bell River, up and running, so often. It feels like a dream to actually be here."

"More like a nightmare sometimes," Rowena said, but she was still smiling, so Belle didn't take it seriously. No human loved a piece of land more than Rowena loved Bell River. "This garden, for instance, is clearly cursed. I got five puny carrots last year, and looks like this year is going to be even worse."

Belle eyed the small vegetable garden, marked off by scallop-edged concrete borders and braced with painted railroad ties. A few leafy green mounds whiffled in the morning breeze, but most of the growth was too undeveloped and low to the earth to be touched.

"It might be the location," Belle said, squinting up at the bright sky. "This spot doesn't have much shade, and if you get a dry spell, your plants are going to experience a lot of water stress." She looked down again, scanning the garden quickly.

"Also, you probably should avoid bark in your mulch. It'll deplete the nitrogen."

Rowena smiled. "I thought you were an artist," she said. "Not a botanist."

"Oh, I'm definitely not an artist." Belle reached down and plucked a ribbon of crabgrass. No gardener ever spotted crabgrass and ignored it. "I haven't painted anything in a year or more, if you don't count doodles on restaurant napkins."

"You haven't?" Rowena frowned. "That's really a shame. Your talent is amazing. Though I probably wasn't supposed to see it, Mitch has a sketch you drew of him that's just fantastic."

"He kept that?" Belle's eyes widened. "I wouldn't have thought he would. He absolutely hated it."

"Why? It was fabulous." Rowena grinned. "It looked exactly like Mitch…only better. A *lot* better."

It was hard to explain, really. Bonnie remembered that night so well. They'd been in North Carolina. He'd been studying for one of the online courses they sometimes took while they traveled, to make up for the days wasted in dead-end jobs. Bent over his laptop, with the screen lighting his face as he concentrated, his hair tousled from running his hands through it—she'd thought he looked gorgeous. She picked up a pad and pencil and drew him for almost two hours straight.

But when she showed him the sketches, he'd

been unexpectedly irritated. "I look like a kid," he'd complained. "As immature as Alec. Dang, Bonnie, is this how you see me?"

It had been. It was still. She saw him as filled with light. Buoyant. Alive with energy and virility and joy. The only difference was she didn't consider that immature. In her mind, it was the state everyone on this earth longed to achieve—and most of them failed.

"Portraits are tricky," she said. "You can only catch people as you see them—not how they see themselves. These days, if I were to paint, I'm pretty sure I'd stick to wildflowers."

"Well, you're good at those, too. The larkspurs watercolor I bought…everyone mentions how beautiful it is."

"Thank you." Belle said. She fidgeted, twirling the grass around her index finger. She didn't want to talk about this anymore. She'd painted quite a few wildflower pieces when she'd lived here before, and she'd been fool enough to sell them at the local wildflower festival. It could easily have exposed her.

"I guess the whole subject of art is a little emotionally tangled for me." She had to say something. Rowena was still staring at her, looking perplexed and disappointed. "But gardening… that's a different story. I hardly qualify as an expert there, either, but I do love to grow things. I like to be outside."

She hadn't meant for that last sentence to sound so wistful. She'd been her own woman for ten years now and could fry under the sun and sleep under the stars if she chose to. The years of being someone's house pet were long gone, and she didn't want Rowena to think she sat around feeling sorry for herself.

She knew how people would react to that. *Oh, brother, break my heart. Poor little rich girl.*

"Well, maybe that works out for the best, then." Rowena finally seemed to shake off her surprise. "We already have a pretty good art director on staff, but we're desperate for someone to spruce up the grounds, because *Colorado Hearth* is doing a piece on Bell River in a month or so. I've always wanted to make it look the way you painted it in the renderings. Remember?"

"Of course." In those months when the project had still been only a dream, Bonnie had loved bringing Bell River Dude Ranch to life on canvas. She remembered every shrub, tree and flower she'd drawn. "But don't forget…some of that was poetic license. Paintings and real life don't always have much in common."

Once again, hearing a note of melancholy, Bonnie felt her cheeks suffuse with the dull burn of discomfort. Did every sentence out of her mouth have to be so laden with self-awareness?

"Yeah, well, that's okay," Rowena said briskly, covering the moment by bending to pick up her tools. "If you can make even half of your drawings translate into reality, that's good enough for me!"

"I'll try."

People had been milling around them all along, guests and staff and horses and dogs, all a bit vague and anonymous to Belle, who'd been concentrating on the conversation. But suddenly one of the figures passing in the distance caught her attention, the one man in sharp focus amid a sea of hazy nobodies.

*Mitch.* She pressed her palms against her thighs, trying to control the tension darting through her veins.

Dressed in jeans, a checked shirt and muddy boots, he was walking toward the stables—and walking slowly, as if he were in some physical discomfort. His head ducked toward his collarbone, as though the sun bothered him. He carried a large brown saddle in one hand, the stirrups swinging as he moved, and with his free hand he reached up to tilt his cowboy hat forward onto his forehead.

Rowena noticed him, too, and both women watched until he disappeared into the shadowy interior. Belle felt sure Rowena watched with a calmer heart. Belle found it difficult to breathe deeply, just watching the elegant slouch of his stride.

"Is he okay?" She turned to Rowena. "He looks…uncomfortable."

Rowena chuckled darkly. "He's probably got a head the size of a wrecking ball, with jackhammers and snare drums going full blast. He was at the Happy Horseshoe last night with Jude. He said Mitch was drinking like a madman."

Belle swung her head around to the stables instinctively, as if there were something left to see. But though other cowboys came and went, Mitch might as well have been swallowed whole by the building.

"That's weird," she said. "Mitch doesn't drink. Not like that."

"Apparently he did last night." Rowena chewed on her lower lip thoughtfully, as if trying to decide whether to say more. "And apparently he wasn't alone."

Belle frowned. "The lawyer?"

"Nope. It's weird, because I had honestly feared he was getting serious with Indiana. But Jude told Tess, who told Bree, who told me, that he was getting cozy with one of the women who works in the tattoo parlor downtown."

Rowena smiled, aware, of course, of how gossipy she sounded. "Her name is Crimson Slash, if you can believe that. Ridiculous, but I figure it's good news. Indiana the ambitious, laser focused lawyer might have actually snagged him. But

Crimson Slash doesn't sound like anyone permanent, does she? That can't even be her real name."

Belle was silent, and immediately Rowena groaned.

"Oh, dear Lord. Those were probably the dumbest words I've ever uttered—which is saying something, considering how often I have my foot in my mouth. I'm sorry. I didn't mean—"

"I know what you meant." Belle put her hand on Rowena's arm to show she had taken no offense. "It *is* significant when a person takes on an alias. It does usually mean they are hiding something or that they might not stick around. But it doesn't mean she's no threat. Mitch isn't afraid of the unconventional, and he isn't a snob."

"Neither am I, honestly." Rowena sighed. "Although if I have to say that, can it really be true? God, can I have left my own checkered past behind so quickly? I've had a dozen jobs more offbeat than a tattoo artist, and I've moved around so much I might as well have been a pinball. I shouldn't be judging her. I don't even know her."

"It's okay," Belle said. "Don't worry about it, really."

But Rowena couldn't quite let it go. "I don't know why I'm being such a jerk. I guess I'm clutching at straws, praying Mitch doesn't jump into another woman's bed—or worse—just to show you he doesn't care."

Belle felt her chest twist, as if someone had

given her heart a rope burn. The idea of Mitch in someone else's bed, whether it was the lawyer who wanted to marry him or the tattoo artist who wanted to booze it up…

It was shockingly painful.

"Well, getting drunk with someone doesn't always lead to sex," she said. "There's no reason to assume it went any further than the Happy Horseshoe."

Again that wistful note had crept in. She was as good as begging Rowena to reassure her Mitch was still being faithful to a relationship he'd openly admitted was dead and buried.

Poor Rowena. She couldn't give Belle what she wanted, and she was clearly caught between her natural preference for candor and her desire to calm Belle's fears.

"No…" Ro spoke slowly. "It doesn't *always* lead to anything. But…but Jude says he left Mitch at the bar, with Crimson at his side. And, well…"

"Just tell me," Belle said. "It's okay, Ro. Really."

"Well, I don't know anything, not for sure." Rowena sighed. "All I know is…he didn't come home last night."

MITCH WASN'T OFFICIALLY Rosie's babysitter this afternoon—Alec was. But of course that was merely make-believe, to make the kid feel valued. Rowena had enlisted Mitch as backup and then sweetly explained that if he let Alec do anything crazy she'd come after them both with a pitchfork.

Mitch had considered maybe resenting the implication he was as reckless as a ten-year-old, but then he remembered a certain incident involving a trampoline and in-line skates…and he decided to let it go.

He even made a point of arriving early. Rosie's nursery adjoined Dallas and Rowena's bedroom, and both led out onto a shared porch overlooking the side garden. Rowena, Alec and Rosie were out there, and through the doorway, he could hear Rowena's voice as she gave her stepson instructions.

"I'll be gone an hour, and if you aren't too noisy, she'll probably sleep the whole time."

Alec's suspicious voice piped up immediately. "Okay, but…I still get paid, even if she sleeps the whole time, right?"

Rowena glanced at Mitch, who arrived on the porch at that moment, and grinned. "Yes," she answered patiently. "In fact, if she does sleep the whole time, you'll get more."

*Clever Ro!* Mitch always admired how well she handled the kid. She didn't try to win his affection with syrupy compliments and crushing hugs. She just treated him with the same affectionate exasperation she used on everyone. Alec adored her.

"And then, since you'll be rich, you can take

me out for ice cream, your treat." Mitch wiggled his eyebrows at Alec, knowing how unlikely that scenario was. Alec was infamous for his stinginess. He was always saving up for some preposterous project.

"The devil I will!" Alec's voice rose, but then, remembering Rosie, he calmed himself, finishing his comment in a whisper. "Do you know how boring it is to babysit? No way I'm blowing blood money on ice cream."

"Well, maybe I'll win it from you at checkers. You bring your board?"

"Of course." Alec gestured toward the pretty wicker chairs set near the railing, where they could smell the roses and soak up the sun. The table between them was already set with a full board. "But you won't win. You never do."

"There's always a first time," Mitch said easily, accepting Rowena's goodbye air-kiss as she moved toward the small gate that led off the porch and down to the garden. With half his mind, he registered she seemed in more of a hurry than usual. He knew she had a kiddie trail ride to lead, but not for another ten minutes.

And then he saw why she rushed. He caught a flash of sparkling red fire coming around the live oak at the corner, and then suddenly Belle was walking toward them.

She wore a faded cotton shirt and blue jeans… and he knew those jeans. His palms tingled, remembering how often he'd cupped that denim in his hands. How often he'd tugged it down, over her hips…

He cursed under his breath, earning a scowl from Alec, which was odd, since the boy didn't have any problem with cursing and in fact did it darned well himself, whenever he was alone.

"Quiet!" Alec frowned and jerked his head dramatically at the bassinet.

Mitch glanced at Rosie, who stirred briefly, pursing her little pink rosebud mouth, but she didn't seem terribly disturbed. Chances were, with her temper, she'd know some choice words of her own in a few years.

He looked back at Rowena, who was talking to Belle, having intercepted her a few yards from the garden. Belle carried a caddy full of gardening tools and was wiggling her fingers into a pair of leather gloves, and she glanced at the porch every few seconds while Rowena talked.

*Damn it.* What was she doing right here, right now? He'd heard the plan was to let her do some landscaping for an upcoming magazine piece. But Bell River was a big spread. Why would she have to be working on the garden right at their feet?

It was obvious he'd been set up. And there wasn't a darn thing he could do about it, because, once again, any protest would expose how affected he was by her presence.

Turning just abruptly enough to catch him

looking at them, Rowena smiled and waved goodbye one more time. Belle hesitated a moment, standing with the sunlight sparking gold and rose highlights in her hair, and then she casually strode toward them.

"Morning," she said politely, letting both Mitch and Alec get a share of the smile. "It's a gorgeous day, isn't it?"

Alec didn't seem to be in the mood for company any more than Mitch was. "I don't know," the boy grumbled. "Isn't it always like this in spring?"

Alec watched with a frown as Belle set her caddy on the ground; the metal tools clinked slightly against each other.

"Hey, you're not going to be making a lot of noise digging around out there, are you?" Alec's torso practically hung off the railing as he peered down curiously. "Because I'm in charge of the baby, and if she wakes up in a bad mood, it's going to make my job a lot harder."

Belle darted a subtle glance at Mitch. She was probably wondering whether he'd put the boy up to chasing her away. Then again, maybe not. She and Alec had always gotten along well, and she knew how blunt he was.

"I'll be as quiet as I can," she said. "You won't even know I'm here."

Mitch laughed internally. *Fat chance.* From the

first day they'd met, he'd always been so aware of her it felt like a sixth sense.

If she was really going to stay, and Rowena was going to play matchmaker, then clearly the sooner he got out of town, the better.

He hadn't told anyone about his decision to leave Silverdell, and he didn't intend to, not until it was a done deal. He had a couple of standing job offers at various ranches, because he was darn good at training horses. He'd worked on some nearby ranches for date and gas money when he was in college. Over the past couple of years, he'd been helping get Bell River's new mounts trained for guests whenever he was in Silverdell.

But he wasn't sure he wanted to work for other people anymore. And thanks to the money from the Garwood Chore Jacket, which should hit his bank account any day now, he didn't have to. He was toying with the idea of setting up his own training facilities.

The big question was...where? His reputation was mostly local—wouldn't help him much in Montana or Texas. Or Ocala, Florida, where there was a guy who raised horses and needed a trainer.

But he desperately wanted to get away from the place where he'd always be seen as the sheriff's punky little brother.

"Hey, are we going to play or not?"

Alec was already at the table, nudging his checkers into more perfect alignment. He sounded impatient. Mitch blinked away his mental fog and arched a brow toward the boy.

"Wouldn't miss it for the world." He pulled out his chair and sat down, taking black, as always, which meant he'd be staring out at the garden. For one paranoid moment, he wondered if Alec, who hated losing, had assigned his uncle the outward-facing position on purpose, so that he'd be distracted by watching Belle and possibly lose his concentration.

Probably not, although such diabolical strategizing wasn't beyond the little demon. Alec was aware Mitch had been in love with Belle and had even badgered Mitch for an explanation of why he'd come home without her last year.

Mitch had found the interrogation irritating—doubly so because he hadn't had a clue what the answer was. Why *had* he found himself alone in Castle Hill, Maine, that god-awful morning? So he'd just said, "We broke up." At least that was true, if vague.

Alec hadn't asked a single question since Belle had returned. That level of restraint, in this particular kid, was shocking. Rowena must have threatened him with his life.

*Thump, thump, thump.* With an unholy delight, Alec jumped three of Mitch's pieces.

"I'm so going to kick your keister," he crowed, then guiltily glanced at the bassinet and lowered his voice. "You're not throwing the game, are you? You know I hate that."

"As if." Mitch found a countermove, taking two of Alec's pieces, and vowed to pay better attention.

For the next five minutes or so, he steadfastly refused to think about anything but the board in front of him—although occasionally, out of the corner of his eye, he glimpsed the strawberry glint of Belle's curls feathering in the wind. She was shaping and pruning the rosebushes that climbed around the porch pillars. Even without looking, he knew every time she moved, because a fresh wave of spiced sweetness washed over him.

Suddenly, he heard her voice. "Hello?" she said.

He looked up, stupidly, as if she were talking to him. She wasn't. She stood behind a curtain of roses ragged enough to let him see she held her cell phone to her ear.

"Evan, I can't talk now. I'm working." Her voice was surprisingly tense…and Mitch found himself listening, trying to read its tone. Tense and something else… Angry? Frightened? He couldn't be sure.

For a few seconds, she seemed to be listening. Frustratingly, the roses split Mitch's view into jigsaw pieces. Pink petals obscured her eyes, and a cluster of green leaves bloomed where her mouth should be. He was left with only her nose, her chin and the phone held white-knuckled against her ear to tell him anything.

"I don't *want* it," she said suddenly, in an eruption so curt Mitch was sure she'd interrupted Evan—whoever he was—midsentence.

"I don't want *any* of them," she repeated, lowering her voice and turning her head away from Mitch and Alec, as if she didn't want to be overheard. "And even if I did, I wouldn't agree to a face-to-face meeting. Even if he were offering to sell me the Mona Lisa, nothing on earth could get me in the same room with that man."

Mitch frowned. *That man...* It had to be Jacob, didn't it? But why would her terrible cousin be trying to set up a meeting? Mitch's gut didn't like it. And obviously, neither did Belle's.

"No, I don't think it's a mistake. I don't care how good the price is. I don't need any more money. I wish to God I didn't have—"

The sentence ended abruptly. Her head turned, she shifted with a puff of perfume that almost smelled like violets and she was suddenly meeting Mitch's gaze directly.

He hadn't realized both he and Alec were gawking at her, their game of checkers entirely forgotten. She took in her mesmerized audience for one silent second, then moved away, putting quick distance between her conversation and the porch.

The last thing he heard was "Tell him? You can tell him to *leave me alone*."

## CHAPTER SEVEN

A FEW DAYS LATER, a crisp Thursday afternoon aglow with spring sunshine, Belle found herself wandering around the moist, earthy, color-laden aisles of Endicott Hill, the best wholesale nursery in western Colorado. She ruffled the bright green tufts of Mexican feather grass, luxuriating in their fine, angel-hair texture.

She had almost two hours to look at plants, and she had Rowena's permission to follow her own vision.... This was just about Belle's idea of heaven.

She'd been surprised, frankly, when Rowena had come out to the porch that morning, where Belle was still digging out dead perennials, and suggested the trip. Between motherhood and the dude ranch, and tomorrow's Mexican Fiesta party, a perfectionist like Ro was run ragged 24/7.

But apparently updating the landscaping really was a priority, and she'd cleared her schedule so she, Rosie and Belle could take the afternoon to order what they needed.

Or rather...Belle would shop while Rowena and Rosie played. Ro's bond with her Colorado ranch land was fierce and primal—but it was all based on emotion and spirit and love. Johnny Wright, the man she'd grown up thinking of as her father, had been a horseman, so he'd given her a great education in handling horses, but he'd expected his hired help to dig in the dirt, not his daughters.

So now, shortly after arriving at Endicott Hill, they were splitting up. Rosie had been immediately enchanted by the display of garden geegaws, birdbaths and wind chimes, and Ro seemed perfectly content to let Belle roam around alone.

"Follow your heart, as long as it doesn't lead you too far beyond our pitiful little budget," she said with a grin.

Belle had already been given the dollar amount—a number she calculated was roughly half what it would take to do the job properly.

But Belle wasn't worried about that. Money was the least of her problems. Maybe Ro wouldn't check too closely, and Belle could slip in the other half without causing a fuss. If not, somehow she'd figure out a way to make Ro okay with a donation. It was the least she could do, after all that Ro had done for her.

"Okay," she said, "but you sure you don't want me to make a list and show you before I actually buy anything?"

"Absolutely sure." Rowena hoisted the baby over her shoulder, allowing her to get closer to the bubbling fountain topped with stone cherubs and butterflies. "I trust you a hundred percent."

Belle felt a small hitch in her heart. Such a simple sentence, and yet...

For Belle, trust was anything but simple. Few people had ever trusted her, starting with her grandmother, who had hired people to watch her constantly, so that she wouldn't "spoil" herself. That had been Ava's expression. "Don't climb trees, Annabelle." Or swim or play tag or eat pizza or chew ice or pierce her ears or cut her hair or even frown. "You'll *spoil* yourself."

And the number of people Belle herself still trusted?

*One.*

Wasn't that ironic? No matter what Mitch did, even if he slept with every lawyer, tattoo artist and cowgirl in Colorado, she would always trust him. He might break her heart, but only because she had broken his. Below that ache, deep in her soul, she knew he was rock solid. He would never exploit or betray another human being to advance an agenda of his own.

"Thanks," she said, trying to sound nonchalant, though her throat felt thick. Ro hadn't meant that kind of trust, of course. She'd merely meant she had confidence that when deciding between ice plant and coral bells, Belle would make the right choice. "I'll come up with something beautiful—I promise."

"I know you will. But remember, we've only got two hours. I'm not sure the archery class is covered at four. Besides, if you take too long I can't promise Rosie and I won't ruin the whole design by buying up all these tacky garden gnomes."

And then, as the baby began to stir, bored with the cherubs, Rowena winked merrily at Belle and strolled away toward the wind-chime display.

The next two hours passed in a blissful blur. Belle could see the design taking shape in her mind. She made little adjustments as she mentally put one plant beside another. She changed her mind a dozen times, comparing the deep red flowers of the Prairie Winecups to the ruddy brown walls of the new stables. Contrast or match? Shade or sun? How much would it cost to put in new drip irrigation? Which ones would draw the butterflies and hummingbirds in summer...without attracting the hungry deer and elk when the snow fell?

She was just putting the finishing touches on her list when she heard a baby burbling with happiness behind her. She turned and, seeing Rowena and Rosie, realized she'd lost track of the time, and Rowena had needed to hunt her down.

She shot a glance at her watch, though the glare from the sunshine made it hard to read. Darn it... She hadn't made Ro miss the archery class, had she?

"It's only three." Rowena was smiling. "And the class is covered. We're good."

Relieved, Belle reached out to tease Rosie's adorable Mohawk of silky black hair. "Did you buy all the garden gnomes? Because I probably could incorporate a few into the design."

"Nope. We resisted, though we did pick out half a dozen wonderful stone benches. I thought maybe we could arrange them out by Cupcake Creek. The view is gorgeous, but there's nowhere to sit."

Belle loved the idea. And though she knew it would put a dent in the budget, she didn't bring that part up. Rowena was an impulsive, fiery creature by nature, but she didn't take foolish risks with her beloved dude ranch. So if she thought she could afford the benches, she could.

"I guess we ought to be getting back," Belle said reluctantly. She had half hoped she could look at the tree section, though it would have been merely self-indulgence, as Bell River didn't need any more of those.

The rolling acres of the ranch surged with stately maples, hawthorns, poplars and mountain ash, all old and full of character. Her efforts, the agave and the yarrow and the ice plants, would simply be accessories bedecking an already gorgeous grande dame.

But even more difficult than missing out on the trees was returning to reality. For these two hours, Belle had been able to forget all her worries. The strange call from her lawyer, the constant badgering to make decisions about the house, the money, the paintings…

She'd even been able to forget Mitch. Mitch, whom she hadn't laid eyes on since that day he'd played checkers on the porch with Alec. That had been days ago. So far, the campaign to win him back was a nonstarter.

Temples aching, exhausted by the hopeless labyrinth of her thoughts, she put her hand up to the blue ribbon that held back her hair and loosened it a little.

"Hey." Rowena put her hand on Belle's arm. "You okay? It's pretty hot out here. Maybe we should go inside. I forget that people with fair skin—"

"No." Belle knew Ro meant well, but instinct rebelled against the warnings she'd heard so often. "No, it's not that. I'm just… I didn't sleep very well last night, that's all."

Rowena bounced the baby softly, her green eyes thoughtful as she scanned Belle's face. "Was it Mitch?"

Belle shook her head. "No. Well, not only Mitch. There are just so many decisions I have to make. The house…the money… My lawyer calls ten times a day trying to get me to deal with it." She took a breath. "But I'm not ready."

"So tell him that. It's *your* house, *your* money, right?" Rowena's black brow arched. "That means you deal with it on *your* timetable."

Belle nodded, grateful for the unconditional support—and, if she were honest, for having Rowena as a role model. Belle would never be the spitfire Rowena was. She'd been trained to obedience from birth, and she sometimes thought she'd exhausted her lifetime supply of courage when she'd decided to run away. She was so tired now. She'd beaten Jacob. And yet…

It felt a lot like defeat.

But whenever she was around Rowena, she always felt a little tougher, capable of fighting one more fight.

"I guess it's mostly Mitch," she admitted. "I haven't seen him in days. He has been awfully creative about avoiding me. Or maybe it's not deliberate. The ranch is so much bigger, and so much busier, than I had imagined. You've worked miracles here, Ro, really. But—"

"But you thought it would be like before, when we were all in one house, all bumping into each other constantly."

Belle nodded. "That was silly, wasn't it? With the whole family working here, the ranch would have to expand, and for the venture to support everyone, you'd have to be attracting tons of guests. It's just that—all those lovely moments I imagined, when we'd suddenly find each other conveniently alone, in the stables, on the porch, out by the waterfall…"

Ro patted Rosie's back. "Yeah. Privacy is a

rare thing at Bell River. But the problem isn't just crowds and space. It's Mitch. You're not running into him because he simply isn't here. No one has seen him much since you arrived."

"Oh." Her cheeks stung, as if the news had been a light slap to her face. She'd driven him away from his own family. "I'm sorry."

Rowena laughed. "Don't be. You may think he hung the moon, but for the rest of us a little break from Mitch isn't always a bad thing."

Belle appreciated Ro's attempt to brush it off, but she knew better. She'd never met a more tightly knit family than this one. Maybe some of the intensity was the result of the years when the sisters had been pulled apart, after their mother had died and their father had gone to prison. But the bond was intense, and every partner they'd brought into the fold shared the same commitment.

Around Bell River, the sisters, their husbands, children and stepchildren obviously lived, worked and played together because they shared common goals, common dreams. Because life made sense together in a way it could never do separately.

It was one of the things she'd always loved best about Mitch. Even when he and Dallas were fighting, even when Alec was driving them all insane, their love for each other glowed like a neon sign.

"It may be hopeless, then," she said. She bit

her lips briefly to steady them and looked down at her hands, brushing off potting soil from her fingertips. "I may have been more naive than I realized, thinking I could just show up here and change his mind."

She half hoped Ro would rush in to say, "No, no, it'll be fine." To assure her that Mitch would come around soon. But Rowena just kept patting Rosie's back absently, her brow furrowed.

"Listen, Belle, I probably should tell you something."

Belle didn't like Ro's tone. It was somber, as if she were at a funeral. Belle didn't prompt Rowena for more. She waited.

"The thing is, he's not there because he's spending most of his time with Crimson." Rowena wrinkled her nose. "I'm sure he's just trying to make you jealous, but—"

"No, he's not like that." Belle shook her head, registering Rowena's expression of disbelief. "Really, he's not."

"If you say so. You obviously know a side of him we've never seen. But if he's not trying to make you jealous, then there's some other reason he's pushing this relationship so hard, so fast. Maybe he's trying to convince himself he's over you. And surely, in a backward way, that's encouraging, right? If he didn't care, why would he have to exile himself from the ranch and throw himself into the arms of a new woman?"

Belle clung to that logic. It made a certain sense…
that was, until the arms of the new woman worked
their own magic, until they became familiar and
sweet and new emotions were born.

"I hope you're right," she said.

"I am." Rowena's voice was so emphatic that
little Rosie lifted her head and stared at her
mother curiously. "Still…"

She rubbed her lips against the baby's little
nose, then looked up at Belle. "Still, we're going
to have to think of *some* way to throw you guys
together, and soon. Because…well, the truth is,
Crimson isn't the worst cloud on the horizon."

"There's something worse?" Belle closed her
eyes for a second, hard, then opened them again.
She didn't want to hear anything worse. "How?
What?"

Rowena shifted the baby one more time so that
she could free a hand. She closed her long fingers
across Belle's lower arm with a gentle strength.

"He just told Dallas last night. He's moving to
Florida, Belle. He's leaving Bell River for good."

MITCH HAD COME UP with a dozen other, better ideas
for spending a balmy Friday night, but Crimson
had vetoed every one of them. She wanted to go
to the Bell River Mexican Fiesta, and she wasn't
backing down.

"What? Are you ashamed for your family to
know you're dating a body modification artist?"

Crimson's sassy hazel gaze scraped his face, looking for guilt.

Chuckling at the thought, he'd tilted back his chair, though Jeff, the boy who ran the Sweet Shoppe's soda fountain, scowled. "Don't be ridiculous. Nobody gives a plug nickel about that. And even if they did, they don't decide who I date."

"Okay, then. What?" She'd sucked hard at the straw she'd shoved into her double-chocolate milk shake, trying to get the last half inch of liquid, while she tilted a bold glance up at him. "Is it Bonnie? I mean…Belle?"

He'd brought his chair legs back to the floor. *Nicely played, Crimson.* That was obviously check *and* mate. They'd known each other for only about a week, and she already had his number.

And so, of course, here he was, with about fifty other people, crowded into the new arts hall at Bell River, listening to a mariachi band and watching a bunch of bullfighters and gypsy dancers twirl around the floor.

He and Crimson had danced the first few songs, but after that he had to do some guest-tending—chat a bit, dance a few of the single ladies around. He'd been seriously neglecting his Bell River duties lately, spending most of his time over at Gray Stables, which was the breeding business owned by Rowena's brother-in-law, Gray Harper. Gray always needed help with his horses.

Rowena was ticked, of course—partly because

she had wanted Mitch to work with *her* horses, but primarily because it ruined her little matchmaking scheme. But he didn't care. He wanted to move on, not sink back into the quicksand of that hopeless relationship with Bonnie...or Belle, or whoever she was today.

Problem was, he didn't trust himself, not if he saw her, if he caught a whiff of her perfume or heard her laughter in the distance. No point pretending he could rely on willpower. He already knew she had a way of making willpower disappear.

So his best bet was to stay away from Bell River completely till she was gone. Whatever mysterious magnetic attraction she held over him, surely it couldn't get him if he was five hundred acres away.

Sooner or later, she'd get the message they were really finished, or, more likely, she'd just get bored. Either way, she'd go home to her mansion and her millions, and he wouldn't have to worry about falling under her spell again. A thousand miles, surely, was enough to keep him safe.

Luckily, Crimson didn't mind being left to her own devices tonight. She could make friends with anyone, and every single man in the hall was eyeing her. She'd already been led onto the floor a dozen times, most recently by the guy who was renting their River Moon cabin. Apparently, the guy had met her while getting a tattoo yesterday.

After a while, Mitch decided to take a break from business socializing. He moseyed to the bar, where Jude, looking like a movie star in a red shirt and white suit, with a spangled green sombrero slung down his back, was helping to serve drinks.

Mitch ordered a ginger ale.

Jude raised an eyebrow, but he knew better than to comment. Mitch had never been much of a drinker, but after making such a fool of himself that night in the Horseshoe—and paying the price the next morning—he was off the stuff entirely.

Jude began putting out more cocktail napkins. "Knocked yourself out in the costume department, I see," he observed drily.

"Don't start." Mitch knew he was underdressed. Around them, the room was a whirling sea of red, white and green, of sombreros and mantillas and castanets. Bell River's activities department always offered costumes to the guests and staff for the big themed parties. But he hadn't planned to attend, so he'd missed it.

Just like he had missed almost everything that had happened on the ranch this week.

"Given the short notice, I think I did fine." And he had. No one with his coloring owned red shirts, but at the last minute he'd dug out a green one, slapped it on over his jeans and dared anyone to say it wasn't a costume.

Jude's smile spoke volumes, but he gazed blandly at the dance floor. "Crimson seems to have done a little better."

Mitch couldn't deny that. She'd done herself up right. She wore a ragingly sexy Mexican dancer outfit—strapless at the top, tight around the hips and a wild ruffled skirt with a slit up one leg, rising all the way to the legal limit.

"And clearly the Lothario from River Moon thinks so, too." Jude angled a curious glance at Mitch. "If you don't reclaim her pretty soon, buddy, you may not be the one taking her home tonight."

Mitch shrugged. The thought had occurred to him. But he couldn't get worked up about it.

Jude made a margarita for a bullfighter and a white wine for his *señorita,* then turned back to Mitch. "I take it that doesn't bother you."

"Not as much as it should." Mitch lifted one corner of his mouth. "Not as much as I wish it did."

"Ahh." Jude nodded. He was Mitch's best friend, his only confidant, and he knew chapter and verse of the Bonnie/Belle saga. "Bummer."

"Crimson's nice." Mitch knew that sounded patronizing, so he tried again. "Really nice. She's smart and fun and funny. But the rest… It's just not there. There's no fire, you know? Because—"

"Because you're a damn fool?" Jude's voice was innocent.

That pretty much summed it up. Because he was a damn fool, he didn't have the slightest interest in sleeping with this very cool, superhot lady.

They were already on date number four. Unless someone turned up his inner thermostat, she was in for a disappointment if they ever got to number twelve.

Half a dozen partiers who clearly did *not* need another drink bellied up to Jude's bar. Callously abandoning his friend to the delicate task of shorting the liquor without offending anyone, Mitch escaped to the buffet table.

He grabbed a fistful of jalapeño poppers, not because he particularly wanted them, but because they were the first dish he came to. But, now that he was here, the guacamole looked pretty good, too. The ranch's head chef, a battle-ax of a woman they ironically called "Cookie," was the most amazing talent. He couldn't understand why she stayed here instead of making it big in New York or L.A.

"Hi, Mitch."

He looked up, his mouth full of jalapeños. *"Belle."*

In the split second it took to recognize her, the floor beneath his feet turned gooey and unreliable. He swallowed the last popper and tried to keep his mouth from dropping open.

How did she do this to him? Her costume was modest—a gathered white bodice that flowed loosely over her breasts, a wide red belt that cinched her waist and a flowing green skirt that hid everything, even her ankles. Only the tantalizing hint of one shoulder peeping from the top could possibly be considered "sexy."

And yet she took his breath away.

*Damn it.* This was why he needed that thousand miles between them.

"Hi," he said, not trusting his voice with any more syllables than that. Even that one sounded slightly cracked and awkward. He hadn't made a sound like that since his voice had changed.

"I was hoping you'd be here," she said, smiling politely. She paused. "I haven't seen you much this week."

"No." He took a chip and dug it into the guacamole, just to force himself to take his eyes off her. "I haven't been here much."

They stood in an uncomfortable silence for several seconds. He wanted to be nicer, but every time he looked at her his heart started galloping like a runaway horse, and he felt his emotions being dragged along behind. Someday, maybe he'd get over her. Someday, maybe he'd be able to talk to her like a civilized human being.

But *someday* was a long way off.

"Mitch." She touched his arm, and he refused to let his body react, though her fingers might as well have been an electric cattle prod. His veins sizzled, and he smelled the burn in his nostrils.

"Mitch, I just wanted to say that if you're staying away from the ranch because of me, you don't have to. I know you meant what you said the other day. I know you're not interested in trying to fix things between us. I'm not going to do anything to make it uncomfortable for you."

*Ha.* He dug around in the guacamole some more, as if he'd lost something in it. "I'm not staying away because of you."

God, listen to him! He sounded like a ten-year-old. Like Alec, who, whenever he missed a bull's-eye in archery class, would lift his chin and announce, "I wasn't even trying."

He met her gaze, holding on to his emotions so he didn't tumble into those amazing blue eyes. She had a red daisy tucked behind one ear, and her red-gold hair glistened around it like satin glass. It might be the sexiest thing he'd ever seen. He ached to kiss that ear.

"I've just been busy, that's all," he said. He had to talk. If he didn't talk, he would kiss her.

*And then what?*

"Okay. I just wanted to be sure. But if it's not because of me, I'm glad." She hesitated, then spoke again with a deliberately casual air. "Rowena told me you're seeing someone. Is it serious?"

"No." Mitch briefly considered trying to use Crimson as a shield, but it wouldn't have been fair to Crimson. And he and Belle had never played games like that. They'd fallen for each other the minute they'd met, and there had never been any point in trying to hide it.

"It's not serious. She's great, but she's just a friend."

Belle nodded. The daisy slipped a little, and she put a hand up to tuck it back into place. The mariachi band rocked into "La Bamba," and Mitch saw Barton James climb onstage with his guitar. He also saw Crimson flash him an apologetic glance as the River Moon guy swung her back onto the floor.

"I was hoping maybe we could be friends, too," Belle said suddenly. Though her voice was soft, he could hear her as clearly as if they were alone in the hall. "It would be very hard if we ended in so much anger. After all we…after everything we…"

She didn't finish. He wondered if she really meant what she was saying. Would that make everything okay for her? All she wanted was for them to part in peace? As *friends?*

"Do you think that's possible, Mitch?"

"Sure." But he realized that, without meaning to, he was shaking his head. "*Friends.* Why not? Sounds like fun."

Her smile wavered, as if she was confused by

the mixed signals. But she didn't say anything, clearly preferring a mixed signal to a no. For several seconds she simply stood beside him in that strangely immobile way she sometimes had. She didn't look awkward—Belle never looked anything but gracefully posed. But her body was eerily lifeless, and her empty gaze looked unseeingly toward the costumed dancers.

"So, tell me something, Belle. Friend to friend."

She glanced back at him. "Okay."

"You know that call you got the other day, by the porch?" He wasn't sure why, of the millions of questions he still had about their knotted past and sticky present, he chose this one right now.

But something about that call had bothered her, a lot. He hadn't been able to put it out of his mind.

"Who was it?"

The mere mention of the call bothered her still. He could see it in the tightening of her features. The question made her uncomfortable, caught her by surprise.

Well, tough. He'd been waiting a long time for this answer. Wasn't this what *friends* did? They asked questions, to which they got answers?

The two of them could either be estranged and silent, or they could be friends who shared. She couldn't have it both ways.

"It was my lawyer," she said. "His name is Evan Dalquist."

"What did he want?"

"He wanted to tell me he'd heard from Jacob. Apparently Jacob has an Annabelle Oil he'd like to sell. Number Fifteen."

Mitch frowned. "To you?"

She still wasn't looking at him. He wasn't sure what she *was* looking at. Her eyes rested on the dance floor, but he had a feeling she saw something very different.

"Yes, to me. I suppose it's his only way of getting his hands on at least a little of my grandmother's money."

"Wow. That's low." For some reason, the idea of that scumbag sneaking his grubby hands into her bank account by selling her a painting of herself… Well, it made Mitch's temples start to throb. Which was an overreaction, he knew. He hadn't ever even met the guy. "Are you going to buy it?"

Finally, she looked at him. "Of course not. I wouldn't take any of those oils if they were a gift. I hate them."

Suddenly, she didn't seem even remotely like a mannequin anymore. Though she remained poised on the outside, heat rose off her in waves, as if she were boiling on the inside.

*Interesting. Hate* was a big word. Why such intensity? The Annabelle Oils were pretty paintings, once you got past the idea that the unearthly fairy girl was supposed to be Belle.

And they had helped to make her a very, very rich woman. Rich enough to come play cowgirl down here as long as it amused her, apparently. Rich enough to agree to landscape the entire ranch for the ridiculous salary of one dollar.

At the ranch's bimonthly budget meeting, Rowena had told them all about Belle's generous gesture. A smattering of applause had risen in the room. Saint Annabelle of the Flowers. No one had been willing to look directly at Mitch, which was doubly annoying.

"We're not broke, for God's sake," he'd said, finally speaking above the clapping. He had taken over the books a few months ago, discovering he had a knack for numbers, so he knew exactly where the bottom line stood. "Why don't you just pay her, the way you'd pay anyone else?"

"Because she isn't *anyone else*." Rowena had glared at him across the table. "She wants to thank us, because we took her in without references, without questions. She wants to thank us because we loved her for herself, and not because she was Annabelle Irving."

He studied Belle's face now, acknowledging it might have been difficult being the flesh-and-blood girl behind the romantic Annabelle Oils. If, from the cradle, you were held up as an icon of mystical beauty, what did you do with the usual growing-up angst, like zits and bony elbows?

And maybe it was just him, but the girl in the

pictures was a little disturbing. That degree of beauty, combined with the eerie poise, the blank, multicolored eyes, somehow suggested the supernatural. Or the cursed. Or the tragically insane.

Boys must have been scared to death of her. He certainly would have been, if, at fifteen, he'd met her in that mansion, with a dozen creepy Annabelles staring down at him from their frames on the wall.

He shook off the odd image. "Why would Jacob try to sell the painting to you, then? Doesn't he know you hate them?"

"Oh, yes." She nodded slowly. "He knows."

Mitch waited. But she didn't elaborate, and suddenly he realized her face had closed off. His chest tightened. He knew that look. He *hated* that look. It was the same one he used to see back when they were together, if he pushed too hard, if he tried to make her tell him why they were running.

The look was the equivalent of a twenty-foot glass wall, electrified and topped with barbed wire. He could still see her, but he couldn't touch her. The look meant he wasn't going to get an answer, no matter what he tried. Threats, bribes, sex, tears, desperation…

But why now? What secrets could she still be hiding, now that she'd supposedly vanquished the bad guy? And how many games of twenty questions would he have to play to tease out even the smallest revelation?

He recognized the same tight spiral of frustrated anger and rejection forming behind his rib cage, and he drew himself up. *To hell with it.* He'd had enough of that look, and that feeling, to last him a lifetime.

Luckily, Mr. River Moon had finally remembered his manners and was delivering Crimson back to her date. The guy was still flirting hard, though, using his last few seconds to make a desperation pass. He lifted his hand and feathered her spiky red hair with his palm, as if he found it irresistible.

Crimson rolled her eyes and gently removed his hand, but she was laughing, and when she caught Mitch's gaze, she winked playfully.

Mitch smiled back at her with genuine pleasure. Or maybe it was relief. He might have been too hasty, deciding they had no future. Her simple what-you-see-is-what-you-get personality suddenly seemed like exactly what he needed.

"It was good to see you, Belle," he said, setting down his ginger ale and holding out his hand to say goodbye.

Belle accepted the handshake uncertainly. "Mitch, I—"

He squeezed her small warm fingers exactly as tightly, and held them exactly as long, as he would have done with any other guest on the ranch.

"And, just for the record, you were right," he said with a smile. "It's much more civilized to end this thing as friends."

# CHAPTER EIGHT

BELLE KNEW SHE wouldn't be able to sleep, so she didn't try. She changed out of her costume, pulling on blue sweatpants and a white T-shirt instead, and then dragged on an old sweater over that. Then, piling her hair clumsily on top of her head with a clip, she went outside.

Her cabin was one of six that had recently been built in a cluster out on the eastern side of the Bell River property. Four of the others were occupied by guests, as seven-night-minimum rentals. The sixth belonged to Mitch. It was where she'd visited him…that night.

Her cabin was at the outer edge of the group, and she had the largest yard because she had no eastern neighbor but the trees. The mowed and manicured garden area bled slowly into uncut grasses, wildflowers and, eventually, a dense copse of golden aspens and loblolly pines.

She stood on the wraparound porch for a few minutes, drinking in the cool, fresh, piney night air. In the black sky, a thousand stars glittered as sharply as glass shards. Far away, but carrying clear on the empty air, a night bird sang.

She loved the nighttime here. Even when her heart was heavy, as it was now, she felt comforted by the simple beauty of the land. Maybe, she thought, she'd plant a night garden over there, using only flowers that would shine in the moonlight. That way, when she was gone, she could think of other guests standing on this porch, watching her flowers glow.

When she was gone...

She realized she could hardly imagine what being "gone" would mean. Where would she go? Back to Greenwood? She shivered, pulling her sweater tight across her chest and chafing her upper arms with her palms.

Suddenly, over in the aspens, she heard a crack, as if something—or someone—had stepped on a branch. She stared at the trees, waiting to see what emerged. Bell River was rich with wildlife.

But nothing came.

Her skin prickled, even under her sweater. She glanced at the other cabins, but their windows were dark, except for the uniform front-porch lights. She'd left the party earlier than most of the guests. After her conversation with Mitch, everything had felt flat and she had no longer felt like dancing.

She glanced back at the trees, but everything was quiet now. And then, into the silence, her phone began to chirp. She looked at the display and frowned. *Evan?* It was ten o'clock at night.

What legal emergency could have him calling her at this hour?

She answered, if only because it was comforting to hear another human voice in the stillness that suddenly felt more eerie than peaceful.

"Hey," he said. "I hope I'm not interrupting anything."

"No. Not at all." She leaned against one of the porch railings, with her back to the trees. "What's up?"

"I just wanted to remind you that the museum board's deadline is tomorrow." Evan sounded uncharacteristically tentative. Maybe he'd learned that bossing her around didn't work. "Look, I know you said you're not ready to decide, but—"

"And I'm not."

She wasn't antagonistic toward the museum board. Of all the overtures she'd received, she liked the museum idea the best. She couldn't imagine Greenwood as a sheik's home or a boarding school or an ironic, anachronistic office space for tech prodigies—though she'd received proposals from all those groups.

The museum board, though, wanted to display sculpture and paintings and eighteenth-century porcelain figurines, and let art lovers wander through the rooms for a modest admission fee. An impersonal, heavily guarded public space. No one would live and eat and sleep and dream at Greenwood ever again.

That idea appealed to her in some inexplicable, primitive way. To know that Greenwood was not her problem—was not *anyone's* problem—would be so freeing, as if someone had lifted a heavy, rotting albatross from her neck.

And yet, whenever she really imagined signing the papers, some amorphous uncertainty held her back.

She couldn't articulate the feeling. It was as if she had something left to do at Greenwood. Something important...which made no sense, considering she could hardly bring herself to set foot in the place.

"I'm still weighing all the options, Evan." She tried to sound completely calm and rational. The last time they'd spoken, when he'd phoned to tell her about Jacob's offer, she might have been a little harsh. It wasn't his fault Jacob wouldn't leave her alone. She mustn't blame the messenger.

"Okay." He sounded resigned. "I just wanted to remind you the board meets tomorrow, and one way or another they'll be choosing their new location. If Greenwood isn't an option for them—"

"They'll have to go somewhere else." She sighed. "I know. I'm sorry, Evan."

"No problem."

His voice was so bland and noncommittal. Always the professional. She wondered sometimes what he really thought of her. She wondered what Jacob had told him about her...

She put her hand against her forehead. No, that was paranoia. Jacob had better things to do than try to undermine her lawyer's trust in her.

"Evan." She bit her lip before continuing. "Jacob hasn't called again, has he?"

His short silence was her answer. Obviously, he had.

"Darn it." She shifted the phone to her other hand. "Why didn't you tell me?"

"Look, Belle, I'm sorry. He specifically asked me not to." Evan's voice was matter-of-fact, a good lawyer voice, just laying out the facts. "He's called a couple of times, actually. He wants me to intercede, to see if I can get you to agree to meet him and to buy the oil."

She closed her eyes and let the crown of her head fall back against the rustic pillar. "No."

"But his price… It's an amazing bargain, Belle. You could turn around and double your investment the next day. I know you don't really care about the money, but… Has it occurred to you he might be trying to patch things up? It can't be easy for him, knowing you think…"

That he'd tried to kill her. The fact that Evan couldn't even complete the sentence told her where he stood. Whether Jacob had poisoned his mind or not, he believed she was what Jacob called her: neurotic, paranoid, as unstable as her mother.

She didn't really care what Evan thought, as

long as he did his job. They weren't friends, just professional associates. But she couldn't help wondering how he could be so blind. Surely, he could see it was beyond ridiculous for Jacob to try to sell her a painting he knew she loathed. It made no sense at all.

Jacob wasn't stupid, and he wasn't crazy. Greedy, sociopathic, narcissistic, yes. But never without a purpose.

So he had to know she'd never agree to buy it. Why, then, did he even suggest it? She wasn't sure why the logical disconnect was so disturbing, but it was. To her ears, something vaguely threatening lurked beneath the seemingly innocent offer.

But apparently it didn't sound that way to Evan's ears. If she mentioned her suspicions, it would only confirm what he already suspected. Annabelle Irving was a little paranoid. A little off.

Well, of course she was. Look at her mother. Look at those paintings, for heaven's sake.

Behind her, another branch cracked, and a current of unfocused fear glimmered up her spine. She whipped around and stared once again at the trees. Nothing moved.

Had she imagined the sound?

Her confidence sagged. Could Jacob be right, after all? Was she perhaps a little paranoid?

Maybe. Maybe paranoia had grown out of her

strange childhood. She didn't really remember everything that had happened in those days, back when her grandmother was alive. So much was a jumble. So much was lost to time, impossible to reconstruct.

Back then, Greenwood had been filled with artists, some genius but most merely hacks, hangers-on who wanted to associate with Ava's greatness—and mooch off her millions.

And Annabelle had been so young, and so sheltered that, emotionally, she'd been even younger than her years. Maybe the black holes, those lost hours that seemed to dot her memory like terrible swamps, were figments of her overwrought imagination.

But why, then, did all that stop when her grandmother died? When Belle was fifteen, Ava Andersen Irving had dropped dead of a heart attack, right there in front of her easel, paintbrush in hand. A guardian was appointed for Belle, a distant cousin who whisked all the sycophants out like so many mice and ran the house like a drill sergeant.

From that moment on, there were no more black holes. Had they somehow been connected to Ava all along? Had Ava, the brilliant artist worshipped by so many, been capable of doing things her granddaughter couldn't bear to remember?

"I'm sorry, Evan." She tightened her voice, so

he'd know she was serious. "I'm not ready. I'll let you know when I am."

But the minute she hung up, her phone chirped again. She frowned. Was he going to argue with her? This time, though, it wasn't a call. It was a text.

Number blocked.

Her backbone starting to tingle once again, she read the short, unsigned message.

You look beautiful with your hair like that.

The back of her neck went cold, as if someone had put an icy hand there. Instinctively, she whipped around, trying to see who was watching her. She'd only put her hair up just now, before walking out onto the porch.

She turned in a full circle, peering into the starry darkness in all directions.

But she saw nothing. She heard nothing. If anyone was out there, he was well hidden...and very, very still.

Instinct took over at that point. Ignoring her bare feet, she flew down the cabin stairs and began jogging across the cold, damp grass. She didn't pick a destination consciously. She simply began running toward Mitch's cabin as if she were following a guideline that had been left to lead her out of a very deep cave.

She didn't see the figures silhouetted against

the curtains until the very last minute. Her foot was poised to touch the first of his front steps when her conscious mind finally registered there were *two* silhouettes where there should have been just one.

She froze in place, trapped between the fear that had driven her toward him and the sudden understanding that she would not be welcome here.

Two shadows. A man and a woman, standing side by side in front of the sofa. Not in each other's arms, but close enough...

The light in the cabin was bright, and it threw detailed shadows. Belle had no trouble at all recognizing Mitch's broad shoulders and Crimson's spiky hair.

"WE NEED TO TALK." Mitch had filled two coffee mugs and carried them out of the kitchen. He handed one to Crimson, who stood in front of the sofa, waiting for him to join her.

She smiled, accepting the mug and inhaling the nutty aroma with obvious pleasure. "I had a feeling you might say that." She waved her mug toward the cushions. "Let's at least get comfortable, though, okay?"

They sat. Immediately, she leaned back against one of the padded arms, lifted her legs and put her feet in his lap. The understanding there would be no sex remained, but she was a very touchy-feely person in nonsexual ways. Like wanting a good foot rub when she'd been wearing high heels too long.

He took one slim foot and began to knead the ball just under her big toe. She groaned with pleasure and shut her eyes. "Nice," she murmured.

He worked his way slowly down her arch, the way she'd taught him. She'd be great in bed, he could tell. She knew what she liked, and she knew how to communicate without words.

After a minute or two, she let her eyes drift back open, though she left her foot where it was.

"Okay, go ahead," she said pleasantly. "Tell me all about how we should stop seeing each other because you're not over your old girlfriend. But use small words. You may have been drinking ginger ale all night, but some of us have a serious case of tequila head."

He couldn't help smiling. That was, indeed, exactly what he'd planned to say. He'd been rehearsing it all the way to the cabin, as he came to his senses and realized he didn't have the right to use her to numb his pain. She was a human being, not a bottle of aspirin.

"Sounds as if I don't have to tell you anything," he said. "What, you read minds, too?"

She lifted her shoulders, the closest thing to a shrug she could manage from that position. "Not exactly. It's more like…thought bubbles. You know, like in comic strips? I see thought bubbles."

He laughed out loud. "Yeah?"

*"Yeah."* She scowled, as if to scold him for the skepticism she heard in that word. "I can tell what people are thinking, as if they had thought bubbles printed over their heads."

"Well, that's scary." He picked up her other foot. "All the time?"

"Of course not *all* the time." She sounded annoyed, as if he were being deliberately dense. "That would be ridiculous. Some people are excellent at hiding their feelings. But other people, yeah. Other people all the time."

"And which one am I?"

Instead of answering with words, she merely twisted her mouth up at one side and rolled her eyes.

*Okay.* Obviously he was one of the "all the time" people.

"So here's what I saw." She yawned and stretched slightly, as unselfconscious as a cat. "I'm walking back from dancing with August…he's the guy who got the phoenix tattoo the other day…and there you are, standing next to Belle, and you're wearing a thought bubble about *this big.*" She held up her hands, as if she were describing a fish she'd almost caught.

He waited, knowing she'd tell him without prompting. She was a talker, a communicator. She didn't seem to see any point in being coy.

"And your bubble is a mess, Mitch. I mean,

*really*. It's saying, 'I'm still in love with Belle, but that's not working, because I'm really mad at her, but Crimson is a nice gal, so maybe I can make that work, because I really could use some sex that isn't complicated, with somebody who won't hurt me, for a change.'"

He dropped his head back against the sofa and chuckled softly. She wasn't kidding. She really did see thought bubbles.

"What are you laughing at?" Using her elbows, she hoisted her head and shoulders up a few inches. "You're trying to say I read you wrong?"

"I wouldn't dare. All I'm wondering is how you think I got from the 'I could use some uncomplicated sex' thought bubble to the one that says, 'We should stop seeing each other.'"

She dropped back, waving his words away with one hand. "Oh, that's easy. See, you're a good guy. You've got a good heart, and somebody filled it with notions of chivalry and Sir Galahad and stuff like that. So in the five minutes it took us to walk to your cabin, you convinced yourself your plan wasn't fair to me. You don't think you should lead me on, given that you can't get over Belle. Besides, you're planning to move to Florida soon. Ergo, it's time to break up."

Mitch was literally speechless, which didn't happen very often. His hands stilled on her foot as a sudden, long-forgotten memory of his mother surfaced. She had died when he was three. She'd been in bed a long, long time, but he'd spent many hours in a chair beside her while she told him stories of gallant knights and damsels in distress.

He looked at Crimson. "You're scary, you know that?" But he smiled when he said it, because, beneath the sassy exterior, she was also somehow very sweet.

"Yeah. I know." Though she'd drunk very little of her coffee, she seemed to have sobered. She swung her feet down and pulled herself to a sitting position. She ran her fingers through her hair, not smoothing it as most women would, but making sure it stood up as spiky as ever.

She reminded him, endearingly, of a baby porcupine he'd found once, a terrified creature that used its little spikes as armor.

He kept that to himself, though. He had a feeling she wouldn't enjoy the comparison.

She gave him a very straight look. "But you're wrong," she said. "We should definitely keep seeing each other, at least for a while, till we find out whether you're gonna be able to let her go."

He smiled grimly. He'd already "let her go." The only thing left to find out was whether he could move on, or whether he'd be stuck in this sour, dysfunctional, sexless life forever.

"Look, we have fun, right?" Crimson still watched him without coyness. "I like you, and you like me. And since we've taken sex off the table, what's wrong with that?"

"Nothing." He shook his head. "I just think you should understand that I—that she—"

"I get it." She leaned over and put her hand on his cheek, letting his jawline rest in her palm. "I do. I know you're all tangled up over her. But it has occurred to you, I'm sure, that you don't have a monopoly on tangles."

He liked the easy way she touched him. It was uncomplicated and undemanding, like the comforting encouragement of a true friend.

He smiled. "No monopolies. But does that mean you've been in a—"

"It means I didn't spring fully formed from the oyster shell, either. It means I come with a history. I come with baggage. Lots and lots of tangles. And it means that maybe, for the time being, a nice guy who doesn't want to jump into bed with me is exactly what I'm looking for."

He studied her eyes carefully, and she met his gaze without blinking or glancing away. She wasn't playing games. She really was content to be just friends—at least for a while.

He didn't kid himself she'd hang around forever, if he didn't pull himself together soon. A guy who dragged around his broken heart like a ball and chain wasn't all that great as a lover *or* a friend.

She dropped her hand and leaned over to pick up her shoes. "So…deal?"

Before he could answer, something happened

outside. He turned his head toward the window. He thought he heard…something. Outside, in the darkness. Footsteps, maybe? But not the other guests. The sound had been nearer than any of the other cabins.

Or maybe he hadn't heard anything. In a way, it had been more like a feeling, a strange sensation that moved the small hairs at the base of his neck.

He leaned back and with two fingers parted the curtains a couple of inches so he could check the yard.

To his surprise, the common area was utterly still. Nothing moved, not even the easy quivers of aspen leaves. Starlight silvered everything, so the scene looked more like a photo than a real living landscape.

"Hey. *Deal?*" Crimson had her shoes on, and she'd stood, but she was still waiting for an answer.

He let the curtains fall shut, confused and oddly disappointed. His instincts didn't often mislead him like that.

"Of course," he said, finding a smile. "Deal."

By NOON, the Saturday-afternoon sun felt vicious, as if it were trying to burn Belle's hair right off her head. *What a day!* Everyone had been complaining about the unseasonable heat wave. It hadn't seemed too bad to her, until today.

She'd been supervising the delivery of fifty

large containers of Mojave sage, but after she signed the invoice and sent the nursery workers home, she decided she'd take the rest of the afternoon off.

Saturday was her free day, anyhow. She had only handled the delivery personally because she was eager to see the plants. The sage came in several shades of purple—lavender, grape, maroon and almost all the way to blue. She'd wanted to be sure they'd brought the right ones.

They had. After inspecting the last feathery violet blooms, she straightened up and arched her back to loosen the aching muscles. She lifted her hair onto her head, then bent forward so the cooler air could blow across her damp neck.

All around her, people milled about, their laughter, shouts and conversation filling the air with a pleasant hum. Staff members wore casual khaki-colored jeans and green T-shirts with the Bell River logo on the breast. But you could have identified them easily, even without the uniform. They were the lithe, athletic ones moving fast, carrying saddles or sports equipment or clipboards—or, like that teenager over by the stables, leading parades of eager children to their pony rides, canoeing and rock climbing.

The guests were usually completely different. Often overdressed, they strolled rather than bustled. They exclaimed over every wildflower and took pictures of the fringe of mountaintops that ringed the land. They carried nothing heavier than beer bottles, volleyballs or binoculars.

"Hey, haven't you ever heard of weekends?"

At the sudden sound, Belle released her hair and lifted her head. Bree, Rowena's elegant blonde sister, who was in charge of all social activities, stood in front of her, smiling. She didn't look at all affected by the heat. "Surely Ro lets you take a day off now and then?"

Belle returned the smile. She liked Bree, though she didn't know her as well as she knew the others—partly because of Bree's natural reserve and partly because she didn't live in the heart of the ranch, like her sisters. Bree and her husband, Gray Harper, ran a horse-breeding operation way at the other end of Bell River's spreading acres.

"It's not Ro," Belle assured her. "It's me. I'm so nervous about getting this right. I'm not a professional landscape designer, you know, so I've got a lot to prove."

"Ah, the need to impress Rowena. We've all been there." Though her blue eyes twinkled, Bree shook her head, as if bewildered and amused in equal measure. "I'm not sure I understand it, but I definitely recognize it."

She took a second to give Belle a calmly appraising look. "Though frankly I wouldn't have thought *you*—" she put a small emphasis on the word "—would really need to impress anyone."

Belle flushed a little. She knew what Bree meant,

of course. But surely the woman didn't really think that having money eliminated the need for love and approval?

"I could say the same about you," Belle countered pleasantly, giving Bree's impeccable, Grace Kelly beauty a quick once-over. "But as far as I can tell, insecurity is just the universal human condition. Deep inside, we're all a little bit afraid we're not good enough."

Bree laughed comfortably, though a quick shift in her face said she knew she'd been subtly corrected.

"Exactly." Bree grinned. "Well, except Rowena, of course. Rowena is the exception to all rules, because Rowena is a law unto herself."

Belle thought about the early days, when Rowena hardly slept for fear she wouldn't be able to pull off the dude-ranch miracle. She would rather have dropped right in her tracks, like a horse flogged to death, than let anyone say, "I knew you couldn't do it."

"Oh, I don't know," Belle said. "I suspect there's a little demon of self-doubt on her shoulder, too."

Bree nodded slowly, her expression losing some of its cool distance. "So…what are you doing this afternoon? Are you entirely booked up? Because Ro and Penny and I are heading out to work on a secret project, and it would be great if you could come, too."

Belle wasn't sure what to say. She didn't have

any pressing chores and had, in fact, been dreading spending the afternoon alone in her cabin. When she was surrounded by other people, even strangers, she found it so much easier to shut off her thoughts.

And ever since the anonymous text she'd gotten last night after the party, she'd been strangely on edge.

"I don't know. If it's something private, maybe it should be family only. I can—"

"Please, don't say no." Bree put out a hand, though she stopped short of touching Belle's arm. "It's not private—it's just secret." She chuckled, obviously aware of how silly that sounded. "And it's fun. Please. Ro'll kill me if she heard I left you behind."

There wasn't an inch of truth in that statement, as Bree had obviously just this minute decided to include her, but Belle couldn't resist. The Wright women could be prickly, independent and demanding, but they could also exert an irresistible charm.

# CHAPTER NINE

AN HOUR LATER, Belle was extremely glad she'd said yes. The four women were in downtown Silverdell, crowded into a small but gorgeous bridal salon, trying on dresses and tiaras and veils.

Ro had filled Belle in on the "secret project" as they drove, all piled into her car. They were going to plan a secret wedding.

Belle's eyes widened. A secret wedding? How was that even possible? And who were the bride and groom? For one ridiculous moment, she feared Rowena had decided to force Mitch to marry her. But of course, even Ro wasn't that crazy. Given how Mitch felt, it would have required a shotgun, the proverbial team of wild horses and maybe some chloroform.

The real answer made much more sense. Tess, their newly discovered half sister, who ran the spa side of the ranch, was planning to marry her fiancé, Jude Calhoun, in a quiet civil ceremony at the courthouse next month.

The couple had rejected the idea of a big wedding. They thought they should downplay the whole thing, they said, given their unusual circumstances.

And then, of course, the sisters had to fill Belle in on those "circumstances," which took most of the short ride into town. Not only was Tess heavily pregnant by her horrible ex-husband, but the creepy ex had actually been killed on Bell River property only a few months ago.

"It was awful. Still, if Tess thinks we're going to let her sneak off to some government office somewhere to get married, as if she's got anything to be ashamed of, she's got another think coming." Rowena sounded merrily indignant. "It's not her fault she married a weirdo. So we're going to throw her a surprise wedding!"

At first, Belle could only sit back and marvel at the formidable tidal wave of energy the Wright women created when they put their minds to something. Luckily, the bridal-shop owner seemed to have known them all their lives and had dressed them for their own weddings. After a few pleasantries, the woman withdrew to her private office, giving them the run of the place.

It was the first time Belle had seen all three sisters together like this, happily playing and cracking jokes. She felt as if she were getting a privileged glimpse of how they might have been as children.

Ro was still the boss, Penny was still the softy and Bree was still quiet, but they were wonderful together. They laughed and argued and snatched veils from one another's heads, until at one point they collapsed together on the small blue satin chaise. They might have been a trio of happy, tumbling kittens.

But soon the wave swept Belle up, too, and she was as giddy as the rest of them. When Penny encouraged her to try on one of the dresses, a simple, knee-length white sheath that Penny said would be perfect for her, she let herself be persuaded.

But the minute she put it on, she felt ridiculous. She walked out of the dressing room reluctantly, miserably self-conscious. The others had tried dresses, too, though all of them were already married. Still, Belle's case was unusual. She wasn't engaged and probably never would be, not to the man she loved.

And she couldn't quite imagine agreeing to marry anyone else.

As Belle came through the dressing-room door, Ro looked up, then groaned.

"Oh, good Lord, why'd you let her do that, Penny?" Ro tossed a tiara back into the display case irritably. But, in spite of the tone, she was smiling. "Now the rest of us are going to look like ugly ducklings stumbling around the swan."

Bree made a tsking sound. "Give the gal a break, Ro. She can't help being gorgeous."

Penny didn't respond, intently absorbed in fuss-ing with the neckline, then the hem, determined to get it exactly right. She was the artistic sister, and she obviously knew what she was doing. When Belle stepped onto the little round platform and looked at herself in the three-way mirror, she almost stopped breathing.

She'd never seen such an exquisite dress in her life—though she hadn't been able to detect anything remarkable when it was on the hanger. But now that it was on a real body, its minimalism—chiffon over satin, with three-quarter sleeves and a ballerina neckline—was absolutely perfect.

If Belle ever did marry, she would want to wear this dress.

Penny's doe-brown eyes shone with triumph. "I knew it. I knew it would suit you. Your looks are so…so extraordinary. You need a simple dress."

Rowena came over, and she met Belle's gaze in the mirror. "It's magic," she said quietly. "The very best kind of magic."

Magic, indeed. What else could it be? Belle had spent so much time looking at paintings of her supposed "beauty" that she'd actually come to hate her otherworldly looks. As a child, she'd prayed every night she would wake up looking more normal.

Of course, she never had. And when her grandmother had dressed her up in the extreme costumes she used in the oils, Belle had ended up resembling some intense fairy-child creature, whose sexuality felt off, unhealthy, and whose hold on sanity was, at best, precarious.

In this dress, though, she looked like a woman. A healthy, happy, *normal* woman. Slim, but fit, even a little muscular and outdoorsy. Messy reddish hair and friendly blue eyes, sunburned cheekbones and a nose full of freckles from these long days in the hot sun.

She smiled at herself, then instinctively covered her mouth with her hand, as if she'd done something vulgar.

Ro laughed. "Don't do that—be proud!" She twitched the hemline, just as Penny had, then grinned. "If I looked like that, I'd be strutting in the street, yelling, 'Hey, mortals! Get an eyeful of this!'"

Bree rolled her eyes. "I'm pretty sure you *have* done that, haven't you?"

And then they were off again, teasing and carrying on and arguing about veils. Belle hoped she could use the distraction to slip back into the dressing room, but Rowena caught her at the door.

She touched Belle's elbow softly. "Hey. I know I'm hovering and smothering, but I can't help it. It's all those mommy hormones, I guess." She rolled her eyes. "Anyhow…I take it nothing has changed with Mitch?"

Belle shook her head. "He's still seeing Crimson, and he's still avoiding me. And I assume, since you haven't said anything, that he's still making plans to leave town."

"Dallas says so." Rowena gnawed on the edge of her thumb, a habit Belle knew she'd tried hard to break but obviously hadn't. She did it every time she was agitated. "What the devil is wrong with that man? We should get him over here and let him see you in this dress. That would bring him around, I bet."

"God, no." Belle felt ill at the thought. "I'm sure he already thinks you're matchmaking. I can't imagine how disgusted he'd be if he thought we'd engineered a surprise sighting of me in a bridal gown."

Rowena wrinkled her nose. "Well, if he wouldn't insist on being such a stubborn fool, no one would *need* to do any matchmaking, would they?"

Belle smiled. Rowena would fight to the death for anyone she cared about, which was lovable. And yet, this was one time her intervention would be a terrible mistake. Mitch needed to believe the woman he loved trusted and respected him. If Belle seemed to be ganging up with his bossy sister-in-law to pull his strings like a puppeteer, he'd hate them both for it.

"I appreciate that you're rooting for us, Ro, but please, don't try anything like that. It would only make things worse." She took a deep breath. "If that's possible."

Ro knocked on the wooden door frame. "Don't

even say that. Of course it's possible for things to be worse." She shuddered. "He could actually *marry* one of those women."

"And he may." Belle thought of the silhouettes on his cabin curtains, the two heads so close together. She laid her hand against a sudden pain between her ribs. Her palm felt hot against the cool chiffon. "I have to be realistic. He waited for me a long time, but he's too alive, too male…" She tried to smile. "Too *Mitch* to wait forever."

Ro didn't answer for several seconds. She clutched a lacy bridal veil in her hands, and she let it sag in front of her, touching the floor. She rested her shoulder against the door frame, as if she needed the support while she thought things through.

Finally, she took a deep breath, raised her head and spoke.

"Look, Belle…I don't want you to take this the wrong way, okay? I love you, and I love having you here. As far as I'm concerned, you could live at Bell River forever. But I know you actually have a real home, and obligations, somewhere else. If you think it's time for you to call it quits and head back to California, you should go. I don't want you to feel stuck here, just because you said you'd help with the grounds."

Belle looked at Rowena, momentarily dumb.

*No. You're wrong. I don't have a* real *home anywhere.*

The words welled up from somewhere deep inside, and they pushed at her throat. But she clenched her jaw and somehow managed not to let them come out.

Greenwood wasn't home to her, and it never would be again—but that was hardly the same thing as being homeless. Why all this self-pity? Did she really think she was the first, or the last, woman to be rejected?

A broken heart wasn't the end of the world. With time, she'd heard, they even mended... stronger than before. And she was so much luckier than many people. She had money. She was young and healthy. Over the past couple of years, she'd even discovered she had her fair share of courage.

She could start over, somewhere else, if she had to. She was so lucky, really. With her assets, she could start fresh in Paris or London or Tahiti. Any sparkling city in the world was hers.

Any city but Silverdell.

"I want to finish the landscaping," she said. "If that's okay with you. But I think you're right. I probably should leave after that."

For answer, Rowena simply hugged her, hard. They were still clinging to each other, with all the unspoken emotion hanging in the air, when the chimes over the salon's front door rang out.

They both turned at the sound, instinctively

looking toward the street entrance. Two men had entered, one carrying a baby.

The bright afternoon light threw them into silhouettes as they entered, but a cold sensation sank to the pit of Belle's stomach.

The larger man was probably Dallas, judging by the way he held the baby with the hilarious Mohawk.

But the other man was Mitch. Belle recognized him instantly—she knew his outline by heart. She had drawn it a hundred times. That easy expanse of shoulder, that rakish swoosh of hair over his forehead, those narrow hips and long legs...

And here she stood, in a wedding dress.

Rowena looked at Belle. "You have *got* to be kidding me." Rowena's eyes were round, but her wide mouth was already curving in a smile that acknowledged the impossible absurdity of their situation.

"I swear to heaven, Belle. I did *not* set this up."

"DID YOU HAVE anything to do with that?" Mitch's voice was tight, and Dallas's truck suddenly didn't seem quite big enough for the both of them *and* the memory of all those women in one room, all decked out in wedding gear.

He didn't bother to explain what he meant by "that." He didn't have to. It was encoded in male DNA to react to the sight of four women in bridal wear.

Dallas, who was driving, lifted his fingers from the wheel, disavowing the entire episode. "That's a big *hell no,* little brother. Definitely not my style. If I wanted to get you two together, I'd probably just siphon off your gas so you'd run out somewhere lonely." He chuckled, obviously reminiscing. "Corny as it sounds, it works, you know?"

Mitch didn't answer. He wasn't in the mood for jokes. He was getting pretty sick of this. He propped his elbow on the windowsill and rested his temple against his knuckles. He needed to calm down.

"But it's not Rowena's style, either, if you ask me." Dallas glanced over at Mitch cautiously. "In case you were planning to be mad at her."

"I'm not *mad* at anybody." Mitch forced his voice into a more normal register. "I just don't appreciate finding myself the main character in an idiotic sitcom. What did they *think* would happen if I saw her in a wedding dress? Did they think I'd drop to my knees and propose to her on the spot? I'm not Pavlov's dog, for God's sake."

Dallas let one corner of his mouth tuck in a little, but he didn't answer the question directly. He drove in silence for a while. They were headed into Montrose to pick up a couple of mountain bikes that had just come in, which was why they'd needed to drop Rosie off with Rowena.

The silence and the hum of the road under the

truck's tires gradually did their job, and Mitch felt his system begin to cool. Now that he was thinking a little straighter, he couldn't see how Rowena could have contrived this charade deliberately. No one knew the bikes would come in early or that Mitch would take a notion to ride along.

He gazed at the ranch land sweeping away on either side of the road. The wildflowers had gone crazy this year, and the grass looked as if someone had let kindergartners loose with pastel crayons. Yellow, blue, pink, purple, red...

This part of Colorado truly was beautiful country. Rugged and bare sometimes, but haunting, graceful and real. He realized he'd foolishly taken it for granted all these years.

He wondered what Florida looked like in the spring. He'd never been there, even when he and Belle were traveling, so in his brain the whole state looked like publicity shots of Disney World.

It would be summer, though, before he started work at the Linebaugh stables—not spring. He wanted to stay here for Jude's wedding, naturally, and then he felt an obligation to help at Bell River through the rest of the spring season, which didn't end until June 1.

After that, he was going to build in a few weeks' vacation, so he didn't have to hop from one job right into another. He probably wouldn't hit Ocala until nearly July, and you didn't need a meteorologist to tell you what the weather would be like then. It would be sidewalk-melting hot.

He shifted on the truck's seat, imagining horseflies and mosquitoes the size of bullfrogs. He tried to recollect why he had chosen Florida. Suddenly it seemed like the dumbest idea he'd ever had.

He needed to think about something else.

They drove in silence for a while, letting the corniness fade. And then, five or ten minutes later, Dallas cleared his throat.

"Belle did look pretty amazing, though, huh?"

Mitch swung his head toward his brother. Dallas's troublemaker dimple was showing, so he knew he was intentionally poking the hornet's nest.

"Don't start," Mitch warned.

"Well, she did." Dallas flicked a grin his way, then returned his attention to trying to pass a horse trailer that was apparently being driven by a dead person. "I mean, come on. You don't have to want to marry her to see how hot she looked. You just have to have eyes."

"Shut up." Mitch was already having enough trouble getting the picture of Belle out of his brain. *Amazing. Hot. Yeah.* Definitely true, but even so, he wasn't sure those were the right words.

In fact, he wasn't sure the right words existed.

Too bad her grandmother couldn't see her in that dress. That was the real Annabelle Irving.

A body that flowed and curved with a natural grace, like a river or a ribbon in the wind. Hair that made a man's fingers tingle just from looking at it.... Hair that would scald him like a brand if it touched his skin. And a face...

He shut his eyes. He wasn't poet enough to describe her face.

All he knew was that when he saw her standing there, all gold and pink and white and wonderful in that dress, he'd had a knifelike flash of premonition. He'd understood with sharp clarity that someday, when she'd left Colorado and given up on him, she'd stand before another man in a dress like that, and she would say, "I do."

"Mitch. You okay?"

Dallas was frowning in his direction, and Mitch wondered if he'd made a weird sound or something. His throat felt tight and oddly jagged, so maybe he had.

*Enough. Stop being such a masochist.* Okay, she'd marry some poor love-maddened fool someday. So what? Just meant she'd drive *that guy* crazy instead. Just meant *that guy* would be the one to sit up all night, trying to figure out how to get his bride to open up and let him in. His beautiful bride with her unreachable silence and her secrets and her inability to share anything that mattered.

Mitch mentally saluted the poor sucker. *Good luck, buddy. You're a better man than me.*

"I'm fine," he said out loud and started trying to think of a way to change the subject.

Then his cell phone rang. He smiled to himself at the cliché. *Saved by the bell.*

He didn't recognize the number, but any distraction would do. He answered. "This is Mitch."

"Mitch, this is Jacob Burns." The caller had an educated, pleasing voice, well modulated and warm. "We haven't met, but you may have heard of me. I am Annabelle Irving's cousin."

*Good God.* Mitch's hand almost went slack on the phone. He hadn't remembered her cousin's last name and hadn't placed him at first. This was the psycho? What the hell was this bastard doing, calling him?

"Oh, dear." Jacob chuckled wryly into the awkward silence. "I suppose that means you've heard the worst about me. None of Belle's accusations are true, but of course you won't believe that. Still, I hope you'll listen to what I have to say. I know you care about Annabelle, and I was hoping you might help me with something. Something that would be in her best interests."

*Her best interests? Right.* Mitch fought down a sudden Neanderthal urge to reach through the phone and throttle the lying son of a—

*Steady.* He wasn't a kid anymore, and he didn't beat up people he disliked.

"I'm afraid you've been given bad information,

Mr. Burns," he said, his voice clipped. "Belle and I aren't together anymore."

"I had heard that," Jacob murmured supportively. "I'm so sorry. And believe me, I sympathize. It can be difficult to maintain a long-term relationship with Annabelle. She's very…high-strung."

He sounded melancholy, as if it pained him to think of his poor, unstable cousin, but also aggrieved, as if he was bone-tired of being portrayed as a bad guy.

Wow, the guy was good. Really good. Mitch had a pretty reliable built-in lie detector, and even he didn't detect a fake note in Jacob's delivery.

"And I also know, all too well, that being estranged from her doesn't necessarily mean you've stopped caring about her." Jacob sighed. "That's why I hope you still might help me."

"Well, you're wrong about that," Mitch said flatly. "Dead wrong."

He might not be able to pin down the phony notes, but he knew he wanted no piece of this, whatever it was.

Burns might be a first-class bastard, but he wasn't Mitch's problem. Why start acting all Sir Galahad now? No matter what stories his mother had told him, Belle wasn't his princess, and he wasn't on dragon duty anymore.

Even when he had been, she'd actively rejected

his protection. She'd ditched him without a word, choosing to fight her battles alone.

So it was a little late, and a little pathetic, to rev into super-chivalry mode now.

"Mitch, please." Jacob's voice wheedled. "I just want to sell her my— "

"No." Mitch shut him down before he could mention the Annabelle Oils. "I said I won't help you. Whatever it is you're offering, peddle it somewhere else."

And then he hung up. He clicked End. He put the phone on mute. When even that didn't feel like enough, he turned the damn thing off and stuffed it in the glove compartment.

He turned to Dallas, blocking the inevitable questions.

"Don't ask," he growled. "Just drive."

BELLE HAD LEARNED that Sunday mornings were the most peaceful time at Bell River. Most weeks, the ranch hosted a Saturday Night Social in the activities hall, at which some people partied a little too hard. So in case anyone needed to nurse a throbbing head the next day, the youth staff always planned a Sunday day trip for the younger guests.

This morning, the children had lined up early, under a huge blue sky, to have their binoculars hung around their necks and their bird-watching journals slipped into their backpacks. Then they were helped onto their horses and clopped off in a parade toward the middle meadows, where they would get a birding lesson from Barton James and a nature photography class from Penny.

Half a dozen young staffers rode along, as well. Keeping track of fifteen kids under twelve years old, most of whom would cry, or fall, or fight, or puke, or wander off, sounded to Belle like a terrifying prospect.

One of the young men—a boy, really…he didn't look a whole lot older than his charges—waved at Belle as they rode past. Seeing him wave, about six of the little kids did the same, calling goodbye cheerily, though they probably had no idea who that lady kneeling in the flowerbed over there could possibly be.

She smiled, lifted a mud-covered hand and returned the salute. Just one of the many things she loved about Bell River. There were no strangers here. Guest or staff, busboy or queen, you were family the minute you drove through the gate.

She bent back to her work, digging up the yarrow that filled the beds between the large paddock and the stables. Rowena had pointed out the areas most likely to be photographed, and Belle was concentrating on those first. In this spot, the yarrow was pretty, but it was old, leggy and just about played out.

She had an idea that Spanish gold broom would work well here. It could handle the dust and activity, and it had the advantage of blooming a little earlier than the yarrow, which would help in the photos.

She dropped another yarrow into her cart, wiped her forehead, which had already grown damp, and had just bent down to dig when she heard the sound of a text message coming in. She pulled off one glove so she could use the smartphone keys, then dug out her phone and looked at the incoming.

You look awesome in blue.

The hairs at the back of her neck prickled, and the same shivery feeling cascaded down her forearms. She rose to her knees so she could scan the area around her. But there didn't seem to be anyone nearby.

She absently tugged at her blue cotton shirt, which had been chosen purely for utility, was at least ten years old and hadn't ever looked particularly good on her, anyhow. It clashed with her eyes.

Her fingertips against the fabric felt oddly cold, and numb, as if she were using someone else's hand. She tucked the phone back in her pocket. If someone was watching her, she wouldn't give them the satisfaction of appearing worried.

She dug by rote, her mind racing. Who could possibly be sending these texts? They weren't threatening, really…except in their anonymity. And in their specific mention of some present condition—her hair, her shirt. It carried a subtle undercurrent of stalking. *I can see you. Right now. I can see you.*

As she pulled up the last yarrow, she heard the sound of horses' hooves again—this time very near.

She glanced up, suddenly tense.

"Hi, there."

Belle breathed more normally. It was Rowena, on her pretty paint mare, Flash.

Rowena glanced at her watch and grinned. "Clearly you haven't recovered from your workaholic problem."

Belle smiled, so happy to see a friend she probably would have hugged her, if she could reach her.

"It doesn't feel like work." She sat back on her knees, surveying the wet ground and her own mucky clothes. It had rained hard last night. "It feels like making mudpies."

Belle knew Rowena understood. Ro felt the same way about her ranch and had been working eighty-hour weeks since the moment the idea was born.

Belle didn't mention the text. She didn't want to seem neurotic. She certainly didn't want to let on that she still dreaded being alone in her cabin. Last night, she'd been restless till three o'clock, then awake again at six. She'd tried everything. Reading, yoga, solitaire, hot milk, counting stars…but nothing put her to sleep.

Desperate, she'd even tried pulling out her sketch pad and attempted to draw the cabins, the trees, the wildflowers, anything she could see from her window. But all the sketches fell flat. And then she did something she hadn't done in over a year. She tried to draw a person.

She had Mitch on the mind, so she decided to see if she could get him safely down on paper instead. She wondered if she could capture his face as it had looked yesterday, when he had spotted her by the dressing-room door.

She still wasn't sure what emotion he had been expressing. She thought maybe, if she could sketch it, she might recognize it, even if it was too complicated and subtle to have a name.

But she scratched through every attempt, then wadded up the papers, tossing them in the trash basket, deeply dissatisfied. The expression had been so fleeting and had been so quickly replaced by cool, shuttered detachment.

Her small talent simply wasn't able to capture it. She wondered whether her grandmother could've done better.

The whole thing had left her frustrated and lonelier, edgier than ever. So she'd put on her jeans, grabbed her gloves and headed out to work.

"You okay?" Rowena shifted a little in her saddle. "After yesterday?"

Belle used her palm to shade her eyes as she smiled up at her friend. "Of course. Turns out no one actually dies of embarrassment after all."

"Nope. We just sometimes wish we could." Rowena chuckled, then nickered softly to Flash, who was growing restless. "Anyhow, I wanted to warn you that Mitch is planning to train one of our new horses today. Good of him to actually grace our presence. He may use the inside arena, but the weather's so nice…"

Belle understood. In this weather, Mitch would probably bring the horse outside, to this wide green paddock just beyond the stable, just yards from where she worked.

He'd be right where she could watch him—and vice versa, if he cared enough.

She put down her trowel. "When's he coming?"

"He's already here. He's saddling Persia right now. And…" Rowena wrinkled her nose, always a sign she was trying to hold back some emotion. "And he's got Crimson with him."

Already here—and not alone. Belle shot a glance at the stables, but they were too big and too well built to reveal any activity within. Some primitive instinct told her to hustle away, right now, before he could emerge. She even put her gloved palms on her thighs, readying herself to rise.

But then she changed her mind.

By heaven, she wasn't going to run. Running would look...ashamed. She couldn't pretend she wasn't embarrassed about yesterday and sorry she looked so disheveled and muddy now. And... okay, she was jealous, too, of Crimson, because the other woman was relaxed and confident and having a wonderful time with the man Belle loved.

But she wasn't *ashamed* of anything.

"Okay," she said brightly as she picked up her discarded trowel. "Thanks for the heads-up."

Rowena grinned. "Good for you. Well, don't work too hard."

She cantered off, so graceful she might have been one with the horse. At the far edge of the paddock, she waved over her shoulder. Then Flash's white shanks churned in the sunlight as Ro urged him into a gallop, and she disappeared into a small poplar grove, her black hair streaming behind her.

As if that was his cue, Mitch suddenly emerged from the stable, leading a large brown stallion who stepped high and lively and tossed his head every few seconds, as if trying to shake free his harness. Belle knew horses only from her months here, and from traveling with Mitch, but she'd learned enough to know this horse was a handful.

Crimson followed them at a safe distance. Belle watched the trio and tried to read the body language. Mitch was revved with an eager energy, as if he couldn't wait to meet the stallion's challenge. The horse was defiant. And Crimson... Well, at the moment she was staring at Mitch's backside. The half smile on her lips was familiar to any female. She was enthusiastically enjoying the view.

As if she felt a gaze on her, she turned her head suddenly toward Belle. When she recognized her, she smiled. Then, rather looking embarrassed to be caught ogling, she held up one hand, waggling the fingers in the universal sign for "smoking hot."

It was too innocently mischievous to be annoying. Belle found herself smiling back before she gave it a second thought.

Mitch still didn't seem to have noticed Belle. Concentrating mostly on controlling the horse, he opened the paddock gate and led Persia in. Crimson didn't follow. She climbed onto the small white fence and arranged herself for viewing. She tugged at her shirt, crossed her legs three different ways before settling on one, then fluffed her hair and ran a forefinger around the rim of her lips. She clearly expected to be both audience and show.

Did that mean they hadn't slept together yet? Belle hadn't ever primped in that superficial way again, not once she'd made love to Mitch. Their connection, their animal need for each other, was so much deeper than lipstick or hair spray. Bare naked, sweating and tousled, flushed and panting and raw—that was when they were the most irresistible to each other. She never cared what she wore, because all he wanted was to strip it off. She never arranged herself in artificially seductive poses, because the primal ballet of their bodies coming together was rough and clumsy, but also exquisitely beautiful and true.

She shoved her trowel into the dirt blindly, fighting a dizzy, swooning sensation in her midsection at the thought of their lovemaking. The earth turned easily, the sides sliding into the hole where the yarrow had been removed. She felt that same loose, sliding emptiness deep inside, in her heart. In the place where Mitch used to be.

She didn't look up again for a long time. She didn't want to see him. He'd be winning Persia over already, she knew. He was wonderful with horses. He was sensitive, patient and gentle, but always commanding, always in charge. He intuited their needs, and he honored their power even as he tamed it.

She'd seen him settle nervous horses in one session and saddle break wild ones that had been written off as expensive mistakes.

So she didn't look up, not even when Crimson cheered some impressive success. It was Crimson's turn to admire, to cheerlead and to swoon. Why torture herself?

"Mitch! Oh, my God! *Mitch!*"

Crimson's voice changed—this cry was obviously one of distress. It rang through the clear air, followed almost instantly by the thud of hooves galloping, so rough Belle felt the ground shimmer beneath the blows.

She jerked to her feet, confused, cold fear shooting through her veins, driven only by instinct. What had happened? Her gaze frantically searched the paddock, but Mitch and Persia were no longer inside it.

Then she saw them.

The horse had leaped the fence and was even now barreling down the grassy area beside the stable, trampling columbine, snowberry and flox. He was white-eyed, frantic and clearly out of control.

A second later, maybe less, the horse reared back, and Mitch lost his balance. He let go of the reins and tumbled hard onto the dirt, collapsing in an ominous splatter of muddy topsoil.

"Mitch!" Belle noticed, numbly, that her voice sounded exactly like Crimson's. Both were composed of pure terror.

She didn't stop to think. She ran to where he lay…

And realized, too late, that Persia had changed course and was coming straight for her. By the time Belle realized her danger, the horse was already above her, his powerful hooves beating the air.

She dodged, but it was no use. One of the legs

clipped her shoulder. The next one caught her left temple. Red pain exploded behind her eyes, and then there was nothing.

## CHAPTER TEN

FLAT ON HIS BACK in the mud, Mitch blinked up at the blue sky, feeling like an idiot. Thank heaven it had rained last night. If the ground hadn't been soft, that stupid maneuver might have been a real problem.

As he scrambled to his feet and realized he was basically in one piece, he started to laugh. "That's what I get for—"

*For showing off.* That was what he'd intended to say. But then he saw Persia racing away from him...and one hideous split second later he saw that a woman stood directly in the horse's manic path.

Not just a woman. *Belle.*

He started to run, even though he knew it was too late. The horse sped past her, *over her,* and she cried out once. She was already in a heap on the ground when he reached her.

"Bonnie," he said thickly. She was moving, thank God. She was trying to rise up on one elbow, but she wasn't going to make it. He knelt in the mud and caught her in his arms as she dropped back down.

Her eyelids fluttered but didn't open. "I'm okay," she said in the monotone of shock. "But…my head."

He feathered her hair back with two fingers. *God.* He couldn't tell exactly what had happened, but there was too much blood.

"You'll be fine," he said. "You're fine."

He scooped her into his arms.

Maybe that wasn't right. Maybe he shouldn't have moved her. But his body didn't consult the first-aid checklist before it acted. It didn't even ask his brain.

As he stood, he saw Crimson next to him, her eyes round as saucers and her hands squeezed tightly against her chest.

"Call nine-one-one," he said.

THE NEXT COUPLE of hours were among the longest of his life. When they were finally over, and the doctor was gone, Belle was resting comfortably in the River Song cabin with Penny, Max and Ellen.

Mitch, who had remained in the big house, walked slowly toward the great room, where Crimson was waiting for him. Barton had delivered her a cup of coffee and said she seemed fine, but though he'd offered to get someone to drive her home, she'd been determined to wait.

As Mitch moved down the hall, he felt as creaky as an old man, his legs as heavy as boat anchors. His whole body seemed to sag, as if he'd been operating on artificial energy that had suddenly drained out some unseen breach.

Adrenaline crash, probably. Still, why wasn't he happy? They'd dodged tragedy today, and he ought to feel lucky as hell. Belle had six stitches, but she was fine. Head wounds bled all out of proportion to the injury, the doctor reminded them.

Mitch knew that, of course. He'd had a few of his own through the years. But his mind hadn't been working well enough to remember random facts. All he'd registered was blood.

The family had picked Max and Penny to take care of Belle tonight, because their cottage, River Song, had already been expanded and actually had its own guest room. Plus, Max's daughter, Ellen, was eleven and could be counted on to help—or at least not to hurt.

Rowena had lobbied to keep Belle with her, but Dallas had finally made her see reason. The baby might cry all night, and Alec...well, Alec was Alec.

Mitch had felt so strange, standing there, listening to the absurd back and forth. Once, he would have told them all to shut up and go away. Belle would stay with him, of course. He would take care of her.

But not anymore. No one even suggested it. He was as irrelevant as a fly on the wall.

He finally reached the great room. Crimson was perched on a big armchair near the unlit fire, an unopened magazine in her lap. She looked up when he entered.

"They tell me she's fine," she said, smiling tentatively. "That must be a relief for you. Especially since it was your horse…"

He nodded. Amazingly, no one had blamed him. No one had even hinted he ought to feel guilty, but he did. Trust Crimson to know that.

"I pushed Persia too hard," he said. "I got cocky."

She shrugged. "Maybe."

He liked that she didn't brush away the idea it might be his fault. He'd never understood that technique. People could tell you all day long you hadn't been a jackass, but if you knew you had, how did that help?

"I should have known he would balk. The minute I got in the saddle, I could feel his frustration, but I told myself I could settle him." He lifted one side of his mouth. "Maybe I was just trying to impress you."

"Hindsight sucks. And who knows? Different day, you might have pulled it off." She tilted her head, the light from the window catching the red tips of her hair-quills. "And about impressing me… Right up to the part when you got dumped on your butt, you were doing great."

He smiled, and some of his tension slipped away. He plopped down on the armchair next to hers and let his head fall against the headrest. He wasn't quite sure why he felt so awful. The doctor had given him a cursory examination, too, and pronounced him bruised but intact.

"You must be starving," he said, a new guilt kicking in. "The doctor says I won't fully feel the effects until tomorrow. So I could probably handle the picnic at Little Bell, if you're still up for it."

Even as he spoke the words, he realized what a struggle it would be. Little Bell Falls was spectacular this time of year, its crystal blue plunge pool ringed with goldeneye and columbine. And Cookie's picnics were always delicious.

But the idea of sitting on a blanket and concocting small talk for hours, even with Crimson, who made it so easy... It seemed like a Herculean task.

But he owed her, so he offered.

"I don't think so," she said mildly. "But serious chivalry points for the gesture."

"Thanks," he said, relieved. "But next time you've got the weekend off, we'll do it, okay? You've definitely got a rain check."

She didn't answer right away, and his eyes were shut, so he let the silence drift for a few seconds... a minute. Finally, he stirred, opening his eyes to check that she'd heard him. *"Okay?"*

"No, I don't think so," she repeated, her voice as mild as ever. "The truth is...I think I was wrong the other night. I think we ought to call it a day, you and me."

Well, that came from nowhere. Hadn't they already had this conversation? He sat up, confused. "Why?"

"Why?" She rolled her eyes. "Because you looked so stupid, lying there on your butt, that's why."

He frowned at her, but then he saw the gleam in her eye. She was teasing, of course. At least about how he looked flat on his back. She clearly had *not* been kidding about calling it quits.

"Darn." He pulled a dejected face. "That's my best trick, too. The gals usually can't resist."

She smiled, then set her magazine on the coffee table next to her almost-full coffee.

"Look, you know why," she said without rancor. "I told you from the start I don't do rebounders."

He gave her a quizzical look. "But…after the party…you said we should just be friends. What happened between the fiesta and today to change your mind?"

"Well, I had been drinking quite a bit that night, for starters." She grinned. "But the thing is, I thought I could handle being just friends while I waited for you to get over her. I don't want to rush into anything serious any more than you do. But I don't want to waste my time like a fool, either, if there's really no hope."

"So...what happened to make you believe there's no hope?"

She shrugged, as if the reason ought to be obvious. "What happened? *Belle* happened."

*Belle happened?* He twitched irritably. He didn't disagree with her, in principle. They probably should stop dating. He had been uncomfortable all along, fearing he might be leading her on. But the illogic of this particular rationale was frustrating.

"Baloney," he said. "Belle happened *years* ago."

"Not for me, she didn't. For me, she happened today." Crimson's smile was tinged with something sad. "I'd never actually seen you two together."

"Sure you did. At the fiesta, you came right up to us."

She sighed. "Are you being deliberately obtuse, Mitch? I mean I hadn't ever seen you *together*. I'd never seen you touch her."

He flushed, which made him more annoyed. He no longer was sure whether he was annoyed with himself or with her. "I didn't *touch* her. I only carried her inside because she needed help."

One more time, Crimson rolled her eyes. "I don't care if you picked her up with the express purpose of ditching her in the Dumpster. You touched her, Mitch, and the minute you did I knew it was time to fold my cards and go home."

He looked for a good retort. But he couldn't find one. He simply glared at her, his eyes narrowed. "That's ridiculous," he said finally.

"Nope. Not ridiculous at all." She stood, adjusting her jeans and the sexy shirt she'd put on over them. Then she fluffed her hair, the motion he knew he'd always connect with any memory of her.

"I know what I saw, Mitch, and so do you. You're so in love with that woman, and so furious with her at the same time, that it's about tearing you up inside." She gazed at him with an almost-maternal sympathy. "The sad thing is, I'm afraid you've got a lot more hurting to do before you're ready to let her go."

He didn't bother trying to deny it. What was the use? Even with their short acquaintance, Crimson could see right through him, as well as Dallas, or Jude, or any of his very best childhood buddies.

He almost said he hoped they would remain friends, but it would have sounded so insultingly cliché. He'd show her his friendship instead, as time went on. He had a feeling she might need a friend a lot more than she needed a lover, anyhow.

So he just smiled ruefully, conceding the argument with his silence. She walked over to his chair and put her hand on his shoulder. With her other hand, she ran her fingers through his hair. The feathering strokes were light, teasing, futilely trying to spike his heavy waves into an echo of hers.

But he didn't have the right hair for it, and she surrendered with a chuckle.

"You're exhausted, Romeo. Even your hair can't stand up. I think it's time to take me home."

AT TEN O'CLOCK that Monday night, about thirty-six hours after her accident, Belle sat in the great room of the main house, listening to Barton James lead the guests in an encore round of "Home on the Range." The large room was packed. Barton's weekly cowboy sing-along had become one of the highlights of any Bell River holiday.

She had taken a chair in the back, letting the paying guests claim ringside. She hadn't expected to stay long, but one song led to another, and Barton's baritone was so authentic and sweet. Now here she was, nursing a warm lemonade and closing down the place along with everyone else.

But even this lovely little oasis wouldn't last forever, and then she'd have to go back to her cabin. All the sisters, in their turn, had urged her to stay one more night, but she knew she should say no. She didn't need nursing. Penny had woken her every hour on the hour last night, just to be sure she hadn't suffered a concussion. "What's your name? How many fingers am I holding up?"

Two, four, whatever. She never had any trouble, because, miraculously, she hadn't been hurt very badly. But it had been fun, anyhow. Sometimes Ellen came with Penny, just for the novelty of it, and they stayed up, gossiping and laughing and talking about art, which they all loved.

If she stayed another night, this kind of cozy camaraderie could be addictive. She couldn't insinuate herself into the family bosom under false pretenses. Though it amazed everyone, she really was absolutely fine. The stitches didn't even hurt.

So she had to go back to her own cabin. There was nothing to fear there. Jacob was a thousand miles away. And an odd text message that complimented her hair or her shirt was not exactly nightmare territory.

Still, she sat, a paper plate of untouched cookies in her lap, and watched the room empty.

It was only when she saw Mitch walk in that she realized what she'd been waiting for. In all these thirty-six hours, she hadn't seen him once, and she wanted to see him. She wanted to know how he felt after his fall. She wanted...him.

And now here he was. The sing-along was over, and Barton was accepting compliments at the front of the room, his guitar slung over his back and his handsome craggy face beaming. Mitch entered from the side with a young staffer in tow. It was a very young, sweet-faced brunette who might have been the same boy who'd waved to her yesterday.

They consulted a few minutes, seemingly discussing some problem with the river-rock fireplace surround, and then, as he turned to gesture toward the other wall, Mitch saw her.

He was in good-host mode, too smooth to show any reaction. He excused himself to the kid and walked calmly to the back of the room, where she still sat, with her mug of lemonade propped atop the uneaten cookies.

He stopped in front of her but didn't sit down, though the chairs all around her were empty, now that almost everyone had drifted out.

"Hi," he said, smiling. "I'm surprised to see you here. I would have thought you might have enough of a headache already, without adding twelve off-key verses of 'Tom Dooley' to the mix."

She hid her disappointment at the glib line. He was giving her Public Mitch, the merry charmer who was so good at buttering up the guests.

"Oddly, I don't have a headache," she replied in good-guest mode. "I was just this minute thinking how lucky I was. It could have been so much worse."

"Yes." His gaze flickered, and his eyebrows tightened. "Yes, it could have."

An awkward silence followed. He dug his hands into his jeans pockets and stretched his shoulders, working off some tension. "I know Penny took good care of you. She's sweet, isn't she? A born nurturer."

"Absolutely. She's wonderful."

He clearly didn't like the stilted conversation any more than she did, and it seemed to be getting to him. He glanced around the room, shifted on his feet, and then, inhaling deeply, he lowered himself into the chair next to hers.

"Belle." He faced her so he could speak quietly. She was glad to see the public-relations grin was gone. "I'm so glad you are okay. I feel terrible about what happened. I'm sorry I didn't come by sooner, to apologize in person."

She shook her head. "Don't be silly. Rowena brought your apologies. And the flowers were very pretty, if entirely unnecessary. It wasn't your fault."

"Of course it was. I lost control of him. I didn't know you were there, but that doesn't matter. I knew Persia had a temper. I really am so sorry that my mistake ended up hurting you."

"But I'm not hurt," she said. "I'm fine, truly." She let her eyes run quickly across his body. What wasn't hidden by his jacket and jeans looked unmarked. He was as ruggedly graceful and gorgeous as ever. "How about you? That was a pretty bad fall."

"Naw, just a few bruises." He waved it off. "My pride took a far worse beating than my body." He smiled at the disbelief on her face. "I'm not being macho, I promise. I'm sure it looked worse than it was."

"It looked *awful*. I thought—" She wasn't

sure how much she should say. She'd thought he might be dead. Lost to her, forever. Her blood had stopped in her veins. Her brain had caught fire with fear. "I was afraid you'd broken something…or worse."

"No." He shook his head, a minute movement. "No. We were both lucky, I guess. Thank God. If I had—if I had caused you—"

"Mr. Garwood?" The young staffer—Belle now saw that his name tag read "Chad"—tiptoed to a spot in front of them, looking nervous. "I'm supposed to be on cleanup tonight, so if you want to tell me anything else about the fireplace…"

"Right." Mitch stood, in an instant returning to good-host Mitch. He'd grown quite slick at this, she realized, in the months since she'd seen him at work. He still had his own quirky style, but it was smoother, more comfortable in the role of adult.

"It was great to see you, Belle. Great to see you looking so well."

"Yes," she said, covering her disappointment. "And you, too."

"Thanks." Mitch smiled and started to move away. After a few feet, he stopped. "Are you staying with Penny and Max again tonight?"

Her heart took a small, stupid leap, then stumbled on itself as she realized she was probably reading too much into the question. She didn't have a clue, really, why he was asking. Probably just more good-host Mitch.

"No," she said. "I'll be back in my own cabin tonight. In fact, I'm going to say good-night to the others, and I'll be heading straight there."

If he heard her subtext, he gave no sign of it. He simply smiled blandly, put his hand on Chad's shoulder and led him back to the fireplace surround.

"Good night, Belle," he said over his shoulder. "Sleep tight."

SHE WAITED UNTIL well after midnight. She didn't get undressed because she belicved…wanted to believe…he'd knock on her door any minute.

She kept most of the cabin's lights burning, so no one could imagine she was already asleep. She stared, unseeing, at a book. She made vanilla iced tea, because he liked it. She ignored a call from Evan, in case Mitch decided to call before coming over. She didn't want him to get sent to voice mail.

He stayed at the main house—or somewhere—quite a while. But finally she heard his motorcycle rumble by. Her heart drummed fast when she saw his front-room light come on. Half an hour after that, his bedroom window glowed with lamplight.

Half an hour later, his cabin went dark.

Even then she waited…a minute, two, maybe

five. But she knew it was over. She walked slowly through the cabin, turning off lamps, flicking switches. She extinguished the porch light last, because that had felt like the lighthouse beacon, sending its signal out to him.

She stood in the shadows, listening to an owl hoot hollowly, answered only by the wind, and felt the anticipation inside her go dark, too. It flickered out like a guttering candle, in a pool of its own melted hope.

And she heard it.

A stair creaked. A boot scraped. And, finally, finally, Mitch knocked softly on the door.

# CHAPTER ELEVEN

SHE OPENED THE **wooden** door and then the screen door, too. He **stood on** the porch, so silent and still he might **have been** a figment of her dream life. The **midnight shadows** almost swallowed him whole, **except** for his eyes. His eyes glistened, **catching some** sliver of moonlight or starlight or **maybe a private** fire that burned unseen inside him.

She didn't speak. Her heart was beating so fast she wasn't sure she could.

"I tried not to come," he said. His voice was dull, like a man in a trance.

"I know," she said.

She stepped back and made an opening wide enough for him to enter. Even then, as his foot touched the threshold, he seemed to hesitate — the way a character in a fairy tale paused at the boundary to the enchanted kingdom, knowing that once he entered there was no going back.

She shut the door behind him. He stood a foot or two inside the room, his arms hanging at his side, his expression a study in emptiness. He looked at every piece of furniture, as if he didn't recognize what any of it was for.

"Mitch." She moved in front of him, reached up and touched his cheek. "It's all right. I wanted you to come."

"It's not all right," he said. He shook his head slowly. His stubble was raspy, yet soft, against her fingertips. "It's all wrong."

*"Why?"*

"Because I'm here for one thing only." He looked at her with those glimmering eyes. "Do you get that? I'm here because I want to make love to you. I'm dying, Belle. I'm burning up with it."

Her breath suddenly went shallow, as if her lungs were too small.

"I want that, too," she said. She put her other hand on his face, her palms cupping his jaw. His pulse beat rapidly there.

"I know," he acknowledged bleakly. "But you want other things, too. And I don't have anything else to offer."

"Mitch—"

"No. Let me say this. If I don't say it now, before we…" His voice was tight. "I'll hate myself. I want to say I understand why you shut me out—I even understand why you left me, that day in Maine. I'm not angry about it anymore, but the damage is done. It's over, Belle. What we had before—it's gone. We can't go back now, even if we wanted to."

She swallowed a hot, jagged lump that had somehow lodged in her throat. She knew what he meant. Pain changed things, changed people, changed hearts. And they'd both been in so much pain, these months they'd been apart. Love hadn't changed for her. But she had to accept that maybe, for him, it had.

"Even if that's true, can't we build something new?" She searched his eyes for anything that might give her faith. "Isn't that possible? That we could take these feelings and start over from here?"

"No." His voice was husky, heavy with hopelessness. "Nothing good can be built over this much bad. I... You know I see abused horses sometimes. People want me to train it out of them. But some of them can't be saved. The damage goes too deep."

"You try, though," she said, her voice suddenly raw with fear. As he talked, he seemed to be coming to life, pulling out of his trance. When he shook off the spell completely, would he turn and walk away, vanishing through the same magic passageway that had brought him here?

"You try anyhow, don't you?" She tightened her hold on his face. "Because sometimes it works. Sometimes you can make it right."

He simply shook his head again. "Not this time. The truth is, I don't even want to. You need to understand that, before you let this happen. I don't *want* to start over. I don't ever want to hurt like that again."

The sentence should have crushed her. It wasn't that he *couldn't* try to salvage their relationship—it was that he didn't want to. That statement was the sheer end of the cliff. Once it had been said, there was nowhere to go. Nothing left but the fall.

But suddenly, with a burst of freeing clarity, she realized she didn't care. Maybe she should. Maybe in the rule book of self-respecting females, there was a law against making love to a man who warned you there could be no future.

But rules like that were made by people who had never felt like this. By people who had never stood in the dark with a man like Mitch, aching to touch him, to taste him, to struggle and sweat and finally explode beneath him.

One more time or a lifetime. She would take whatever he was able to give.

"It doesn't matter," she whispered. She let her hands slide down to his shoulders and then pressed them desperately against his chest. "Let it go. It doesn't matter."

When she found his heartbeat, she began to move her hands, kneading the muscles of his chest as the mindless hunger grew. She couldn't help herself. She couldn't be this close to him…couldn't inhale the familiar scent of him, all pine and mint and male….without catching fire in her core.

His breath was shallow now, too, and she knew

he was fighting for control. He said he had changed, but she still knew him. She knew every breath, every heartbeat, every twitch of helpless need. She knew the hungry flare of his nostrils, the rapid exhalation of warm breath and the jagged inhalation...

"Listen to me, Belle." For the first time, he lifted his hands and gripped her shoulders tightly. His fingers were hard, and she knew them, too. "I'm leaving Silverdell. In a few weeks. Have they told you that? I'm moving. I'm leaving for good."

"Yes," she said. "They told me. But you're here now. Please stop talking, Mitch. Make love to me."

She was afraid he might resist her, but he must, finally, have exhausted his willpower. The only sound he made was far from a protest—it wasn't even a word. It was a groan of pure surrender.

He scooped her up, as if she weighed nothing at all, and carried her into the darkened bedroom. She expected their lovemaking to be wild—rough and urgent, the kind of sex designed to drive away all conscious thoughts, all doubts. But when he laid her on the bed, to her surprise he was infinitely gentle.

He kissed her deeply. His lips were tender. Reverent. And, oh, so deliciously slow.

From the first moment, he was so present... so conscious and unhurried as he removed her clothes, then his and spread her across the quilt, to see, to taste, to touch. Maddeningly unhurried, he stroked her naked body. Achingly deliberate, he lowered his lips to her hot skin and teased it with his tongue.

He was right, she realized—it should be slow. If this was to be their final night together, it was right to stretch time, to make it last, to postpone the inevitable end.

As her breathing grew faster, he lightly touched the bandage at her temple. He gazed at her, his eyes dark. "Will it hurt you?"

She shook her head. She was hardly aware of it.

He kissed the skin around the wounded area softly, and then he trailed his lips back down her body, one inch at a time. Her neck, her shoulder, her breast...

Ahh...he knew her so well. Within minutes, she shimmered. She melted. He kept going, until she began to shift restlessly, grabbing the quilt in tense fingers, then releasing it, then squeezing tight again.

He knew her *too* well, perhaps. He could bring her to the edge over and over and never let her fall. He knew exactly where the limits were, when a nibble was too much, when a fingertip not enough.

She couldn't bear it. "Please," she said. "Please, Mitch. Now."

His lips, which were sliding across her breasts, curved into a smile. But he obviously had no intention of setting her free. He took her into his hot, wet mouth…. Then, as she whimpered, he released her and blew lightly on the moist peaks.

Satisfaction slipped away one more time, not far…but tormentingly beyond her reach.

"Please," she said again, twisting as he let one finger touch the fiery throbbing spot between her legs.

"Shhh" was all he said, and he lifted the finger, letting the surging waves subside.

For a while, she continued to struggle. She twitched under his hands, made small anguished sounds at the fire of his mouth. She arched, and she panted, and she reached for him, but nothing she did could break through to the other side of this beautiful torture.

Every single second, she was sure she couldn't bear it for even one more. Eventually, the elegant agony claimed her mind, as well as her body, and she couldn't fight it anymore. She accepted her impotence, her inability to free herself, and let him do as he would.

By the end, she was not a human body, but a tight, delirious, floating ball of pulsing light. When he moved into her, rigid and thick and wet with his own need, she cried out his name, letting it float out of her on a rhythmic wave of helpless joy.

But even then, though he, too, must have been half-mad, he moved with the same excruciating deliberation. She was unbearably aware of every millimeter of his slow plunge forward and every fiery second of his equally measured pulling away.

In, then out, then in again. Dragging fire through her, a slow torture. He was steady, powerful, unstoppable… She had no choice but to match his pace, rocking slowly, hot fire, slow pain. She whimpered, her whole body alive with quivers and flames.

"Bonnie, look at me," he said. He slipped his hands behind her back and lifted her up toward his naked chest. Their gazes locked.

He thrust hard once, twice…and then faster, harder. She lost count as she suddenly felt him filling her with a golden, pulsing warmth.

"Yes," she whispered. "Yes." She cried out with relief as he finally brought her home, ending her long torment in a cascade of rippling, glittering spasms and a torrent of streaming bliss.

ORDINARILY, MITCH LOVED dawns at Bell River. They could be pale and misty, or they could be full of splash and sparkle, but they were always clean, always quiet, and they left him glad to be alive.

But this dawn was different. This was the dawn that, deep in the night, cocooned in Belle's arms, he'd allowed himself to believe would never come.

It always did, though, didn't it? You could have

the worst night in the world, or you could have the best. Either way, the dawn would still break, and it would end.

He'd been awake awhile already—he always woke early. Training went best, he'd learned, when the horses had fewer distractions. So though he wasn't in his own cabin, and he'd slept only an hour or two at most, here he was, pulling on his jeans and walking barefoot into Belle's kitchen to grab a glass of water while she slept.

He drank it standing up, near the kitchen window. He wondered where he'd left his watch. The height of the sun said it must be at least seven. The morning light had already climbed over the mountaintops and was streaming in through the aspens. It picked up a golden-yellow from the leaves and twinkled on the glass as he tilted it to finish off the water.

Seven. Guess he hadn't opened his eyes quite as early as he'd thought.

He ought to leave now. He should have left an hour ago.

But he hadn't been able to. When he had woken, it had taken the first half hour just to make himself get out of the bed and leave her there alone.

He walked back to her bedroom door now, though he knew she still wasn't awake. She always yawned, extravagantly, when she first woke up.

He leaned against the doorjamb, his bare shoulder registering the chill of the glossy painted wood, but he didn't care. He had always liked to watch her sleep.

It was strange, this time, to see all that red-gold hair tumbling across the white sheets, across her pale skin. She lay in a shaft of sunlight, and the sheets had slipped down nearly to her waist, but her hair draped over her exposed breast, as artfully arranged as if some television censor had decided their show should be family-friendly.

*Ha.* Good thing the censor hadn't been here last night.

*Last night.* The memory touched his mind for only a second, as light as a butterfly wing, but it was enough. His body hardened, instantly ready for more.

He turned away, trying to put his mind somewhere else. Which horses had he agreed to work on today? Or was this the day they were supposed to pick up the flowers for Jude's wedding? No... wait...hadn't he told Alec they'd do something after school?

Darn it, he couldn't even think straight anymore. He ran his hands through his hair, wondering if he'd knocked a few brain cells cockeyed after all when Persia had tossed him.

Irritated, he wandered into the front room and shoved aside the drapes so he could survey the outside common area. He was too grown-up to sneak out of a female's room in a dash of shame anymore, but he was human, and he dreaded facing the third degree from the family.

He hardly knew himself what had happened last night. He darn sure wasn't ready to explain it to anybody else.

But the grounds were surprisingly empty, except for a bunch of squirrels who were comically attempting to shinny up the bird feeder's slick metal pole.

It would be a good time to make his exit. No witnesses and no morning-after awkwardness with Belle. He could write a note. That was the time-honored way of escaping without all the drama, right?

Though why there should be drama, he wasn't sure. He'd been honest. He had made his feelings very clear at the outset. He hadn't even lied by omission. He'd told her the truth, and he'd given her a choice. So surely he'd inoculated himself against the typical recriminations.

But suddenly that bachelor's checklist of deniability sounded oddly hollow. If she'd been burning, aching for this, the way he had, how much "choice" had there been, really?

His mind spun with the circular debate, and his legs felt strangely rooted to the spot, as if they might not cooperate if he told them to walk away. That scared him, so he forced himself to hunt down his shirt, his shoes, his watch and put them on.

Once dressed, he grabbed a pen and the refrigerator magnet pad, and he sat down at the kitchen table to see if he could cobble together some kind of note that didn't sound sleazy and clichéd.

His pen hovered over the pad, but the right words didn't come. Then he noticed that her sketch pad lay on the edge of the table. He picked it up, out of habit more than anything, and had already begun flipping pages before he remembered he probably didn't have quite the same carte blanche with her possessions anymore.

But what he saw in the pad made him keep going. Page after page was filled with aborted attempts to sketch people. Apparently, since she'd been here, she'd tried to draw almost everyone at Bell River. There was Cookie's cartoon fury, and next, Rowena's maternal fire. Then Jude's movie-star glamour and even Rosie in a fit of temper, her face as scrunched as an old man's beneath her ridiculous Mohawk.

But none of the people were even half-complete. Some had been scratched through with bold, rough lines that proclaimed Belle's frustration. Others had been abandoned with half faces, half bodies… one leg, no mouth, no eyes. They floated on the pages like ghosts.

Why couldn't she finish them? He heard a soft noise—was she awake? He turned toward the bedroom door, instinctively knowing she wouldn't want him to see these.

But then, from the corner of his eye, he spotted one of the young staffers climbing the front steps. Looked like Chad, he thought. Probably delivering the mail. Guests didn't get much out here. They weren't here long enough, for one thing. But also, most of them had come to this remote spot specifically to get away from all that.

The kid loped onto the porch, then bent down and slid an envelope under the door. He was gone in five seconds, out of sight in ten.

Mitch hesitated. Then he scraped his chair back softly, went to the door and picked up the letter. Handwritten address, with big, looping letters. He flipped it over and read the return address embossed on the back of the envelope.

*Jacob Burns,* he read. *Sacramento.*

He frowned down at it. *Burns?* He remembered the smarmy voice on the phone and felt a rush of annoyance. Jacob was undoubtedly frustrated that Mitch wouldn't play go-between and was now resorting to an entreaty by mail. He must really, really need the money he thought he could get from that painting.

Why couldn't the guy get the message? Belle didn't want to hear from him. And why, of all the bad luck, did the bastard have to come insinuating himself into her life *today?*

Mitch had an irrational urge to hide the envelope, his sixth sense telling him the letter would upset her. More trouble. *Damn it.*

Why today?

He ran his hand through his hair again, knowing he wasn't making any sense. Why *not* today? Was Mitch the only person who was allowed to hurt Annabelle Irving today?

*"What is that?"*

He turned, surprised to see Belle standing there, fully dressed, her hair pulled back in a careless knot. Her voice was oddly tense.

He held out the envelope. "Mail," he said.

She took it with tight fingers, and for a moment she stared at the front of the envelope. She went blank, turned right before his eyes into the mannequin Annabelle. He knew what that meant. Without question, she recognized the handwriting.

"Who is it from?" He posed the question as casually as he could.

She glanced up. She hesitated a fraction of a second too long, and then she shrugged. "It's nothing. A charity requesting money, probably."

*A charity?*

His temper sent up a warning flare. If he'd believed for one single second she really didn't recognize the sender, he might have let it go. But he knew, beyond any doubt, that she was deliberately lying. And suddenly he couldn't stand being shut out anymore.

Not after last night.

Without saying a word, he extended a hand

and, slowly, carefully, used the edge of the envelope to swivel her hand, turning the envelope over. The embossed return address now was visible to both of them.

She flushed, but she didn't speak.

"Don't you want to read it?" He said the words slowly, like the challenge he meant them to be.

She stared at him for a second. Then she raised her chin. "No. Not while you're here."

He laughed, a short, bitter sound. "Why not? I thought he wasn't a threat anymore. I thought you were through with hiding and running and keeping secrets." When she didn't answer, he tightened his jaw. "But you still don't know how to share anything important, do you? Not with me, anyhow."

"I guess not." She looked at him for a long second. "But then, why should I?"

The cold question blindsided him, and for a second he wondered if he'd misheard. She must be joking.

He tilted his head and gave her an appraising look. "Maybe because you said you wanted to start over. Remember? You said you came back to Bell River to see if you could make things right." He shook his head, unsure whether he was angry or just plain disappointed. "And because last night—"

"*Last night?*" She shook her head, her brows driving together with a sudden intensity. "No,

Mitch. Just…*no*. Don't you dare mention last night."

He stopped talking. She was going to have to explain that one. He wasn't going to try to guess what she meant.

She folded her arms over her chest. The envelope made a light crackling sound as it folded up against her body.

"Last night you couldn't have made your feelings plainer. You wanted to have sex with me, but you weren't interested in anything else. No relationship, no commitment, no future." She took a deep breath. "And I accepted those impossible terms, because—"

She broke off, as if she honestly didn't know how the sentence should end. She'd accepted his terms because… Because why? She had no answer, which meant that, in the light of day, she'd realized she'd made the wrong decision. She meant that if she had it to do over again, she'd tell him no.

"I accepted your terms," she repeated simply. "You wanted a no-strings-attached plaything, and you got it. But surely you didn't think that kind of deal included a free pass into my heart, my soul, my secrets. Those things come with love. When all you're offering is sex, all you get is a body."

Her contemptuous tone stung. He felt himself closing off, putting up defenses. He raised one eyebrow and gazed blandly at her flushed cheeks.

"I tried *love* the last time," he said. "Unfortunately, that didn't work, either."

Her eyes were bright, almost feverish. "It didn't work because what you wanted wasn't possible. I couldn't share everything with you. You just don't understand. You think every family is like yours, every home is like Bell River. But it isn't. You have no idea what I'm dealing with."

"No, I sure don't." He held one hand out, palm up, indicating he couldn't deny that basic truth. "And why is that? Oh, yeah. It's because *you won't tell me.*"

"Oh, please, don't. We're going in circles." She rubbed her forehead, as if the argument was causing her physical pain. "I *couldn't.* I couldn't put you in danger, too. God, Mitch, do you think I wouldn't have loved to have someone at my side? Do you think I didn't want to share the struggle with someone? With you?"

He looked at her, a heavy feeling spreading through his chest. It felt like defeat. It felt like giving up.

"No, to be honest, I don't think you did. Because I don't think you know how to trust anyone. You didn't trust me, obviously. And maybe I deserved that, back then. I wasn't as strong or as mature as I could have been. But I've grown up since the day you left me in Maine. Maybe *because* you left me in Maine. I've changed, but it doesn't make any difference to you. And I think

I know why. Do you want me to tell you what I think?"

She didn't answer. She merely glared at him with feverish blue eyes.

"Because you don't trust *anybody,* Belle. Not anyone. Not ever. No matter how hard they try to prove they're worthy. I've tried to figure it out. And I've decided there's only one reason for paranoia that goes so deep. There's only one thing it could mean."

Her chin rose even higher. "And what is that?"

"It means the person you *really* don't trust, the person you're *really* afraid isn't worthy, is yourself. You can't believe anyone will be true to you and protect you, because you don't think you're good enough. You don't think you deserve it."

The accusation fell into the air between them with an unexpected emotional violence. She almost physically recoiled, and he knew he'd hit a nerve. For a minute, he thought those sparkling eyes would overflow with tears. He almost wished she would do it—cry, break down, fall apart. If the dam that hid all those emotions finally ruptured, maybe a path would open, and he could get inside.

But she didn't break down. The dam held. She shut her eyes for a long minute, and when she opened them, they were dry.

"I think you should go, Mitch. And I don't think you should come back."

"I know," he said, unsurprised that he'd crossed some invisible line. Maybe he'd been trying to do that. Either way, it was something that had to be said.

He gestured toward the table. "I was just about to, when the letter came. I was already writing you a note."

She glanced at the rectangular strip of magnetic notepad. Her small smile was caustic, and he knew why. The piece of paper was so pathetically narrow. It could never hold any real feeling or offer any real goodbye.

"It's funny, isn't it?" She reached out and touched the back of the kitchen chair, as if she needed a crutch to help her stand. "Turns out you were right all along. I was a fool to come back here. What we had was so special, I couldn't believe it was gone. But it is. We buried it under this avalanche of hostility and hurting each other and fear."

She gazed at him from under exhausted lowered lids. Her face was pale, and the contrast made her amazing hair seem brighter and stranger than ever. A dark spot had bloomed in the center of her bandage, as if their lovemaking might have caused her stitches to bleed.

She looked very young and unnaturally fragile, like a fairy…a wounded fairy.

Like one of the Annabelle Oils, he realized

suddenly. And the thought sliced him somewhere deep and unseen.

"Belle," he said, but then he stopped, because he didn't know where the sentence had been going.

"It's dead," she went on, as if he hadn't spoken. "And the saddest part is…if we try to bring it back to life, all we'll get is some pitiful, deformed version of what it used to be."

She shook her head, slowly, as if it hurt to move it even an inch. "All we'll get is something like… last night."

# CHAPTER TWELVE

"I'LL LEAVE RIGHT after the wedding." Belle met Rowena's troubled gaze and tried to smile. "The landscaping will proceed just fine without me. The bulk of the planting will be done today and tomorrow, but I'll leave detailed notes about which plants go where, for the smaller stuff."

Rowena frowned. "I'm not worried about plants."

It wasn't noon yet, but Belle had wanted to tell Rowena the news first. She owed her that much.

She'd found her in the stables, overseeing a couple of new employees and some stall shifts for horses who had shown decided preferences in neighbors.

Ro gestured to one of the new stable boys, showing him which stall to clean next. "Let's not move Night Owl until we get Earl Gray settled. He's happy out in the paddock right now, so just muck out in here for the time being."

Then she touched Belle's elbow and urged her toward the door. "Come on. Let's go somewhere we can talk."

Belle followed her reluctantly. She wasn't sure

she could handle a private heart-to-heart right now. After Mitch...and the letter from Jacob...

She loved Rowena, but too much TLC would only weaken her. She was holding her emotions together with little more than pride and duct tape, and like all patched-together things, it wouldn't stand much pressure.

Once outside, Ro maneuvered through the cluster of buildings that included the stable, the indoor arena and the old barn, above which Belle had lived when she'd first come to Bell River. She hoped Rowena wasn't going up to that old apartment. The ghosts of Mitch and Bonnie O'Mara undoubtedly were everywhere in there.

But then she remembered.... The new head wrangler lived in the apartment now.

Ro kept going, off toward the small wooded area that abutted the buildings. Before the expansion, this copse had seemed much more remote, Belle remembered. Ro stopped at one of the few truly ancient trees on the property, a plains cottonwood with a thick knobby trunk and spreading green canopy.

Belle had suggested putting one of the new stone benches beneath the tree, and it stood there now, shady and welcoming.

"See?" Rowena grinned. "I knew I needed to buy these things."

They settled on the bench, which turned out to be quite comfortable. They sat side by side, facing back toward the main house. The view was gorgeous, like a picture postcard. The sprawling wood-and-stone lodge under its clear blue dome of sky. The pastures green and peaceful, with horses grazing. Fresh landscaping and wildflowers everywhere.

If Rowena hoped to talk Belle into staying, this was an effective opening gambit. It was almost May, so the air was crisp but warm. The sun had drawn the subtle cinnamon scent out of the nearby ponderosa pines. Who wouldn't want to stay on this healthy, gorgeous land?

Who wouldn't want to belong? To have the right to call it home?

Rowena leaned back and sighed. "Okay. I figure I have about five minutes, maybe ten, before somebody tracks me down and needs something." She glanced at Belle, smiling wryly. "So tell me what I can say to make you change your mind. Do you want my firstborn child? Seems unlikely, since you've seen her epic temper, but you never know."

Belle laughed. She should have trusted that Rowena wasn't going to turn sentimental. Ro hated showing emotion and weakness more than anyone Belle had ever met, so she wasn't likely to go all mawkish about this.

"I'd take Rosie in a minute, if it weren't so patently clear she belongs with you."

Belle fondly pictured the adorable little tyrant,

whose looks and coloring grew more like Rowena every day. Belle had instantly been so enchanted with her that she'd felt a compulsion to get her charm down in a painting.

And then it had hit her. Maybe that was exactly how her grandmother had felt the minute she saw baby Annabelle's preposterous red hair and blue eyes. Maybe her grandmother hadn't meant, at first, to do anything but honor her.

"The truth is, Ro, I can't let anything talk me out of leaving. I *have* to go. It's time."

The breeze blew against Rowena's loose black hair, and she tilted her head back, obviously enjoying the feeling. She rarely sat down, so she luxuriated in any respites that came her way.

"So. Is it just my idiot brother-in-law driving you away, or are there other reasons, too? Because if it's just Mitch—"

"It's not. That hasn't worked out, as you probably know. But I have so many things to take care of back in California. I've been avoiding them too long. I'd avoid them forever, if I could. But I can't."

Rowena nodded slowly. "Weird, isn't it, how hard it can be to go home and face…" She shrugged. "I don't know. The memories, the ghosts, the truth about yourself, whatever. I spent fifteen years running from mine, so you can't really impress me with your avoidance skills. It hasn't even been a month for you."

Belle smiled. "But look what a happy ending you got. If you'd come back sooner, you might not have married Dallas."

"True." Rowena let her gaze drift over the Bell River beauty, obviously still deeply in love with her land and her life. "Dallas and I both had a lot of growing up to do. Well, okay, mostly me. And of course, if we hadn't traveled these roundabout paths, we wouldn't have Alec. So maybe the cliché is true. Maybe everything does happen for a reason."

"It would be lovely," Belle agreed quietly. "If it were true."

But she wasn't so sure. She'd learned so much about the real world in those eighteen months she'd been on the run. She remembered too well the people she'd met out there—working hard and often suffering hard through no fault of their own. Maybe you earned your happy ending, but maybe some of it was luck.

And not everyone was lucky.

She had been, though, at least financially. That meant she was in a position to help other people. Maybe, at the same time, it would give her life some kind of meaning. It wasn't love, and it wasn't Mitch, but it was worth doing.

The only other thing she knew, amid all the uncertainty and dread, was that she would never live at Greenwood again.

The unwholesome world of the estate no longer made any sense to her. It was like living in an ornate carnival fun house, where mirrors distorted your reflection and doors led only to other doors. Nothing—and no one—was entirely as it seemed.

The letter from Jacob that morning had been one more confirmation of that. Yet another request for a meeting, of course, with the same thinly veiled warning that she'd regret it if she refused. But this letter had included something even more disturbing. It had included a line about Mitch.

About Jacob and Mitch and a conversation they'd had about her. A conversation Mitch had never once mentioned to Belle.

A tightness burned her throat, and suddenly she had to work hard to swallow.

"You know, when you first came to work for us, people thought I was crazy to hire you." Rowena's voice sounded reflective, as if she were merely musing out loud. "Girl out of nowhere, no references, no known address. And me living alone in this big haunted old house."

Something in Rowena's tone of voice, mild as it was, made Belle look up.

"They thought I'd rob you in the night?"

"Or worse." Rowena rolled her eyes. "*Idiots*. But my point is…do you know why I hired you in spite of what they thought?"

Belle smiled, glad of a new topic. "I did wonder why, at first. Later, when I knew you better,

I got it. Your number one hobby is doing things other people tell you not to do."

Rowena laughed so merrily it scattered a few nearby doves that had been nibbling on a piece of apple core someone had discarded in the copse.

"Okay, that, too. But the *main* reason I hired you was that you reminded me so much of myself."

Belle tilted her head. Timid Belle and fiery Rowena? The girl who desperately needed to remain anonymous and the girl who shook the apple tree just to watch the fruit fall?

"It's true," Rowena insisted. "I knew you were on the run, and I'd spent so much of my life on the run. I knew exactly how it felt to approach a total stranger and ask for a job, any job, just so you'll have a roof over your head at night."

Belle sat silently, thinking how difficult that must have been for someone as proud as Rowena. At least Belle had brought along enough money to pay for a cheap motel. She hadn't been afraid of the rain or the weather. Only Jacob.

Even now, the sight of his name on an envelope could make her blood run cold. Even now, she read a veiled threat behind everything he said or wrote. "I honestly believe you'll regret it for the rest of your life, if you refuse this meeting, Belle." That sentence could have been sincere, rather than sinister, couldn't it? But she'd shivered when she'd read it.

She was shivering now, too. She kept her gaze on Rowena, trying to absorb some of her courage.

Rowena was biting her lower lip, concentrating hard on her words. "So, anyhow, I think you and I have probably been on similar journeys, no matter how different they seem on the surface. So I'm going to say something I probably shouldn't say." She smiled, a one-sided, self-aware humor moving through her face. *Imagine that.*

"Okay," Belle said carefully, but a new squirm of anxiety moved behind her ribs.

"The thing is, I know something terrible happened to you back in California." Rowena raised a hand to stave off explanations. "I don't know what it was, and it doesn't matter. Something terrible happened here, too. And because of that terrible thing, I believed I could never trust anyone again. But the truth was, the only person I didn't trust was myself. In a lot of ways, I blamed myself for what had happened, and I hated myself as much as I could ever have hated my father."

Belle smiled wryly, and Rowena saw it.

"Oh, phooey." She groaned and put her hand to her forehead. "I'm not expressing myself very well. It's just that, since I didn't love myself, I didn't believe anyone else could love me, either. And…heck, I'm oversimplifying it, of course, but—"

Belle put her hand on Rowena's arm. "No, no. You're saying it exactly right. I'm only smiling because Mitch said almost the same thing to me just this morning."

Rowena's eyebrows went up, and she cocked her head in surprise. "Well, I guess the boy has some common sense after all."

Belle hesitated. Then she decided that, since she was leaving anyway, she might as well speak her mind.

"He's not a boy, Ro. He's a man." Her voice was mild but firm. "And I suspect he's leaving Bell River because it's so hard to prove that here."

Rowena seemed speechless for a second or two. And then, slowly, as the message sank in, she nodded.

"Fair enough," she said. "I hear what you're saying. And I'll keep that in mind, if you promise to remember what I said. What Mitch *and* I said."

"I promise," Belle said sincerely. "I'm not sure I know how to change any of it, but I'll remember."

"That's good enough." Ro stood briskly. "So it's a deal, then. I'll get back to work, and you get back to California."

Suddenly, as she smiled at Belle, Ro's green eyes blazed with unshed tears. Reaching out, she hugged Belle fiercely, then ruffled her hair as affectionately as she might have tousled Alec's carroty mop.

"See if you can meet those ghosts of yours head-on, Annabelle Irving, and vanquish their sorry asses for good. And when you're done, make sure you come back to Bell River and tell us all about it."

"FRANKLY, I DON'T KNOW how much give there is in the price." Realtor Ralston Dunchik, still a little winded from the climb up the wooden staircase, gazed at the foundation slab in the middle of the Putman property and sighed. "The divorce is nasty, and, well, you know how that goes."

Mitch glanced at Dunchik, a large blond thirty-something who could have been a twin of his sister, Indiana, and made a noncommittal sound. No, actually, he *didn't* know how divorce went. But he assumed it could be an emotional train wreck, just like any love affair gone sour.

Now, *that* he knew about.

"Still, it's a very desirable piece of property." Dunchik, who had been recommended highly by Indiana, slapped an aspen trunk approvingly, the way a used-car dealer might pat the hood of a Chevy. "I've got a list *this long* of people who have been waiting for it to come on the market."

Mitch, who was gazing out over Silverdell, didn't bother looking back to see how long. The list of hungry buyers might just be salesman hype, but it easily could be true. The property was very special.

He'd mentioned his dream of owning it to Indiana a long time ago, back when they were discussing what he'd do with his windfall from the chore jacket.

Apparently she had a memory like a steel trap—especially when it concerned something she might turn to financial advantage. He hadn't told her about his upcoming move, so when the property had hit the market, she'd assumed he still wanted to buy it.

He should have told her to forget it. Even now, as the three of them stood on the side of Sterling Peak, with superlatives about the land spouting from Ralston's mouth like water from a garden hose, he wasn't sure why he'd said yes.

He glanced back at the brother–sister team. If he'd known Indiana planned to tag along, he might not have. It had been a tightrope walk, keeping their professional association on an even keel while backing away from anything personal. But he'd succeeded—or so he'd thought, until she'd showed up with her brother this afternoon, dressed in jeans so tight he wondered why she didn't pass out.

"Oh! Hello, there." Indiana's voice sounded very surprised, and not in a good way. "I'm sorry.... I didn't know anyone else was showing the property this afternoon."

Mitch turned to see what the bother was.

It was Belle. She stood at the top of the stairs, in a golden stream of light sifting through the aspen leaves. She looked shocked to discover the property so crowded. Her face was blank, her hand frozen on the last inch of railing.

Ralston, who apparently noticed Belle had no Realtor in tow, moved toward her with all the charm his sister had lacked. He'd already yanked loose a business card and was holding it out.

"Hi, there," he said. "I'm Ralston Dunchik. I'm sorry—I'm showing the place to another client right now, but if you're looking to buy property in this part of western Colorado, I'd be delighted to work with you."

Belle quickly recovered from the surprise of finding them on-site. She smiled as she approached them, leaving the staircase behind.

"Thank you," she said, lifting a hand to decline the card politely. "But I'm just here to look around. I'm not planning to buy anything. I actually live in California. I'll be going back home tomorrow."

*Tomorrow.* So it was true. Mitch ignored the swoop of dismay in his gut, because it was just old instinct at work. He'd already known she was leaving soon, so what did it matter which day it was?

He'd seen the Herculean push to get the last week's worth of landscaping finished in just three or four days. Nursery deliveries came just about every hour on the hour, and she was always outside, supervising planting or digging holes and lugging fertilizer herself.

Still, he was surprised that she'd be finished and gone tomorrow. Apparently, she planned to stay for Tess and Jude's wedding, then leave the very same day.

*Wow.* She didn't let moss grow once she'd made up her mind.

"Well, take the card anyhow," Dunchik urged. "I'd be happy to help you look in California, too. I keep up on all the important residential properties west of the Rockies."

Mitch shook his head internally. Dunchik had that glassy, poleaxed look he'd seen on men's faces a hundred times when they first glimpsed Belle. The poor guy would have declared himself an expert on crater-front property on the moon, if she'd said she wanted to live there.

She took the card and slid it into her pocket. Mitch noticed, belatedly, that she wore jeans and a faded T-shirt, and she looked smudgy, as if she'd been working outdoors all morning. To be honest, he was surprised Ralston hadn't written her off as too poor to fawn over, no matter how pretty.

And yet, maybe Ralston had a sensitive eye for good breeding. She had something in the way she held herself…something refined, gracious and unconsciously elegant.

That indefinable something—the Cinderella factor—must have been what told Ralston she wasn't here to pull weeds, in spite of the grass stains on the knees of her jeans and her dirty fingernails. It told him she might actually have the bank account to buy this place, if she wanted to.

He'd seen it himself in those earliest days when she'd first arrived at Bell River, a complete mystery to them all. He remembered telling Rowena she looked like the kind of girl who had grown up with cheerleading camp and etiquette class.

*Cheerleading camp.* It made him laugh now, but that was as high as his imagination had been able to take him. He didn't think in terms of mansions and fame and inheritances immense enough to kill for.

"And I'm Indiana, Ralston's sister." Indiana put her hand out, more polite now that she realized Belle might be useful. "I'm in patent law, but one of my partners specializes in real estate, and I'd be happy to recommend him if you're looking for representation."

"Thank you," Belle repeated, a rote courtesy. "Not right now, but I'll definitely remember your name."

Then, for the first time, Belle turned her smile toward him.

"Hello, Mitch," she said pleasantly, though he couldn't quite read her expression. "Looks like you heard the property is for sale even sooner than I did. Are you thinking of buying it?"

*Awkward.* If he said no, Ralston and Indiana

would think they'd been strung along. If he said yes, that gave the wrong signal to Belle.

So he straddled.

"Well, hey," he said with a noncommittal cowboy grin. "I've dreamed about buying it for the past five years. Now that it's finally for sale, I figured I'd be crazy not to at least come take a look."

Her smile didn't falter, though something in her eyes didn't like the answer. Or maybe just didn't like *him*...

"Of course. That makes sense," she said neutrally.

"Then this is definitely the moment to make those dreams come true," Ralston said enthusiastically. He gestured toward the foundation. "I've seen the blueprints the Putmans commissioned, and the house was fabulous. I wonder if they'd be willing to include that in the deal."

Indiana oohed admiringly, as though her brother had just been touched by brilliance. The two of them moved off together and began pacing the perimeter of the foundation. Ralston gesticulated, as if he was illustrating where all the elements would have been.

Mitch instinctively glanced toward Belle. However grand it was, the Putmans' house was unlikely to seem "fabulous" to either of them. They'd built their dream home here in such detail—from the picture windows to the wraparound porch—

that anything else would jar like a bad note in a symphony.

But Belle didn't seem to be listening. She was biting her lower lip, and her thoughts seemed to be turned inward. Then she spoke quietly. "Would it be okay if we take a minute? I need to talk to you about something."

"Sure." He kept his surprise to himself. He double-checked Ralston and Indiana, who were deep in their conversation, and then he walked slowly off to the side.

He didn't notice where he headed, just that it was toward privacy. She followed him without speaking, and when they were adequately out of earshot, they stopped.

The stump of a very large spruce was right in front of them. He put one foot up on the edge and waited. But she didn't seem to know where to begin.

"I have to admit I'm surprised to see you here," he said, to get the conversation going. "Are you thinking of buying it?"

The question wasn't as dumb as it sounded. Just because she'd stonewalled the Dunchiks didn't mean she wasn't interested in the place. It might just mean she had her own professionals and didn't want the other vultures circling.

"Of course not," she said. "I came up to look around one last time. I leave immediately after the wedding. And since it seems unlikely I'll ever get back to Silverdell..."

She let the sentence trail off. He couldn't hear any hint of sadness in her voice, though. She sounded oddly matter-of-fact.

"Anyhow, that's not what I wanted to talk to you about. I didn't know you'd be here, of course..." She subconsciously touched her cheek, where a small streak of mud ran under her eye, like the grease a football player would apply to reduce glare. "But it's easier to just ask you now."

"Okay." He kept his voice agreeable. "What's up?"

She paused for another second, studying him. Her gaze was steady but cool, as if he were a total stranger she didn't much like the looks of.

"I want to know if you've been talking privately to Jacob."

*"What?"* He frowned. Of all the things he'd imagined she'd say. "Of course not. Why would you ask me that?"

She narrowed her eyes. "Because in the letter he sent me, he says you have. He says he talked to you on the phone just the other day. He says the two of you were discussing how to persuade me to buy Number Fifteen."

Mitch was already shaking his head indignantly...and then he remembered. *Aw, heck. That call.* That one brief, insignificant call, while he was driving to Montrose with Dallas. The day he saw Belle in the wedding dress.

"No. Wait. Jacob *did* phone me once. He said he wanted my help with something, and I told him to go to hell. I don't call that 'talking to Jacob.'"

She eyed him coldly. "What *do* you call it?"

"I call it *nothing.*" He waved a hand. "It was so pointless I had almost forgotten it. The only memorable thing about the conversation was how bad I wanted to climb through the phone and kick his ass. Hanging up on him was far less gratifying."

*Oh, for Pete's sake.* She didn't believe him. She hadn't softened her expression by so much as a flicker.

"That's not how he tells it," she said. "He seems to think you're quite an ally."

An *ally?* And suddenly, just like that, Mitch was mad as hell.

He laughed, the sound so loud and harsh it made Ralston and Indiana turn their heads toward him.

"Wow," he said. "Just *wow.* I always knew you didn't trust me, but this really takes the cake. You don't believe what *I'm* telling you, because your homicidal, psychopath cousin says something else?"

Finally, her eyelids flickered, the first hint of doubt. "I didn't say I didn't believe you. I don't know what to believe."

"Just as bad," he said.

She tilted her head. "When were you going to tell me about it?"

"Honestly?" He was too angry to sugarcoat this. "Probably never."

She widened her eyes.

"Look, Belle, I know the very thought of him upsets you. Why would I bring it up, when it was so completely meaningless? *Nothing happened*. I probably said ten words in the whole conversation, and eight of them were curse words. The other two were 'get lost.'"

She shook her head, as if she still couldn't be sure. She turned her face away. She slid her fingers into the front pockets of her jeans, hunching her shoulders in a move that looked suddenly vulnerable, like someone bracing against the cold. She looked very alone.

His anger died down a little, but he refused to feel sorry for her. If she was alone, it was by choice.

"Belle, why is this such a big deal, anyhow? You said he wasn't a threat anymore. You aren't still afraid of him, are you?"

She shook her head, but if she had intended to answer, she never got the chance. The sound of a cell phone chirping cut into the silence. Instinctively, he touched his jacket pocket, but it wasn't his. At the same time, she pulled out her own cell phone, which was lit up, receiving an incoming text.

She glanced down at it, and her face went pale. Her fingers on the phone were white-knuckled.

He couldn't read the words, but he could see it was a very short message. Surely no one sent seriously bad news via text, did they? Not even that bastard Jacob.

"Belle?" He felt an illogical pinch of worry. "What's wrong?"

Instantly, her lips tightened, and she tilted the cell phone toward her chest, like a poker player who thought someone was looking at his cards. It happened so fast the movement couldn't possibly have been voluntary.

"God, did I really just ask that?" He laughed again, this time entirely at himself. "When will I *ever* learn?"

She turned toward him, making a low unhappy sound. "No, I wasn't… I didn't mean to hide it from you. I don't know why I did that. It's nothing. Really."

He let the laugh die down to a sardonic chuckle. "Nothing you plan to share, anyhow."

She gazed at him mutely, then extended her phone, face up. He flicked his gaze down, not meaning to actually read it, but so few words were printed there, it was impossible not to absorb the whole thing with one glance.

I wish I could make you stay.

But... His glance whisked up to her face. He was confused. That really *was* "nothing." He didn't know exactly what he'd expected, but that benign little text wasn't it. It could have come from Rowena, Penny, any of the sisters. Heck, even Alec was fond of her and wouldn't want her to leave.

"Seems pretty innocent. So why did you go pale when you got it?"

She blinked a couple of times, then took a breath. "Because I don't know who sent it. They always say 'Number Blocked.'"

He darted a glance toward the Dunchiks, who were now watching them from a distance. Finished with their own discussion, they were clearly growing restless. They probably had an algorithm to determine how many minutes they could spend with any one client without losing money.

Mitch bent toward Belle slightly, turning his back to the siblings. "What do you mean, *they?* You've received other texts from this person?"

She nodded. "I assume it's the same person. There were just two others. Equally innocent. And yet..." She scrolled through her texts, then handed him the phone, a liberty he recognized as unusual.

He read them quickly.

*You look beautiful with your hair like that. You*

*look awesome in blue.* They did seem entirely innocent, unless you were allergic to compliments. He stared at them a few more seconds, trying to see them through her eyes. What was so unsettling about these little anonymous love letters? He'd sent many a note like this in class, when he was a kid.

And then it hit him.

"It's as if…" He tried to put his finger on the precise element that carried the creep factor. "As if he's watching you."

"Exactly. But I never see anyone else around, so it ends up being very…unsettling. Still, the tone isn't really threatening in any way."

"No, but—" He stopped himself from continuing. Fool that he was, he'd been about to say, "Why didn't you tell me about them?"

She slipped the phone back into her pocket. "I'm sure it's nothing to worry about, particularly since I'm leaving so soon. It's just strange, that's all."

"I'll look into it," he said. "If they—"

But they'd run out of time. He heard Ralston's heavy footsteps approaching from behind them.

"You know, that's a top-notch, frost-protected foundation," Ralston said, his confident voice a little too loud. "The Putmans put real money into it, and I bet your architect could work with what's already here. Save you a bundle."

Mitch turned to meet the Realtor's smooth, toothy smile.

Ralston gestured toward the foundation. "And the footings are at least half again as deep as required for this air-freezing index."

Mitch had to give the guy credit. A man who could hype a concrete slab with no house on top was pretty good at his job. Behind him, though, Indiana was *not* smiling. Either she was tired of waiting, or she'd heard the gossip, too, and had figured out who Belle really was.

"Impressive," Mitch said. Then he put his arm around Ralston's back. "Hey, I know you guys need to get back to Grand Junction. I've kept you far too long."

Ralston denied any inconvenience with every fiber of his being, but Mitch insisted. Within seconds, they all began descending the Putmans' charming wooden staircase to the parking area. Indiana led the pack, followed by her brother, who continued to talk, as if he were personally selling Mitch every aspen they passed on the way down. Mitch walked in front of Belle, just in case she tripped.

As they reached the first landing, he realized she had dropped a good bit behind. He turned, wanting to be sure everything was okay. She was simply standing there, staring back toward the property. That stair was, he knew, the very last spot at which the land was still easy to see.

She didn't turn around for several seconds, and then she gazed down at him somberly. Her eyes glistened, as if they were damp, and he felt a quick sympathetic burning behind his own lids.

*No.* None of this nonsense. They'd made their decision, and it was the right decision. It was over. These flickers of sentimentality were just the death throes…or, more precisely, the after-death twitching. They would cease soon enough.

As he stood there, looking into the sun that streamed over her like honey, he tried to think of something light to relieve the tension.

Below them, Ralston was still talking, talking, talking. So Mitch decided maybe he could just grin and say, "Funny how once the world discovers you have money, all kinds of weirdos crawl out of the woodwork, hoping to get some of it."

But then he remembered. She already knew that.

# CHAPTER THIRTEEN

BELLE HAD ALWAYS cried at weddings, even as a little girl. Even before she understood the real reasons for tears—the innocence of two souls setting sail together, prepared to weather storms; the poignancy of a tale just beginning, to which no one knew the end—she'd found weddings almost unbearably sad.

In the earliest years, she'd cried because her grandmother had dressed her in something scratchy or stiff, and she'd wanted to leave. Later, she'd cried because everyone seemed to be in costume, and she associated costumes with misery. Toward the end, when she was in her late teens, she'd cried because she couldn't imagine such a lovely, innocent thing ever happening to her.

But today, at Jude and Tess's wedding, held in the front room of Bell River, she cried because they looked so happy, and their joy, after they'd endured so many difficulties, was a ray of hope anyone could cling to.

The room looked like something out of a fairy tale, overflowing with yellow roses, daisies and daylilies. The sisters had considered an outdoors wedding, but they had decided that an illegitimate sister probably had felt on the outside all her life—and so they brought her in.

The guests were almost all immediate family—Dallas and Rowena, Alec and Rosie, and Ro's natural father, Atherton-Reese; Gray and Bree, and Gray's grandfather, Grayson; Penny and Max and Ellen. And, of course, Mitch.

Belle and ranch manager Barton James were the only guests not blood related to someone in the family. Embarrassed at what felt like an intrusion, Belle had tried to bow out gracefully, saying she needed to hit the road anyhow, but Rowena wouldn't hear of it.

"We don't make our decisions based on blood around here, thank goodness." Rowena's eyes had momentarily been shadowed, and Belle knew she was thinking about how fragile her own blood status was, now that everyone knew Johnny Wright wasn't really her father. "It's about love. And I love you. *We* love you. So book a later flight. You *must* stay."

Now Belle was glad she'd said yes. What a beautiful, romantic exchange of vows it had been. The vows they'd written for themselves and had planned to speak, even at the courthouse, were simple and touching. Tess's yellow-and-white lace dress, which her sisters—and Belle—had picked out for her amid so much laughter and love, was exquisite.

Tess resembled a ray of sunshine. Jude, whose good looks were legendary in Silverdell, was dazed with happiness, as if Tess's beauty had struck him blind. Belle had worried about their future, given that the baby Tess carried wasn't Jude's. But she didn't worry anymore. Any man who loved a woman that much would inevitably love her child.

When the rings were safely on their fingers, the minister granted permission for the groom to kiss the bride. A chuckle rippled through the room, because Jude definitely hadn't waited for an official okay. Tess was already in his arms, being kissed so thoroughly Belle felt sure everyone watching ended up a little light-headed, too.

Well, with the possible exception of Alec, who turned to Ellen and gave her the universal signal for "gross"—an index finger toward an open mouth. Ellen, all dressed up and looking older than her eleven years, stood on her dignity and didn't stoop to respond.

Belle smiled, thinking what fun it would be to watch those two grow up. Ellen clearly had a head start, but Alec had...well, he had what Fitz used to call "pizzazz." Fitz had used the word to describe the splashiest, most glamorous flowers, but it applied to stubborn, witty, handsome little boys, too.

"Awwww." Penny leaned her head on Max's shoulder as she watched the kiss go on and on.

She smiled at Belle. "So what do you think, Belle? All things considered, I'd say we pulled it off."

"You certainly did." Belle could hardly believe they'd kept all this secret. The barns and stables and outbuildings had been bursting with flowers, decorations, food and supplies for the past several days. The sisters had been like kids, whispering, giggling and making ridiculously unsubtle references to their secret mission.

"Good thing the spa was slammed this week." Max hugged Penny with one arm, while trying to wrestle a bored Alec with the other. "If Tess hadn't been so busy, she would have seen right through you three stooges in a heartbeat."

Penny grinned. "Shows what you know, buster. Who do you think arranged all those massages, anyhow? We were going around town, handing out free spa treatments like Santa Claus."

The sisters had obviously loved every minute of the intrigue. And last night after the family dinner—the night before Tess believed she would be going to the courthouse for a simple ceremony—the sisters had delivered a huge sparkling silver-and-white-wrapped box to the table. When Tess had opened it and glimpsed the gorgeous dress inside, she'd understood immediately. She'd laughed, even as she'd burst into tears, jumping up to hug the others.

Within minutes, there wasn't a dry eye in the room. Not even Alec's.

Yes, Belle was very glad she'd stayed for this.

She glanced toward the mantel, where Jude was thanking the minister, and saw Rowena beckoning to her. Ro had been Tess's maid of honor, and Mitch had been Jude's best man—decisions they'd made back when the plan still called for that courthouse quickie.

At first, Belle had pitied Tess for having to pick just one of her new sisters to stand by her, risking hurt feelings in the other two. But then Belle recognized the beauty of Tess's choice. Not only was Ro the eldest, and because of that was the simplest choice…but also she was the other "outsider" in the group. She'd been glad she wasn't related to Johnny Wright, of course, but the news had also turned her sisters into half sisters and changed her status to *illegitimate love child,* just like Tess.

Belle excused herself to Penny and Max and made her way to the front. "Well done," she said as she reached Rowena, who luckily no longer had Mitch beside her anymore. Belle hadn't seen him since the kiss, though she knew he must be nearby. She hugged her happy friend. "It was absolutely perfect."

"Thanks." Rowena beamed, clearly thankful it had gone off without a hitch. "Can't you stay for food?" Rowena and Belle had been over this a dozen times already, so she didn't look hopeful. "I know what you said, but—"

"I can't risk missing the plane. Fitz is meeting me at the airport when I arrive, and he's arranged his schedule around it."

"That's good," Rowena said. "And you're staying with him when you get there, right?"

"In the gardener's cottage, yes. At least at first. I might be able to help them a little."

Rowena seemed to be searching for another argument, so Belle jumped in to forestall it. "Ro, it's okay. It's time for me to go. I said my goodbyes to everyone last night, and it would just stir things up again if I hung around now. It's the right thing. You know that."

Rowena set her mouth mulishly. She knew Belle was right, but people as stubborn as Ro didn't like bowing to anything, even logic. "All I know is you always seem to be leaving us right after a wedding. There's something messed up about that."

Belle smiled. The day she and Mitch had run away was the day Dallas and Rowena had gotten married. It could seem sad, if you looked at it that way. But Belle had vowed she wouldn't let herself view life as half-empty anymore. She was going to look for the good. It had to be there.

"Well," she suggested, "you *could* say I'm always sticking around here just a little longer than I otherwise would have, so I can be here for the weddings."

Rowena wrinkled her nose. "Don't you dare turn Pollyanna on me. Besides, all of us are hitched now, so how will we lure you back next time?" Her eyes widened, full of sudden mischief. "I know. We'll marry Alec off early. It'll kill two birds with one stone."

Belle's answering laughter felt a little mechanical. They both knew what the next Bell River wedding would be. The only unmarried member of the family was Mitch, and as soon as Belle was out of the picture, the Indianas and Crimsons and all the other women who lusted after him would slither in to make the kill.

And where in that scenario was the "good" she was supposed to be looking for? She swallowed, knowing the answer. In Mitch's happiness, that was where. If he fell in love, if he married someone else, whether it was tomorrow or ten years from now, she'd have to find a way to be glad for him.

But that was tomorrow's battle. Today, she had to get out of here without a scene.

She hugged Rowena and then, with a bright smile, she maneuvered her way slowly out of the room. She congratulated Jude, kissed Tess and continued hugging and promising to phone until finally she opened the back door and breathed her first gulp of fresh air.

It had been like running an emotional gauntlet, but she'd survived it. The parking lot was only fifty feet away, and her rental car waited there, its hood winking with sunlight.

"Okay if I walk you to your car?" Mitch spoke from somewhere to her left. Heart thudding, she glanced over. He was sitting on the porch swing, slightly angled, with one knee cocked up on the seat. His head caught the sunlight, and all the rich, amber strands he disliked so much blazed out from the brown like a corona of fire.

He looked so casually elegant in his beautifully cut gray suit, with his yellow tie loosened and his top button open, that he might have been part of the upcoming magazine photo shoot.

"Thanks," she said with a smile. "My suitcases are already in the trunk, though, so there's really no need."

"I know." He unfolded himself and stood. "But there are a couple of things I'd like to say before you go, if you don't mind."

She hesitated, trying to think what this might mean. But she had no idea, and she couldn't think of a reason for saying no, anyhow. She shifted the keys from one hot palm to the other. "Okay."

They walked down the back stairs, silent as if by agreement until they reached the car, where no one could possibly overhear. She clicked the remote, then put her hand on the sun-warmed door handle and faced him.

He didn't waste time. He knew when her plane left.

"The first thing is…I want to tell you what I found out about the texts."

She moved her head a little, surprised. "What did you find out?"

"I know who sent them."

"You do? How?"

He hesitated a few seconds while a waiter with a handcart carrying a case of champagne rattled past, then bumped his cargo up the stairs.

"I started with the suspicion that it might be someone who worked here, because they're the only strangers who could easily find your cell number." Mitch shrugged at her look of confusion. "It's on your contact sheet, for the rental."

"Oh." She frowned. "Oh, dear. But you have a huge staff these days, don't you? So many wranglers and kitchen staff and runners and youth counselors and…"

"Yeah, but I figured it had to be someone young. Really young, because the tone was so gawky, like a kid with his first crush. That narrowed it down to about five boys, and after that, all I had to do was ask around. Who talks about Annabelle Irving a lot? Who seems fixated on your every move?"

She laughed, so relieved it had been nothing sinister that she suddenly found it kind of endearing. "And someone admitted it?"

Mitch smiled wryly. "*Someone* didn't have much choice. It was Chad—nice kid. Turns out, he'd been so love-struck he was driving all the other youth counselors crazy, going on and on about you. They ratted him out instantly."

"Aw." She groaned, thinking how humiliating it must have been. "How awful for him."

"Yeah, he's got his tail between his legs." Mitch tilted his head, as if to read her face better. "I told him he should be ready to come apologize to you himself, if you say the word. He doesn't want to, naturally, because he feels like a total chump, which he is. But he knows he has to do it, if it would make you feel better to hear it from his own lips."

She knew what Mitch meant by that. If she didn't trust Mitch to be telling her the truth. She shook her head.

"Let's not put him through it," she said. Poor kid was probably wishing he could fall through a hole in the earth right about now. She wouldn't dream of dragging him out to have his emotions and his pride flayed in public. "Just try to make him see it might have really frightened me. Although...I'm sure Chad's mortified enough he'll never do anything like that again."

"No, I don't think he will." Mitch let his gaze wander over her face, her hair...and then, just for a flicker of a half second, down her body, too. "For one thing, it's unlikely he'll ever meet another guest who presents quite the same level of temptation as the famous Annabelle Irving."

She played with the chrome trim on the hood so she didn't have to look at him. She chuckled softly. Best to laugh that off as a joke.

"Oh, I don't know," she said. "What about the famous Haley Hawthorne?" Haley was Jude's childhood sweetheart, the woman he'd left when he fell for Tess, and a rising Hollywood starlet. "I hear Haley's a fan of Bell River, too."

Mitch smiled, but thinly and only with his lips. His eyes remained fixed on her.

"Haley," he repeated thoughtfully. "I guess it's possible. As I said, the kid is *very* young, and his palate might still be that immature. But I doubt it."

She flushed, but the compliment was subtle enough she could continue pretending they were only teasing. Still, she appreciated that he was trying to keep things pleasant, right to the very end.

"Thank you for tracking down the truth," she said. "I wasn't terrified or anything, but…it probably would have lodged like a little thorn in my subconscious, making me edgy, if I hadn't ever found out."

And heaven knew she didn't need any more of those little thorns. She hoped he could tell she really was grateful.

He didn't say anything for a few seconds. Awkwardly, she clicked her cell phone to check the time.

"I really should get going, or I'll miss the plane." She glanced at two young waitresses who were going up the stairs, balancing the wedding cake on a tray between them. "And you'll miss all the fun."

"I know," he said. He put his hand on the car hood, too. Their fingers ended up only an inch or two apart. She could feel the warmth of his skin emanating toward hers, subtly different from the sun heat of the metal. "But there is one more thing I wanted to say before you go."

She held her breath. This was how it had been in her dreams, of course. In those dreams—day and night—he stopped her at the last minute and refused to let her go. He spoke the magical words that would unravel all the knots and make all the anger and confusion blow away, leaving only their old love behind, miraculously unchanged.

Her rational mind knew that wasn't what would happen next. It couldn't, because there were no magical words. But her dream mind began to hope, and hope made her pulse quicken. She fought to keep her breathing even.

"What is it?" She hoped her rational mind was in control of her face. She hated to think her pitiful childish fantasy, in which reality was replaced by a fairy tale, could be read there.

He took a breath. "I just wanted to say…take care of yourself. And, if you possibly can, let the past go. Don't let that bastard take any more from you than he already has. You deserve to be happy, and I hope someday you will be."

Her eyes burned, and a lump of something that

felt like hot twisted car metal had lodged in her throat.

But she managed to smile anyway. *Sunny side up, remember? Find the good.*

But where? How? Her heart was so heavy she could barely hold herself straight.

"Thank you, Mitch." She opened the car door and prepared to get inside. "And please know…I wish the same for you."

TWO DAYS LATER, Mitch was once again dining on fine peanuts at the Happy Horseshoe. Jude wasn't with him, of course—he and Tess were off on their honeymoon. But some of the wranglers from Bell River and Gray Stables got together every Monday night to crack dumb jokes, flirt with the ladies and trade the same fifty bucks back and forth over heated games of eight ball and darts.

When they'd invited him tonight, probably expecting he'd decline, as usual, he'd surprised them by saying yes. Why not? The Horseshoe seemed like as good a place as any to pass the time. Better than listening to Barton James play sad cowboy songs all night in the great room, while the family covertly eyed Mitch, watchful and worried, as if he were a time bomb set to explode at some undisclosed, but imminent, hour.

And a heck of a lot better than sitting in his cabin, supposedly shuffling his new money around on the computer, but more often pulling up a search engine and typing in words like *Annabelle Oils* and *Jacob Burns* and *Get a life, loser.*

It was only eight, but it seemed much later. Crimson was here, too, over in the corner, cozy with a guy who looked as if he might wrestle lions for a living. Mitch had smiled at her as he entered, but he hadn't joined her, not wanting to spoil whatever mojo she might have going with the he-man.

He swirled his ginger ale, waiting for his turn to shoot, and told himself one more time that there wasn't anything pathetic about a twenty-seven-year-old millionaire hanging out in the local bar, sucking down ginger ale because he was afraid that even one beer might knock him off the willpower train.

He smiled wryly into his glass as he took a swallow. He was like any recovering addict, wasn't he? Only instead of tallying the hours he'd been sober, he was tallying the hours he'd been able to stop himself from calling Belle.

Fifty-two and counting.

"Hey, are you going to play or not?" Conrad Avarti, the new head wrangler at Bell River, poked him lightly in the arm with his cue. "You can't zone out just because you're losing."

He was *losing?* The old Mitch wouldn't have taken that lying down. He slid off his bar stool and tossed Avarti an evil grin. *Not feeling it?* No problem. *Fake it.* He knew this script by heart.

"And *you* can't really believe you're going to beat me with a lopsided stroke like yours." He leaned over the table and tried to remember whether he was stripes or solids. Solids, he assumed, but he'd honestly forgotten.

Oh, well. *Just hit one.* If he got it wrong, at least something interesting might happen. He'd never seen a good bar fight in the Horseshoe.

He picked a yellow one and tried to calculate the angles. But it seemed like way more effort than it was worth.

Hadn't he once enjoyed this pointless game? Once, way, way back—like a whole *month* ago? What the heck had happened to him in one lousy month? He shook his head and aimed his cue again. Maybe it had been more exciting when he really needed the twenty dollars he'd bet on it.

He missed, of course, and Avarti whistled softly. The other man moved in, then ran the table. Pretending to be grouchy about it, Mitch peeled off a twenty, then headed back to the bar.

This wasn't working. Maybe he should head out and go home before someone else challenged him to a game. Avarti was probably already spreading the word that Mitch Garwood was an easy target tonight.

Speaking of which...

A great-looking blonde in a red jumpsuit swung up and arranged herself on the stool next to his. The bartender arrived instantly, of course. The woman ordered a fuzzy navel, then gave Mitch a smile inviting him to think about that.

Mitch smiled back.

"I know it's a girlie drink," she volunteered with a small pink pout. "But I can't help it. I'm a girlie girl."

*Ho, boy.* Toying with his glass, Mitch wondered what her story was. She had a pretty face, but he thought her eyes were a little sad—which might account for the compulsively flirtatious manner. It didn't feel quite natural for her.

Or was he just projecting?

"I'm Andrea Fringle," she said, holding out her hand. And, if only because, for once, he felt fairly sure that was her honest-to-goodness, momma-given name, he extended his, too.

"Mitch Garwood," he said. "You're not from around here, are you?"

"No. I'm from Crested Butte. I've always wanted to come to Silverdell for the Wildflower Festival." She lifted her shoulders, as if this next bit embarrassed her. "I'm a botanist."

He smiled. Belle could easily have been a botanist, if she hadn't been a millionaire.

The blonde's hand was small, but her shake was firm, which he liked. He might do worse, he thought, than to spend the evening with Andrea Fringle. Maybe they could exchange stories about why their eyes were so sad and their flirting skills so rusty.

At the very least, it might numb him for a few hours.

But as they released hands, he caught a glimpse of himself in the mirror behind the bar, his reflection splintered by the shimmer of upside-down cocktail glasses. There seemed to be an infinite number of Mitches…and an infinite number of blondes.

He stared, suddenly feeling as if he were receiving a message from the universe. And the message was: *Go home, you idiot.*

The sad truth was—he could play this game forever. He could let one nice, smart, well-intentioned woman after another pick him up, take him out and try to coax him into their beds.

But it wouldn't change anything. Not even if he could be coaxed, and that seemed fairly unlikely, given his track record with Marianne Donovan, Indiana and Crimson. Even if a miracle occurred, and he could feel passion for one of them, it wouldn't make his heart stop aching.

Nothing would fix that bunged-up heart but time. *Damn it.* He was going to have to sit with this loss, and he was going to have to let himself feel the pain.

For how long? he wondered. Idly, he drew an infinity sign with the condensation ring left on the bar by his ginger ale. However long it took.

He shoved his glass across the bar with two fingers, signaling he was done. He pulled out the first bill he came to and tossed it on the counter for a tip.

"Well, gotta get home," he said evenly, giving the blonde his warmest smile, the one that said, "It's not you. Really. It's me."

"Good to meet you, Andrea. Have fun at the festival."

She looked disappointed but covered it well. "I will!" She picked up her fuzzy navel and tilted it toward him in a goodbye toast. "You take care now, Mitch Garwood."

As he turned to go, stuffing his wallet back in his pocket, his gaze just happened to fall on Crimson and her burly date. She was watching him, and from her smile it was pretty clear she'd been doing so for quite some time.

She let her eyes flick pointedly toward the blonde, then back to him and raised her eyebrows, signaling her surprise.

He responded with a sheepish grin and ruefully lifted one shoulder. *Beats me,* his shrug said. *I'm not sure I understand it myself.*

But her smile broadened, and, nodding so faintly her date couldn't possibly have noticed, she lifted her hand, thumb up, in a small but emphatic gesture of absolute approval.

## CHAPTER FOURTEEN

"ARE YOU *SURE* this is a good idea?" Fitz had been sitting on the edge of his chair in the mansion's front parlor, supposedly preparing to head back to work, for the past twenty minutes. His weather-beaten face was furrowed and somber, and he'd asked the same question at least five times.

He obviously couldn't get comfortable with Belle's plan to sleep in Greenwood tonight.

"No," she said with a smile. She leaned back in her Queen Anne chair and let her hands stroke the arms. She'd sat in this chair for Number Fourteen, the first year she threw a tantrum and tried to refuse to pose. She had a powerful tactile memory of this cool, slick gold satin under her palms. She'd wanted to dig her fingernails in, like an animal, and shred it.

She turned her head and saw the same butter-cups dancing in the wind now that she'd been forbidden to look at then. Or if not the same ones, ones exactly like them, planted and protected all these years by the man in front of her.

Just as he had tried to protect Belle. Just as he *still* was trying.

"I'm not sure of anything, Fitz. I simply don't have any better ideas. Once I sign those papers tomorrow, Greenwood isn't mine anymore."

That was the one thing she'd accomplished in the weeks she'd been back that she felt whole-heartedly happy about. She'd just returned from meeting with her lawyers and the lawyers for the art museum, where they'd hammered out a deal. Greenwood would soon become the Greenwood Portrait Gallery.

Thankfully, the board had voted to table the vote on location acquisition, hoping she'd make up her mind. They'd welcomed her return to Sacramento with grateful delight, and they'd walked her through the plans, blueprints and financial documents with pride. She loved everything they had in mind, from the children's art wing to the free public days.

For their part, they'd been shocked and thrilled when she'd offered to donate Number Seventeen, the last Annabelle Oil her grandmother had ever painted, to the cause. It hung at the fork in the double staircase, the first thing anyone saw when they entered Greenwood. She'd almost laughed at the board members' pleasure.

If only they knew. If they hadn't wanted it, she would have burned it.

They parted great friends. The revised agreement was being created and printed tonight. She'd return to sign in the morning.

But that meant her time as custodian of Greenwood was almost over. She'd packed and stored the few things she wanted to keep. It hadn't even filled a small van and had mostly been clothes, books and a few knickknacks her mother had loved.

The appraisers, architects and art restoration experts would arrive by noon tomorrow.

"So if I'm ever going to try to unearth anything, it has to be tonight, doesn't it?"

"We could *make* Jacob tell you." Fitz, the gentlest man she'd ever known, looked fierce. The afternoon light caught the side of his eyes, and, for a minute, they looked like the eyes of a feral cat. Ever since she'd told him she believed something bad had happened to her in this house, something she'd blocked and wasn't able to remember, that primitive, volatile air had clung to him.

He leaned forward, his hands between his knees, dangling his sun hat. "If there's anything to know, Jacob knows it. I would bet my life on it. He was always snooping, even as a boy. Never respected anyone's privacy."

She remembered that all too well. If she ever disobeyed an order, if she ate an extra piece of pie or climbed out of her window to play in the garden, Jacob had been certain to appear nearby. And he'd always ratted her out, instantly and with relish.

She'd been so wrapped up in her own distress

it hadn't occurred to her Jacob had targeted others, too. She'd always thought of him as her own personal demon.

"Did he snoop through your things, too?"

Fitz snarled under his breath. "Of course. He couldn't let anyone keep a secret, even an innocent one." He wrung his hat, his eyes downcast, not meeting hers. "How do you think he found out about Marlene?"

Belle waited a minute before answering, aware this was risky turf. They had spoken about this only once before. Fitz had been married to the same beautiful woman, Marlene, for fifty years. But when he first came to work at Greenwood, he had lied, telling Ava he had no wife, just a spinster sister who kept house for him. Typically eccentric and willful, she'd insisted on a single gentleman gardener, and he had wanted the job desperately.

Overbearing to the end—and beyond—Ava had left instructions that if he married, he must be replaced by a single gardener who would always put Greenwood first. Not until Belle had inherited and gained full control of the property would he be able to tell the world that Marlene was his wife.

But before that happened, Marlene was diagnosed with late-stage breast cancer. Fitz had only a pitiful insurance and no nest egg to get her top-notch care.

Jacob had let Marlene's health deteriorate a long, sadistic time. Then he'd come to Fitz and offered him a huge sum to reveal Belle's location. At the same time, Jacob made it clear that if Fitz didn't agree, he would be exposed and fired, as per the terms of Ava's will.

Fitz hadn't been able to resist.

Belle was careful to keep her voice gentle as she probed. "How long ago did he find out?"

"Several years before your grandmother died." Fitz's mouth pulled down hard at the corners, the leathered flesh folding on itself. "Six, maybe."

She was astonished. She would have thought Jacob would tell Ava instantly, the same way he had handled the dirt he collected about Belle. Find it, fling it and enjoy the fallout.

"You mean Jacob didn't use it right away to get you fired? He held on to the information all these years and did nothing?"

"He didn't do *nothing*. He waited." Fitz's strangely altered voice made her shiver. "That's what he's like. He collects these things, these little deadly bullets. And then he waits."

*He waits.*

Belle stood up, suddenly chilled by the big ornate room and the hard chair. She paced into the adjoining front hall, moving across its checkered pink-and-black granite floor like a pawn across a chessboard. At the last minute, she realized she was heading toward the front door and stopped herself before she touched the huge brass handle.

*He waits.*

She took several deep breaths, then moved back across the chessboard, carefully avoiding looking straight at the fifteen-year-old Annabelle who stared down at them from the landing. That Annabelle, dressed in a blue ball gown that had been too hot, too tight and far too old for her, was sly. Secretive. Flirtatious. A far more disturbingly sensual person than Belle had ever been at any age.

She got as far as the staircase and let herself drop onto one of the lowest steps. The cold marble seeped through her skirt as if she'd sat in ice water. She clutched one of the scrolled banister railings, just for something to hold on to.

Fitz plodded slowly out of the parlor after her, his black tennis shoes making little sound on the granite.

"I'm sorry, BonnyBelle," he said. Though he spoke quietly, the cavernous space created an eerie almost-echo of his words. "I know it doesn't change anything, but I am. It was terrible, having to choose between the two of you. I chose Marlene, not because I love her more, but because I had done wrong by her all those years. And she was suffering so."

Belle shook her head firmly. "You don't have to apologize, Fitz. It was an impossible situation, and you did the right thing." She managed a smile. "Look at Marlene, all rosy-cheeked now and so happy. There is no question you made the right decision."

He nodded, but he continued to rotate the brim of his hat in his hands, turning it in an endless slow circle. He was mute but clearly tortured, unable to forgive himself.

She wished she could help, but she'd offered her forgiveness and understanding from the start. There was no more she could do. The truly dangerous guilt wasn't the kind others tried to place around your neck but the kind you hung there yourself.

That was the kind that would bow you down and break you.

"Anyhow, when I got upset just now, it wasn't because of Marlene." She tucked her knees to her chin and pulled her skirt down to cover more of her legs. The stairs were so cold.

"I was thinking about Jacob, about how long he waited to use your information against you. I think that must be why he wants to meet with me, alone. He's been storing up a bullet, and he's finally ready to fire."

Fitz's hands on the hat tightened, his knuckles whitening. "You think he's going to try to hurt you? We should hire another guard. *Two more.*"

"No." She shook her head. The one guard she'd stationed out front was more than enough. She couldn't say quite why she didn't feel physically threatened, but every instinct told her Jacob's plan was very different this time. "He's tried that, and he failed. He has moved on. Now it's about making me pay."

"But you did offer to pay! To share all of this with him. He turned you down, because he wanted the whole thing, the greedy son of a—"

"Not that kind of payment," she said. She crossed her arms over her chest to stop the goose bumps and stared up into the shadowy second floor. Its rooms lined up along a gallery overlooking the entry. A quadrangle of ten airy studios her grandmother and her protégés had used to make art, talk about art, study art. The family bedrooms were all on the third floor, floating there like the topmast sail of a huge white sailing ship.

"BonnyBelle, I probably shouldn't ask, but… what about your man?"

Belle frowned. "You mean Mitch?"

"Yes. Mitch." Fitz said the name as if the sound of it pleased him. It had pleased Belle, too. *Mitch* sounded so easy, so unaffected, so kind. Like a foreign object she'd stumbled onto. A fragment from that other world, the mirage world, the *normal* world.

"Mitch," he repeated. "He could come. He could stay with you. The two of you could do this together."

"No," she said, trying not to imagine how much

easier it would be if Mitch were by her side. He wasn't willing. And he wasn't hers to summon.

Besides, in some ways his presence would have made it harder, not easier. It all depended, didn't it, on what memories, if any, she unearthed? She might remember nothing, or she might remember things she would never want another living soul to know.

"No," she said again. "I need to do this alone."

MITCH WAS HAVING a bad morning. One of the guests had come in late last night, apparently after having way too much fun somewhere, and had overshot his parking space. When he had finally come to a stop, softly kissing the trunk of the sycamore tree, he'd driven his Mercedes over about twenty yards of Belle's gorgeous, brand-new planting.

These things happened, of course. It probably wouldn't have raised blood pressures to the danger level on a normal day, though Rowena would no doubt have given the guy a piece of her mind.

Problem was, this was not a normal day. This was the day of *Colorado Hearth* magazine's photo shoot, the very moment for which all this landscaping had been done.

Rowena was hopping mad, and, in the interests of saving the poor, hungover guest's life, Mitch and Dallas had come streaking in like superheroes to save the day.

Dallas had sprinted to the nursery while Mitch

dug up the dead soldiers, and now both of them were sweating and grunting like workhorses, getting the new plants put in.

"Your wife's got a temper, you know that?" Mitch dropped his shovel and sat on the ground with a thud that jarred his tailbone, but he didn't care. It was a hundred degrees out here, and he was pooped. "And your daughter has one, too. In about fifteen years, you're going to be in a mess of hurt."

Dallas squatted beside a sage and wriggled it out of the container. He grinned over his shoulder at Mitch. "Yeah, but between now and then I'm going to be the happiest man in Colorado."

Mitch grunted. He unscrewed the cap from his water bottle, then held it up to watch it sparkle like a magic elixir under the unnatural sun. With a groan of pure happiness, he tilted it back. He drained it in one long, fantastic chug.

Now that the work was done—just cleaning up remained—neither of them seemed to be able to move. The only sounds for several minutes were their labored breathing and the plastic crack of water bottles being sucked dry. Mitch gave up the effort to say erect and fell onto his back. He couldn't be any dirtier, anyhow.

When he looked up again, Dallas had joined him on the dirt. He sat with his arms on his raised knees, his hands dangling and his head bowed. Wouldn't you know they'd get premature summer at a time like this?

Rowena had already told Mitch she and Dallas had been up all night with Rosie, who was teething. And now here Dallas was, working himself like a quarter horse to get his wife's posies back the way she liked them.

And Mitch knew that, if hc asked, Dallas would be surprised that it seemed odd. He would do much more than this for the woman he loved. He sure didn't take after their dad.

"Hey," Mitch said, rising onto one elbow. "I want to ask you something. It's about Mom."

Dallas set his water bottle down. "I thought you didn't really remember Mom."

"I don't. I just had this odd piece of a memory the other day. I'm not even sure it's real."

"What is it?"

Mitch wondered whether this was even worth saying. But he didn't get all that much alone time with Dallas, and he really wanted to know.

"I remember her telling me stories. From her bed, after she got sick. I sat in that flowered chair in her room, and she told me about knights and dragons and stuff like that." He laughed. "Anything like that really happen?"

"Of course." Dallas smiled. "Only every night for maybe six months straight."

As if his memory had merely been waiting for the confirmation, Mitch could suddenly remember other details, too. A song she'd taught him. A book about Sir Lancelot. Not many details, even now, but when they were so rare each one was precious.

She'd had blond hair, like Dallas, and their eyes were the same blue. She'd worn a blue nightgown, with a pink ribbon threaded in and out of a lacy part at the top. Her perfume smelled like flowers packed in baby powder.

And when she'd died, their father, always a hard man, had turned wolverine-mean overnight. He'd taken his fury out mostly on Dallas, who looked so much like their mother. Mitch had been too little, too insignificant even to bother smacking around.

What a self-centered brat he must have been! He'd actually felt insulted, snubbed because his dad didn't notice him enough to beat him up.

*What an idiot.*

He wondered if he should apologize to Dallas. Seemed to him a sincere "I'm sorry for being such an insecure little jerk" was way overdue.

But Dallas had already moved on.

"Time to fill the holes," he said, clambering to his feet. "And we might even have time for a shower."

Mitch groaned, but he stood, too. "We need to give our yard guys a raise," he said, with feeling. "A *big* raise."

They worked in silence for a while, shoulder to shoulder, putting back all the dirt they'd just displaced. They got into a good rhythm. They would have made good partners on a roadside chain gang, Mitch thought with an internal chuckle. Not all that different from working for Rowena.

Then, out of nowhere, Dallas spoke. "Okay, it's my turn to ask a question. As long as you've brought up white knights and damsels in distress…"

Mitch made some kind of sound. It wasn't words, but it was clear enough. It meant *No. Shut up.*

Dallas chuckled. "Yeah, like *that'll* stop me." He tossed another shovelful of dirt onto the next plant. "Have you heard anything about Belle?"

"I said *no.*"

"No, you didn't. You grunted. Anyhow, I'm asking because I was thinking about getting in touch with Jeff Shafer. I might ask him to poke around a little, make sure everything is all right out there. He's in California now, you know, and he is connected. If there's anything we should—"

"I already did."

"You already—" Dallas didn't complete the sentence, but the silence was loud with his surprise as he waited for Mitch to elaborate.

Admitting defeat, Mitch finally propped his arm on the handle of his shovel and looked at Dallas directly.

"Yeah, that's right," he said. "I already did. The day she left, while you guys were stuffing cake. I know she said there was no physical danger anymore, but something's wrong—anyone could see that. So I asked Jeff to look into it."

Dallas nodded. Though he'd seemed surprised at first, this clearly made sense to him. "And?"

Mitch smacked briskly at his elbows to get rid of some dirt. "And…he seems to think she's fine. Better than fine, in fact. He said she's moving like a tornado, giving away money and disposing of her estate."

Dallas smiled. "Good for her. And what's her cousin doing about that?"

"Supposedly, he's just smiling and pretending he doesn't care. What else can he do? Even if he were the vindictive type who wanted to punish her for outsmarting him, he wouldn't dare. Jeff says there's plenty of suspicion about him. Always has been, apparently. They couldn't ever nail him, but sounds like they'd dearly love to. He's probably savvy enough to know that."

Dallas nodded. "So everything's fine, then? You're not worried about her out there alone?"

"Well, hell. Of course I am. I worry about her all the time."

Maybe Mitch was just too tired to keep up a facade of indifference, or maybe he was finally ready to admit he needed some advice from his big brother. "I've worried about her since the day I met her. Partly because she seemed to be in trouble. But mostly… Well, you know how it is."

Dallas smiled grimly. "I do."

"But there's nothing I can do to help her. There never has been. She won't let me." He swiped angrily at the grass bits that littered his knees. "I get what Mom was trying to teach me with those stories. She didn't want me to grow up like Dad. She wanted me to know how a man is supposed to care for his wife. But damn it. I can't fight her dragons if she won't even tell me what they are."

"No." Dallas looked thoughtful. "But you know what? That's pretty much true with everyone. Do you think Rowena lets me fight her dragons for her?"

Mitch gave that a half second's thought, then smiled. "No way."

"And do you think Belle is any less determined and independent than Ro?"

Mitch shook his head slowly. "No, I guess I really don't. The surface is different. But on the inside…" He shrugged and simplified. "No."

"Right." Dallas took a deep breath, and Mitch knew that meant some kind of speech was coming. A lecture, he would have called it once. But now he waited eagerly. If Dallas had insight, Mitch wanted to hear it. He was in dire need of insight.

"Look, Mitch, the truth is, we all fight our own battles. The people we love—whether it's a woman or a child or a brother—they all walk through their own hells alone. The best we can do is let them know that, whenever they come out, however wounded they are, we'll be here. And we'll still love them, scars and all."

Mitch didn't respond. There really wasn't much to say.

Except…it made sense. And Mitch hadn't been very good at that, had he? He'd been immature, self-centered, more concerned about his hurt pride than anything—or anyone—else. He'd let his own scars, from his own battles with his ego, cover over his heart, the way a bramble thicket could smother and kill a snowdrop.

And, because his heart was calloused and scarred, he'd hurt the woman he loved.

No, not just hurt her. He'd *lost* her. She was marching through her hell right now, and doing a pretty damn good job of it, by Jeff's account. But when she came out, she wouldn't be coming to Mitch.

He wanted to thank Dallas, for the wisdom, for the guidance, for waiting while Mitch grew up and never giving up on him.

But he had just discovered this embarrassing lump in his throat.

Luckily, at that moment Rowena appeared on the back porch. She wore a nice dress and she even had on lipstick. Her black hair was shining and tamed instead of the usual fierce, tumbled mane. But her expression was all crazed thunder and blunt force.

"Dallas! Look at you! They'll be here in ten

minutes. Are you going to pose for pictures looking like that?"

"No, ma'am." Dallas bowed in mock humility. He knew how to handle his wife. He adored her fire and was willing to be singed occasionally rather than risk snuffing it out. "I will shower in five and be your adoring, photogenic cowboy-sheriff husband in ten."

Rowena made a growling sound. "Make that nine," she said, but her voice carried the smile she refused to allow on her lips.

Then she glared at Mitch. "Don't let him dawdle," she snapped. And then she stomped back into the house.

"Guess the dirt, sun and sweat are all yours," Dallas said with a grin. "Gotta go get handsome."

He started to move away, but at the last minute, impulsively, Mitch called his name. Dallas turned, one brow raised.

"You were a good big brother," Mitch said, knowing Dallas would hate the mushiness but needing to say it anyway. "And I was a royal pain in the ass. I'm sorry. It must have been rough."

Dallas didn't answer for a minute. But finally he smiled again and looked Mitch straight in the eye.

"Nope. Sometimes it was hard being a good son. You know how the old man could be." He cocked his head. "But being your big brother? That was a piece of cake."

AS DAWN BROKE with a watery, old-fish-colored sun, Belle made one final round of the house. She spent a few minutes standing quietly in each room, watching the shadowy corners fill with light. It was as if she wanted to ask each space, one last time, to please surrender its secrets.

She wasn't actually expecting any lightning bolts of revelation. The house had been silent all these years, refusing to divulge anything...or even to confirm there was anything to divulge in the first place.

It had been similarly silent throughout the long, sleepless night. She hadn't heard her grandmother's ghost holding forth on the best technique to create the rich shimmer of silk on the canvas. She hadn't heard the echoes of cocky laughter from the students who had populated these rooms for years, stroking Ava's ego and living off her largesse.

Belle hadn't even heard any remnants of that repressed and angry little Annabelle.

But then, perhaps that was because Annabelle had barely been allowed to speak.

She had found a few long-forgotten memories here, of course. Some sad, some happy and some just pointlessly odd.

In this room, for instance, where the Louis XV chaise lounge stood, covered in flocked gold silk, she'd once come across a young woman lying completely nude except for a piece of red satin that had been draped across one shoulder, across her belly and then down the opposite leg.

There must have been an artist in the room, painting her, but Belle didn't remember that part.

Belle must have been six at the time. It was a hot summer, but her grandmother was working on Number Seven, which featured a wintry fantasy. Annabelle had been dressed in a red velvet coat and hat, both trimmed in ermine. The costume had been stifling.

One particularly hot afternoon, she had fainted. They had put her in one of the second-floor rooms to nap, but she hadn't wanted to waste her rare freedom and had crept out, roaming curiously in her white cotton slip.

When she'd entered this room, she'd frozen in place, not sure what was polite when confronted with a naked stranger.

Unembarrassed, the woman had laughed, very loudly. "You're Annabelle?" she'd said. "Good grief. You're a mousy little thing in real life, aren't you?"

But memories like that weren't what Belle had been excavating for when she'd decided to spend one last night under this roof. They were just emotional debris, bits and pieces regular people might have floating about in their past.

She was looking for something far more important—and, she suspected, buried far deeper. She pulled shut the door to the Louis XV room, then stood on the gallery, gazing down onto the checkerboard front hall, and tried not to feel too disappointed.

She'd known it was a long shot. She wasn't simply looking for a needle in a haystack. She was looking for something she had never seen and couldn't describe, which might not exist in the first place.

On top of that, her subconscious was clearly working against her, trying to prevent her from finding it…if it even existed. Was it any wonder she'd failed?

She started down the staircase, her keys warm in her palm. In minutes, she would walk out the door, lock it behind her and hand the keys to the hired guard, who would remain there until the museum curator arrived to take possession.

And she wouldn't ever be coming back. Not even to see the new museum. She hoped others would enjoy it, learn from it, treasure it.

She would never return.

But at least she could surrender the house with peace today, knowing she'd done everything she could to sort out her past. If an explanation for her fears couldn't be unearthed, she'd find a way to deal with that. She'd set her mind to letting go and moving on. As long as she could say she'd tried everything.

Halfway down the staircase, she paused, struck by one last idea. Her scalp tingled, and the banister under her hand felt suddenly cold.

Had she, really, tried *everything?* Wasn't there one more possibility, so disturbing she had almost blocked it from her thoughts? Wasn't there one more place the truth might still be found?

*Jacob.*

Her instincts had been telling her for a long time that he knew something. And after what Fitz had told her…

She was more convinced than ever. As ironic as it sounded, Jacob was her final hope. Even if he told her nothing, even if he ultimately knew nothing, she must try. If she wanted the peace that would come only with knowing she'd done everything she could, she had to try Jacob, too.

And so she would. She squeezed the banister until the cold went away. She hadn't come this far just to balk at the last bridge.

She used the Greenwood phone, the one by the front door. She decided not to go through his secretary, but to call his private line, and he wouldn't recognize her cell. She'd given her lawyer strict orders not to share that number with anyone.

Jacob wouldn't answer an unidentified call, but he would never, ever ignore a call from Greenwood.

She remained by the door as she dialed, though it was a cordless phone, and she could have moved somewhere sunnier, somewhere warmer. Her heart was going a little too fast, and she liked knowing she was near an exit—and only a few feet from her hired security guard, who stood, even now, on the front stoop.

"This is Jacob Burns." He sounded busy but cordial. That was his favorite act—the high-powered lawyer who still found time to be charming to even the lowliest janitor.

"This is Annabelle Irving," she said.

And then she simply enjoyed the momentary silence. She pictured him sitting at his desk, the pen frozen in his fingers, his eyes moving around the room blindly as he tried to guess why she was calling.

"Belle." He recovered well, of course. He was no fool. "I'm so glad to hear from you, though I have to admit I'm surprised. Evan led me to believe you were implacably opposed to any contact between us."

"I've changed my mind," she said blandly.

He waited for more, and when she offered nothing, he chuckled. "All right. You're interested in buying the oil, then?"

"Yes." She didn't allow her gaze to flick up toward Number Seventeen, smirking down at her from the staircase landing. Best to keep this simple.

"And you are willing to meet?"

"Yes."

"Face-to-face?"

She stiffened her resolve. "Yes."

"Just you and me?"

Suddenly, her blood turned to ice water, and she couldn't do it. Without realizing she was going to, she said, "No. Not alone. I want Mitch to be there, too."

He hesitated. "Who is Mitch?" And then he laughed. "Oh, right. *Mitch.* He's the boy you were living with? Freckles? Ginger-headed?"

She gripped the phone. How dare he speak of Mitch so dismissively? *The boy?* Mitch couldn't be more than a few years younger than Jacob.

And he was a million times the man.

"Yes. The boy I was living with. I would like him to be there, too."

She could almost hear his brain ticking through that scenario, playing it out, deciding whether it suited his plans. If he said no, she would have learned something important. She would have learned that her sense of security had been a false one, because the meet was a trap. A potentially deadly trap.

He cleared his throat. "At Greenwood?"

He hadn't actually okayed including Mitch, but the fact he'd moved on to another question seemed tacit agreement. He didn't like it, obviously, but he wouldn't balk at it.

Her shoulders relaxed a little. She had no idea whether Mitch would do this one last favor for her, but she'd feel better just knowing Jacob believed she wouldn't be alone.

"No, not at Greenwood. That wouldn't even be possible, after today. You may have heard I've granted a long-term lease to the art museum. It will soon be the home of Sacramento's new Greenwood Portrait Gallery."

"Yes. I did hear that." For the first time, his voice betrayed his fury, growing thin and metallic, like the edge of a razor blade. "How philanthropic of you."

"Thank you," she said politely. "Now, about where we'll meet."

"Yes?"

Emboldened, she decided to press her luck. "I want to meet in Silverdell. That's where the Garwoods live, in Colorado. There's a downtown café called Donovan's Dream. The food is lovely, and we will be able to talk undisturbed."

He was silent much longer this time. Annoyed, she hardened her voice.

"I won't meet you in a dark alley, Jacob, or in the woods or at your house. I'm not a fool. It's Silverdell, three o'clock, day after tomorrow... or it's off."

"It's Silverdell, then," he said curtly. "Three o'clock."

She heard the sound of papers being swished across his desk. "I assume," he said drily, "that this burg is big enough to show up on my GPS?"

"I assume so," she said sweetly. "But if you get lost, don't worry. We'll wait for you as long as it takes."

# CHAPTER FIFTEEN

"I'VE TURNED DOWN the job in Florida."

The stark announcement, made in the middle of their biweekly finance meeting, brought absolutely none of the shock that Mitch had been expecting from the members of his family.

Dallas smiled at him. "Good," he said. "Glad to hear it." Then he went back to tallying up the occupancy percentages for April.

Mitch scanned the table. Rowena hadn't even looked up from her calculator. Gray and Bree were exchanging annoyingly smug "I told you so" glances. Penny was smiling as if she were pleased, but she continued to doodle on her legal pad, so obviously she hadn't quite passed out from the surprise.

Barton James had turned his printed agenda over and was scribbling musical notes onto a homemade staff. Mitch tilted his head.... The old goat was writing a song called "The Curly Cowgirl I Can't Forget"?

Max wasn't here. So that was everybody. *Well, wow.*

Finally, Alec, who'd been sitting in the corner trying to be good so Rowena wouldn't kick him out, seemed to wake up and understand what he'd heard.

"Whaaa? You're not? I can't believe it!" The boy sounded really shocked, and Mitch smiled warmly at his beloved nephew. At least *somebody* cared.

"No fair, Uncle Mitch! You promised if you moved to Florida you'd take me to Disney World!"

Everyone looked up then, and Mitch could see they were all fighting back laughter.

"You bunch of bums," he observed drily. "You never believed I'd ever go to Florida in the first place, did you?"

"Nope," Rowena said unequivocally, still punching numbers into her machine.

"Not for a single solitary second," Dallas agreed.

The rest were shaking their heads, too. Gray had begun to chuckle so hard that trying to swallow made him choke, and he had to reach for the pitcher of water in the center of the table. Bree patted his back, her blue eyes twinkling.

Looking from one to the other, Mitch made a low growling sound, pretending to be deeply offended.

Once, he knew, he *would* have been. He would have taken their amusement as a sign they thought he was still a kid or he didn't know his own mind. It would have felt like when you were ten, and you ate too much birthday cake, and everyone said, condescendingly, "Lookie there! *Someone's* eyes are bigger than his stomach!"

But now something was different. And it wasn't in them—it was inside himself. His perspective had inexplicably changed.

Today, he saw what their easy acceptance really meant. It meant they knew him. They knew him well enough to be certain he didn't want to live in Florida. He didn't want to work for some other rancher. If he had wanted those things, they undoubtedly would have supported him and cheered him on.

But, because they knew him, they understood his decision to move had been simply a reaction to unbearable pain. They trusted their family was solid, their ranch was amazing and that, in the end, Mitch was stronger than he thought and wouldn't need to run away.

They had always had faith he would come to his senses in plenty of time.

It meant they *did* trust him, not that they didn't. Wasn't it strange he had ever been able to interpret these things so differently?

"Now look here." Alec put his hands on his hips. "You're saying there's no Disney World after all? You mean to tell me all this time I've just been barking at a *knot?*"

Bree laughed, turning it belatedly into a cough.

"You've been hanging out with the wranglers

again, son?" Dallas's dimples were showing, but the question was posed mildly.

"Yes, sir." Alec chewed on the inside of his cheek, suddenly worried. "Why? Is 'barking at a knot' dirty? I wondered, but Wanking Joe promised me it wasn't."

"It's not," Rowena assured him, her voice oddly muffled. "It's just…colorful, and your dad was surprised."

Mitch settled back in his chair. Lord, he loved this messed-up family.

"I'll take you to Disney World for your twenty-first birthday, squirt. How about that?"

"My twenty-first—" Alec squinted while he did the math. "Are you kidding me? You'll be too old to go on the rides!" He looked around the table, obviously searching for backup, but found none. "To heck with it. I'm going to save up my money and walk there, if I have to. No way I'm waiting for you to be all old and boogered up before I go."

He turned to Rowena, defiance in his eyes. "Yes, I know that was vulgar, and I don't care. Don't bother kicking me out. I'm leaving."

Hesitating only a fraction of a second to see if anyone begged him to stay, Alec stomped out.

In the amused silence that followed, Dallas announced wryly, "You know, whenever we start feeling sad about how Mitch is so grown-up and sensible now, we can simply remember this moment. Rest assured, Bell River family. We have all the wild and crazy man-child we can handle."

"And Rosie right behind. I think we're good." Rowena set her calculator on the table. "Okay, even allowing for the unexpected costs of the wedding and the landscaping, we're still in the black for the first four months of the year. If we can just—"

She broke off as the door to the meeting room opened again. "Yes?" She was edging toward cranky. "What is it?"

"It's Mr. Garwood." The sweet-faced boy standing there looked breathless and deeply upset. "Mr. Mitch, I mean. I have a message for him. A private message."

Mitch stood, wondering what could have upset poor Chad this much. The boy, one of their nicest youth counselors, a kid they'd known around Silverdell for years, was a real rule follower. His only transgression, probably in his whole life, but definitely in his tenure at Bell River, was sending those dorky text messages to Belle.

*Belle.* Suddenly, Mitch's heart pounded against his ribs. *Damn it.* Was Jeff calling to tell him something had gone wrong after all?

"Keep going," he said to Rowena. "I'll be back if I can. Or you can fill me in later."

The minute he got Chad out in the hall, he pulled him aside. "What's the message?"

"Someone wants to see you." Chad's face went

red, as if he had just run ten miles. "I couldn't help it, Mr. Garwood. I was just out there, doing my work. I was setting out the inner tubes for the river run, and I looked up, and there she was. I almost passed out. There wasn't anything I could—"

Mitch took the boy by the shoulders gently, hoping he wouldn't have to slap him to break the hysteria.

"Who?" He locked his gaze on Chad's, so the boy couldn't drift into more babbling. "You looked up, and *who* was there?"

"Miss Irving." Chad said the words in a whisper, as if he weren't allowed.

Mitch's face must have looked blank, because Chad frowned.

*"You know."* He pulled his phone out of his pocket and tapped it, his face twisting strangely as he tried to make Mitch understand without actually speaking the name again. "Remember, Mr. Garwood? *Her.*"

THE LAST TIME Belle had felt half this nervous at Bell River was two years ago, when she had first knocked on Rowena's door, hoping against hope she might land a temporary job here, doing housework or yard work or anything at all.

Her heart had been in her throat that day. But today, waiting for Mitch to come out, was even more nerve-racking. Amazing, given that, two years ago, she'd been homeless, friendless and fearing for her life.

Just proved the old adage, didn't it? Money wasn't everything.

She glanced toward the house. Two middle-aged ladies in denim and cowboy boots shared the swing, chatting and laughing as they gently rocked. They seemed so content, so at ease with their lives. She almost wanted to go up and ask them how they'd achieved it.

The minutes dragged on, and she wondered whether Mitch might refuse to come out. Or maybe he wasn't at home. She'd been gone almost three weeks—for all she knew, he was out with the new version of Crimson Slash.

Rowena's vegetable garden was only a few feet away from where Belle stood. It was clearly doing much better now, with a healthy frill of green rising at least six inches above the borders.

Belle walked closer. A few dandelions and sprigs of crabgrass had sprouted, so she bent down and began plucking them out. She was glad she'd worn jeans and hadn't succumbed to the cowardly instinct to armor herself in linen and jewels.

She was free to act naturally, to be herself in jeans. Touching the earth calmed her nerves, and it helped these anxious minutes pass.

After what seemed an eternity, but was in reality probably only a couple of minutes, she heard the back door open. She straightened, transferring the last weed into the batch she held in her left hand, and watched, heart racing, as Mitch came down the steps.

She wasn't sure whether the pounding was from relief that he was actually home or just the usual physical response to seeing him. As always, he looked wonderful. He looked tanned and muscular and healthy. He looked like Mitch.

He must be doing office chores today. His indoor work "suit" was a broadcloth dress shirt over khakis. When he worked with the horses, he usually wore a soft T-shirt over old jeans.

She had sometimes sketched him both ways, trying to decide which was sexier. It would have come out dead even...except the old jeans knew his body so well and clung so comfortably to all the lovely mounds and ridges.

His face was guarded as he approached. In fact, everything about him was subdued today, from his moss-green shirt to his thoughtful pace. The gray sky over Bell River threatened rain, so even his hair seemed muted, browner than usual, with no sunlight to spark off the auburn strands.

"I know this must be a surprise...and probably not a pleasant one." She offered what she hoped was a reassuring smile. "But I promise, I'm honestly not stalking you. I haven't come back to insinuate myself into your life again, and I'm not trying to get you to rethink the decision we made. I'm in town for one day only."

His brows twitched together, such a brief flicker she might have imagined it. "All right," he said evenly. "What is it, then?"

"I've come to ask a favor." She squeezed her fingers into her palm. In her left hand, the fingers closed over the dirt and bits of crabgrass, which felt spongy and odd. "It's a very big favor. I probably don't have any right to ask. But I don't know who else to trust."

He angled his head an inch or so away from her, frowning slightly and tucking in one corner of his mouth at the same time. It was a universally recognized pantomime of disbelief. Simply hearing her speak the word *trust,* apparently, made him suspicious.

Of course it did, given that trust had been at the heart of all their problems. He probably thought this was pandering...as if Belle's plan might be to toss his ego this crumb, and then another crumb, until he was placated and ready to forgive.

His cynicism came as no surprise, but even so...her heart ached to see how instantaneously bitterness surfaced. This kind of immediate mistrust, reading the worst into the simplest statement, was the reason they had no future. She'd made such a mess of things they couldn't even have one conversation without stirring up old wounds.

"I'll do whatever I can," he said after a minute.

He said it without reluctance or enthusiasm. He simply stated it as a fact.

"Thank you." The words came out on an exhalation of breath she hadn't realized she was holding. She was terrifically relieved to hear it—although she knew that, once he learned her plan, he might change his mind.

"Still." She swallowed. "Maybe you'd better hear what it is before you commit yourself."

He nodded. Toward the parking lot, a half-dozen children filed by behind their counselor, all of them dressed in bathing suits. They called hello to Mitch, some shyly, some boisterously, and the counselor waved, too.

The little group didn't go far. They stopped at a stack of shining black inner tubes. Belle could hear the children badgering their counselor. "How far is the river? What if it rains? Do we still get to go tubing if it rains?"

Mitch glanced at the noisy little crowd, then turned back to Belle. "Do you want to go somewhere more private?"

"It's all right," she said. She might actually do better with an audience. It would be another layer of protection, preventing her from falling apart or making a fool of herself. "My request isn't exactly a secret. It's just unpleasant. The thing is… I'm meeting with Jacob this afternoon at three. We'll be at Marianne's café. I was hoping you might be willing to come with me."

Either he didn't try to hide his surprise or it was so great he simply couldn't. His lips opened, and his brows lowered. "Why?"

"Why did I agree to meet him? Or why do I need you to come with me?"

He shook his head impatiently. "Both."

Had she thought he wouldn't ask? Had she dreamed he'd just tag along without requiring an explanation first?

Besides, the whole point of the meeting was to force Jacob to reveal whatever secrets he'd been keeping. If Mitch sat at the table with them, he would hear those secrets, too.

And yet, letting go was hard. She'd held this strange, unhappy fear inside her for so long, had protected her secret terror the way she might have hidden a crime. It was difficult to let it out, even now.

Yes, she'd vowed to do everything she could. But could she really do *this?* She'd rather have her secrets broadcast to every other human on earth than have Mitch see her as ugly, dirty and...*yes, Ava*...spoiled.

But if she were ever going to find courage, this was the moment. And he was the man. Her lover, her friend, her one true thing...even if he wasn't hers anymore.

She took two deep breaths, tightened her shoulders and took the plunge.

"I agreed to meet him because... Well, he clearly

has some private agenda beyond selling me his painting, and I'd like to know what it is. I think it's just barely possible that he knows something. Something about me. Something that might have happened to me during those years at Greenwood."

Mitch jerked forward slightly, then subsided. "What are you talking about? I know he tried to attack you once, when you were a teenager. But you fought him off, right? The police report said you stabbed him with the pruning shears."

"No. It's nothing like that." She frowned. "At least I don't think so."

"You don't *think* so?" His voice was slightly rough, incredulity in every syllable.

"Right. It sounds crazy, doesn't it? And that's why I haven't ever told anyone. But I feel as if there might be…I don't know what to call them… blank spots. Empty places in my memory. Everyone forgets things, especially from long ago, but this is different. It's not just forgotten—it's *gone*."

"I don't understand what that means."

She bit her lower lip. "Neither do I. That's just how it feels. When a memory isn't there, it's hard to tell why. Does that make sense? Is it gone because I've blocked it or because it never happened in the first place?"

He looked confused and maybe a little alarmed. Oh, God, no wonder she'd never tried to explain it before. There were no words.

She wasn't even certain, in her own heart,

whether anything sinister did lurk in her past. Perhaps she'd taken the generalized unhappiness of her childhood, the strange, long hours of enforced immobility that often ended in tears or fainting or falling asleep in her poses—and turned all that into some phantom menace.

"The truth is, I've always been afraid to find out. I thought if I ignored it long enough, it would go away. It hasn't, though. In a strange way, it's left me worse off, with an almost-insurmountable paranoia."

"Well, you did have some people in your life who..." Mitch's eyes were very dark. "Who were supposed to protect you, but didn't."

"I know. But isn't that true of everyone's life? You get hurt, but you move on. You find better people, people who don't betray you. And you let them help you forgive and forget. But I can't do that, not if I never know who the bad guys were, really, or what I'm forgiving them for."

She felt her eyes burn, so she blinked hard. Small spatters of rain had started around them. Maybe he'd think it was the storm that made her eyes so damp.

She could finish this. She met Mitch's gaze, fiercely determined to hold nothing back.

"I don't even know what my part might have been in...whatever happened. Maybe the person I really need to forgive is myself."

Mitch's eyes narrowed. "Don't be ridiculous, Belle."

"It's not ridiculous. Something's wrong with me, Mitch. You've said it yourself. Something's made me feel as if I don't dare trust anyone. As if no one could love me, not enough to put my safety and happiness above their own interests. Isn't it just barely conceivable I feel that way because, deep in my subconscious, I know I'm not worth loving?"

"No, damn it. It isn't even *remotely* conceivable." He shook his head relentlessly. "It's not that complicated, Belle. In fact, it's hideously simple. You think everyone will betray you because everyone *has*. From the day you were born, they used you."

His voice had risen. She glanced around them uneasily. Though the tubing kids were gone, several other guests were in earshot, trying to enjoy the last few minutes before the storm.

He saw them, too. He lowered his volume but not his intensity. "Have you ever thought maybe your rotten grandmother left you all those millions because she felt guilty, because she *knew* she'd exploited you? Because she *knew* she'd robbed you of a normal childhood? Have you ever considered that?"

"Of course I've considered it," she answered softly. "But the two things aren't mutually exclusive."

*"Gah,"* he muttered in frustration, running one hand through his hair. "Look, we can't argue logically about something we aren't even sure is real. All I'm saying is…the idea that you're to blame for anything that happened to you in that house is preposterous."

He sounded angry, or maybe just sick of the whole melodrama. She looked down at her hand and realized she'd squeezed the weeds into a pulpy mush. She opened her fist and let them fall.

"Does this mean you won't go with me to the meeting?"

His brows twitched irritably. "What? No. Of course it doesn't mean that. Believe me—I'd like nothing better than to meet that son of a bitch, up close and personal."

"Thank you." She breathed again. "But… Mitch…"

She hesitated. When asking for a favor, it seemed pushy to add stipulations. It even seemed reckless, because you might lose the yes you'd worked so hard to get.

But she couldn't risk the meeting degenerating into violence.

"You'll hate him," she began carefully. "He's everything you're not. He's fake, and he's glib. He's arrogant."

"And he's a sociopath," Mitch added sardonically. "I'd say that's probably the trait that'll keep him from getting my Mr. Congeniality vote."

She smiled. "True. But I want you to promise me that, no matter what we learn, you won't get…" She searched for a neutral way to put it. "You won't let things get out of hand."

He laughed once, darkly. "You mean you want me to promise I won't kill him."

She shook her head. "You couldn't kill anybody. Not even him." She put her hand on his arm. "It might feel good to beat him up, but I need you to promise you won't. It wouldn't avenge me, or help me, or prove anything about me, even if it feels that way. I don't want violence. I don't want any more trouble, any more pain."

She shivered as a fat, cold raindrop splatted against her collarbone. "And I definitely don't want any more publicity."

His mouth twisted, betraying that he was biting back comments he knew wouldn't be appreciated. With those dark eyes, he seemed to be studying her face, as if she still confused him.

"Mitch?" She realized her hand remained on his arm. She should let go. But her palm felt so comfortable there. The hard warmth of his muscle was so familiar.

Some habits were going to be very, very hard to break.

"Will you promise me?"

He didn't answer for a minute. He clearly didn't

want to lie, but it was equally obvious he found himself unable to offer any facile guarantees.

"I'll promise to try," he said uncomfortably. "Will that do?"

She pictured how easy it would have been for Jacob to promise whatever his audience wanted to hear. And then, when the moment came, how easy to act exactly as he pleased, as if his vow had never been uttered.

She looked at Mitch's troubled, earnest face. And her heart spasmed tightly. Oh, how she loved this man.

"It's all I could possibly ask," she said.

"I'd like to tell Dallas." Mitch chewed on the inside of his lip, obviously thinking through the logistics of the meeting. "He's the law around here, and even with my best intentions, it's possible things could get ugly."

"Okay."

He smiled slightly. "I'd like to promise he'll be the only one who finds out about it, but you and I both know he tells Rowena everything."

"I don't mind," she said. "I've failed miserably at solving the Jacob problem on my own. I'd be glad of any help that's offered."

Suddenly, the rain began in earnest. She didn't mind getting wet, but he wasn't dressed for mud.

"I should go," she said. "I'm sure you have work to do. I'm sorry this is so rushed—no warning, no notice. I was just so eager to get it over with."

"I don't need notice," he said grimly. "I'll be there."

"WHERE'S DALLAS?"

Mitch stopped Isamar, one of their full-time housekeepers, on the staircase, barking the question. Then, realizing he'd probably scared the poor lady, who was already skittish because she "saw" ghosts all the time, he softened his expression and his tone. "Sorry. I'm just in a hurry. Have you seen Dallas?"

She'd already flattened herself against the landing wall, as if he'd been a rabid Doberman. She widened her eyes and shook her head. "I don't know. I don't know. I haven't seen Mr. Dallas today."

*Great.* She could see the ghost of Brad Pitt, Hercules and even Rowena's dead mother, Moira. But she couldn't see the one person Mitch really needed right now.

He thanked her, encouraged her to peel herself off the wall, then loped the rest of the way upstairs. It was already two o'clock. Where was he? Gray had said Dallas had come up here to repair some crown molding that had been damaged when a guest decided to practice his long shot in the room. But when Mitch had looked, ten minutes ago, he hadn't been anywhere in sight.

Someone else had seen Dallas with the horses, so Mitch had wasted ten minutes scouring the stables. But this time, at the top of the stairs, he finally found his brother, high on a ladder in one of the guest room's walk-in closets.

Rowena was with him, apparently holding the ladder—or admiring the view. The two of them were a real poster couple for marriage. They thought they were being discreet, but even the looks they gave each other should have been X-rated.

"There you are! Can I talk to you a minute?" Mitch glanced at Ro and started to add "in private," but realized immediately what a mistake that would be. She'd be mad, and Dallas would just tell her later, anyhow.

Dallas, who was pushing on a square of ceiling that obviously led to the attic, looked down at Mitch over his shoulder. "Sure. What's up?"

Rowena eyed Mitch curiously. Her antennae, which were way too sensitive to family troubles, clearly had caught a vibration of something interesting in the air.

"I need your help," Mitch said, marveling at how easy it suddenly was to say those words, even to his big brother, the man he wanted most to impress. Guess all it took to lose the chip on your shoulder was the appropriate incentive.

"Yeah, well, get in line," Dallas said wryly. "You'll be right behind Rowena, Rowena and... let's see...*Rowena*."

Rowena smacked her complaining husband on the butt playfully, but her curious gaze never quite left Mitch's face.

"What's wrong?" she asked.

"It's Belle." He might as well just lay the situation all out there at the start, rather than let Ro interrogate it out of him one detail at a time. "She's here, in Silverdell. She's meeting that psycho cousin of hers at three o'clock. At Marianne's place. She came here just now to ask if I'd tag along as backup."

Rowena's mouth opened into a surprised round circle. Even Dallas backed down a step on the ladder and swiveled as far as he could so he could see Mitch's face.

"Seriously?" Dallas frowned hard.

"Seriously."

"And are you going?"

"Of course." Mitch wondered why Dallas had even asked. "She seems to think it's safe enough. But I have no idea what that creep might be planning, or what he's actually capable of doing. Frankly, I don't think it's wise for me to try to handle this alone."

Dallas shot a glance over to Rowena, and Mitch almost laughed out loud, their unspoken dialogue was so easy to read. "Awww, look, honey," their glance said. "Our little boy said *wise*."

It lasted only a second. Then Dallas shifted his

gaze to Mitch. "So…you think maybe the backup should have backup?"

"Yeah." Mitch nodded. "I do. Got time?"

Dallas began climbing down the ladder. "I wouldn't miss it for the world," he said.

Rowena smiled at Mitch, as if she was very, very proud of him, then eased past him in the doorway.

"Just let me phone my father," she called back to Dallas. "I want to be sure he can keep Rosie a few more hours."

"Whoa." Dallas caught his wife by the arm. "Hang on a minute there, partner. You're not invited to this shoot-out."

Rowena raised herself to her full height, then tried to add an inch or two by lifting her chin. Dallas still towered over her. But she stared at him without blinking.

"I invited myself," she said regally.

"Ro," Dallas began, but she interrupted him.

*"I invited myself,"* she repeated. She glanced meaningfully at Dallas's hand on her arm, then transferred the sparkling, irrepressible green gaze to Mitch. "And I have just one question for you two gunslingers. Who round here is stupid enough to try to stop me?"

# CHAPTER SIXTEEN

BELLE MET MITCH at Fanny Bronson's bookstore, just down the block from Donovan's Dream. He had called her a few minutes before three to set that up and to suggest maybe they didn't need to arrive precisely on the hour.

"Let him stew," he'd said. Belle knew what Mitch didn't—that people like Jacob didn't stew. But she'd agreed anyway. For herself, she simply wanted to have the whole thing behind her.

But she'd asked for Mitch's help, and she intended to take it. As she'd told him, handling the Jacob problem herself hadn't really worked out very well so far, had it?

Yes, strictly speaking, she'd "won." She had survived. But she wasn't free and never would be unless she could put these old fears to rest.

Elk Avenue wasn't terribly busy on a rainy Thursday afternoon with no special events to liven things up. The Wildflower Festival had ended over the weekend, so most of the tourists had headed home.

By three-fifteen, the storm had come and gone, leaving a steady drizzle behind. They didn't bother with an umbrella—Donovan's was only a couple of storefronts from the bookstore, and they walked under awnings most of the way.

As they neared the café's green door, Mitch slipped his fingers through hers. She glanced at him, surprised, but he smiled calmly.

"United front," he said with a wink. And then, before she could overthink it, he opened the door.

At Donovan's Dream, the door chimes rang out the first four notes of "Danny Boy," and the regular customers always sang, "The pipes, the pipes are calling" in response. On busy days, it caused quite a commotion and could even make conversation difficult. But on a slow day, the singing could sound fairly puny, with only two or three voices warbling out of tune, self-conscious and out of sync.

Subconsciously, Belle must have been expecting that kind of trailing-off misfire. But what rose up on their entrance sounded more like a full-blown choir. At least twenty customers lifted their voices, and the words rang out clear and sweet.

Startled, Belle scanned the packed room. Why so full today?

Wait…was that—?

*Oh, no.* How could she be so unlucky? Penny was here with Max. And wasn't that Bree, sitting next to Gray?

And Ro and Dallas?

And Barton James?

And…

She stiffened, but a quick pressure on her hand told her Mitch didn't want her to react.

"Steady," he said. "Just reinforcements. You did say you'd welcome any help. But don't worry— the orders are to hold fire unless you give the command."

Yes, she had said she'd welcome any help, but she had never imagined anything like this. She took a breath, absorbing the situation. The room was crowded with her good friends, and Mitch's family, all studiously examining their menus or chewing on their burgers, pretending they didn't see her.

And then, with a lurch, she spotted Jacob. He sat alone at a far back booth, his ostentatiously expensive suit and sour expression setting him apart like a neon sign.

Mitch squeezed her hand, and they walked toward him. Behind them, someone else entered the café, and the "Danny Boy" game started all over again. Belle forced herself not to turn and look.

No doubt it was Alec and Ellen, in coonskin caps, toting their BB guns.

By the time they reached Jacob, the music had stopped, but he still had his eyes shut, as if the music pained him.

When he opened them, he shook his head. "Now, *that* could get old," he observed to no one in particular.

And then, as if he'd just noticed them, he glanced up and smiled.

"Hello, Annabelle." His gaze took in her T-shirt, her jeans, her boots. "You're looking...sporty. But then, you always did have a penchant for costumes."

Almost as an afterthought, he turned to Mitch.

"Hello," he said neutrally. Then, as he finished his quick appraisal, his voice changed subtly. "*You're* Mitch?"

"I am."

Jacob glanced at Belle. "This is Mitch?"

She nodded. "He just said so, didn't he?"

"You sure he's not the other one? The other Garwood boy? The older one? I said you could bring the one you'd been living with."

"Of course I'm sure," she said, not quite clear what Jacob was implying.

But then, as she looked over at Mitch, she got it. Jacob's investigation must have unearthed stories about the cute class clown, the cavalier younger brother. Based on that, Jacob had assumed Mitch would be a weakling, an easy target for the suave and sophisticated attorney from Sacramento.

Instead, what he found in front of him was a poised and powerful man. Mitch had never come close to being a weakling, but he had changed, she realized, over the past months.

He had matured so gradually she had taken it for granted.

"Whoever I am, I'm here now." Mitch guided Belle into the booth. "So let's get on with it, shall we?"

"Of course."

As they seated themselves on the comfortable vinyl bench, Jacob made a fuss of rearranging a large blue plastic tube beside him in the booth. It was propped on the floor, and the top reached just about to his shoulder height. Its previous position had been in no jeopardy, and Belle suspected he'd simply wanted to draw her attention to it.

*Number Fifteen.* He'd brought it with him. And he had rolled the unframed canvas up...something that would have made Ava scream. She wondered why he'd done it. Just for convenience, so he could carry it in and leave it behind, all in one go? Or to demonstrate his disrespect for the painting?

He waved his hand to indicate the coffee cup in front of him. "Shall I call the waitress? I've been here awhile, so..."

"We're fine."

This was the first time she'd seen Jacob since the day of the auction, when she had returned from exile. Even then, she'd seen him only briefly. Suddenly, sitting two feet away from him, with opportunity to study him at leisure, she asked herself if he, too, had changed over these past two years.

But no...he hadn't, not much. Maybe some

lines around the mouth, maybe a hint of fleshiness beneath the chin. Mostly, though, the same insect in human clothing he'd always been.

Mitch, she saw, was sizing him up, too. She looked again, trying to see her cousin through Mitch's eyes.

It wasn't easy. She'd known—and loathed—Jacob for so long that the sight of him affected her the same way a glimpse of a big hairy spider did. But, more objectively viewed, she had to admit he didn't look like a monster at all.

He was tall and fit, and his face, to be fair, was perfectly normal. Even features, good skin. Brown eyes, brown hair. He'd always had plenty of women around, and Belle suddenly understood why. He wasn't hideous, and he projected an air of complete confidence.

And of course he had money. That mattered to a lot of women. It might even have mattered to her, she realized with a surprising flash of insight, if she hadn't learned so early that a lot of money was, at best, useless and, at worst, quite dangerous.

"I'm glad you decided to meet me, Belle." He sounded so sincere, as if her years-long rebuff had wounded him. He toyed with his cup. "It's been difficult, remaining estranged, knowing what you were saying about me. It's long past time for us to patch things up, don't you think?"

*Ah.* She'd been waiting to see which script he'd

be using today. Now she knew. He would be mild, down-to-earth, concerned. The kind of loving cousin who tolerated his difficult, volatile relative as patiently as he could.

She wished she could warn Mitch how dangerous this script was. If he'd been oily, sarcastic Jacob, they might have been able to slip him up. Sometimes, in that mode, enjoying his own clever barbs, he said too much. But in this charade, he was slow to speak and always very careful.

"Okay. Enough small talk." Abruptly, Mitch took the conversational reins. He put one hand on the table, palm down, and the motion caused Jacob's coffee to shimmy in its cup. "I understand you want to sell Number Fifteen. How much do you want for it?"

Jacob seemed pained by the too-crass question. Touching the blue plastic tube protectively, he looked out the window, his gaze unfocused. While he tried to formulate his answer, that averted face said he needed a break from looking at them.

Finally, he turned back, exhaling wearily. Not quite a sigh, which might have seemed theatrical, but close.

*"Well..."* He drew out the syllable and traced invisible circles on the tabletop with his finger.

He was so good, Belle thought. This was how he'd skated by all these years, never getting caught for anything he did to her. It had always been the same, even back when he'd pulled her hair or fried earthworms with matches.

"I think Belle should decide what it's worth to her." He turned to Belle with patient eyes. "It's a beautiful painting, Annabelle. And, as the only one I own, it's very precious to me. If I didn't need to liquidate——"

"Sorry about that. But——" Mitch raised his eyebrows "——your financial woes aren't really her problem, are they?"

"I suppose not." Jacob's somber face was full of injured sorrow. "But, Belle, in the past, you have admitted you recognize the profound inequity of Ava's will. You even offered to make reparation. I didn't accept your offer because I wanted to honor Ava's wishes, no matter how unfair they seemed to me. And I don't ask for any gifts now, either. Just a fair transaction, with satisfaction on both sides."

"Belle hates those paintings, and you know it." It was another confrontational jab, but Mitch managed to keep his tone light. He leaned back against the booth, one elbow on the ridge and his knuckles casually against his temple. "How does spending a fortune for something you don't want translate into satisfaction?"

Jacob smiled.

"Oh, I never take a teen at her word, do you?" He tilted his head. "Teenagers hate many things they later learn to love. And once Ava was gone, surely Belle realized that these oils—" he touched the tube again "—are her closest link to her grandmother."

It sounded so plausible. With a sinking feeling, Belle understood that Jacob had probably spent months, perhaps years, thinking this through. He would have a blocking move for every gambit Mitch could think of.

"Problem is, Belle's little change of heart is merely a figment of your imagination." Mitch shrugged. "She'll give you ten thousand for the thing. It's that high only because she feels sorry for you."

He leaned forward and tapped the edge of Jacob's cup, making the spoon rattle in the saucer. "But I tell you what, Jake. If you're really strapped, I'll spring for your coffee. I happen to be flush at the moment."

Something primitive flashed behind Jacob's eyes. Belle almost laughed. Mitch had just played the eternally powerful male-competition card.

*Yes, yes,* she thought, mentally giving him a high five. Though Mitch never seemed to feel competitive over money, he had grown up with a brother, so he obviously knew the rules. And he'd sized Jacob up perfectly.

Jacob immediately quit making eye contact with Mitch, as if he recognized he'd underestimated the man and needed time to reevaluate. Instead, he looked Belle straight in the eyes.

"The thing is...ten thousand unfortunately won't do the job." He sounded genuinely sorry to be a bother. "I'm afraid I need at least..."

More dramatic stretching of the significant pause. Belle wasn't impressed. If he thought he had her on tenterhooks, he was wrong. She wasn't going to give him a plug nickel, so he could name any number, as high as he liked.

"I'd need about a hundred times that."

Mitch laughed out loud. "You got the Mona Lisa in there, buddy?"

"I have Number Fifteen in there." Jacob still held Belle's gaze. He might have been a snake charmer, trying to hypnotize her. "And...well, there's a little something else in there, as well. A surprise, so to speak."

Belle felt her breathing go very shallow. There it was. Just like that, after all these years, she'd found the truth she'd been looking for. It was, even now, waiting inside that blue plastic tube.

Her skin sizzled all over with the shock of recognition. Here was the bullet, the one he'd held on to until he found the perfect use for it.

She opened her mouth, but no words came out. That unsettled her, because she hadn't realized there was such a thing as being shocked speechless.

Mitch took over smoothly, touching her thigh with a light hand.

"What kind of little something?" He eyed the

tube cynically. "For that money, it better be *little* like the Hope Diamond is little—you know what I mean?"

"Not at all like that." Jacob smiled. "It's another painting of Annabelle, that's all."

"Listen." Mitch leaned forward, the pent-up anger seemingly ready to slip its chain. "I told you. She *hates* those paintings."

"But she's never seen this one." Jacob's expression had turned somber, as if they were chatting at a funeral. "No one has. And, to tell you the truth, no one ever should."

*No one ever should...*

Belle could feel a fire building in Mitch, and that brought her back to life. She laid her hand over the one he still rested against her thigh. She pressed softly, and the thrumming muscle under her palm relaxed. Just a little, but enough.

Oddly, now that Jacob had put his cards on the table, she felt calmer...almost serene. Whatever he had in that tube would be terrible. His face was too smug, too delighted with the bomb he was about to drop into her life, for it to be a bluff.

But she could handle it. Her biggest fear, she'd realized, was that he *wouldn't* ever tell her.

"Sincerely, no one should see it. And, if I can possibly help it, Belle, I want to make sure no one ever does." Jacob drew the tube closer and tucked it under his arm, as if it were a child. "Unfortunately, it's by far the most valuable asset I possess. And given my circumstances…"

She didn't speak, didn't help him to complete the thought.

He sighed. "Be reasonable, Belle. I have to sell it to someone. Isn't it enough that I came to you first? I want to sell it to you, if you'll let me."

*"What is it?"* Mitch sounded angry.

Jacob didn't even flick a glance his way, so Mitch said it again. This time his voice was dangerous, crackling with either fire or ice…or both at once.

"What is it a painting of, you son of a bitch?"

Jacob turned, and for the first time in her life, Belle glimpsed a shadow of anxiety on her cousin's face as he faced a furious Mitch. She was stunned. She hadn't thought he had the fear gene in his DNA.

"It's a nude," Jacob said, taking only a few seconds to recover his poise and adopt that same graveside voice. So hypocritically heartbroken. "Tragically, it seems that, at least this once, our beautiful…*shockingly* beautiful…Annabelle posed without any costume at all."

Mitch's breathing was heavy. "Who painted it?"

Jacob shook his head, as if he'd love to help, but he couldn't. "No idea," he said. "Sadly, I have no artistic talent whatsoever, in case you were thinking it might have been me."

"How did you get it?"

Jacob smiled slightly. "I found it."

"Are you trying to say she posed for this?"

"Oh, no. I'm afraid it's fairly clear she wasn't... in full possession of her senses. It's quite shocking, really. The position, you know...and the detail. And of course, she's very young. Fourteen, perhaps? Or a little younger? You'd have to compare it to the official oils to be sure."

"Who painted it?" Mitch fired the question one more time, like a machine that wouldn't stop until it got the answer. Cold, metallic, inexorable.

"I told you, I don't know. It definitely isn't Ava's style, but it's quite good. Ava had so many young people around her, you know. Protégés, students... whatever you'd like to call them. She never allowed them to paint Annabelle, though. Annabelle belonged to her, and she didn't want to dilute the market."

So it hadn't been her grandmother. It made no sense, really, because it was still terrible. Unthinkable, really. But, even so, Belle felt washed by a cool wave of relief.

It hadn't been her grandmother holding the brush.

"As you can imagine, a painting like this would cause quite a stir in the art world. For more than two decades, the Annabelle Oils have been seen as the epitome of innocent girlish beauty. If this picture went public, and people got a glimpse of the debauchery, not to mention Ava's criminal neglect, letting one of her depraved protégés visit such a thing on her granddaughter..."

Jacob raised his eyebrows. "The book deal alone could easily solve all my problems. So surely you can see the number I asked for is actually quite reasonable. I'm selling at a loss, I promise you."

Mitch looked at Belle. Even though she'd heard his dangerous voice, the fire in his eyes and the tension in his face shocked her. Somehow, he held himself in check. He waited for her sign.

And then, slowly, she shook her head. *No.*

"Damn it, Belle," Mitch groaned. "You can't really be going to give this—"

Mitch broke off the sentence with a curse and whipped his head back toward the other man. The volcano, growling and surging and spitting flames, was gone, replaced by a deadly, concentrated poison.

"Here's the new deal, Burns," Mitch said tightly. "First, forget your delusions of getting rich off that painting. I hate to break it to you, but the average guy on the street isn't as obsessed with the Annabelle Oils as you seem to think."

Jacob snorted. "Maybe not your clientele at Bug River Ranch, or whatever—"

Mitch lifted the edge of his hand to shut him up.

"And for the people who do care," he went on, "if you published that crap, you'd be an instant pariah. You'd go down in art history as the creep who stood by and watched an innocent girl be exploited and then tried to capitalize on her pain."

He smiled coldly. "So, like I said. Forget the ten thousand. We'll give you a dollar for both paintings. A whole crisp dollar bill. You'll take it. You'll leave that tube and walk out of this restaurant, and Belle will never hear from you again."

"Is that so?" Jacob chuckled. "And if I don't?"

"If you don't, then I summon that guy over there. See the one in the sheriff's uniform? Just for the record, *that's* the other Garwood boy. We call him over here, and we repeat this lovely story to him, and then he arrests you."

"For what? I'm afraid possession of this painting isn't actually a crime, much as you might like it to be."

"I don't care for what." Mitch lifted one shoulder. "For being too bloody scummy to walk around with decent people."

Jacob shook his head. "I'd hate to see you waste your time, Mitch. Because he's your brother, the sheriff may harass me for a little while, but then he'll have to let me go. And I'll still have the painting, a lawsuit against the Silverdell County Sheriff Department *and* a book deal."

He swiveled his supercilious gaze to Belle. "For God's sake, Annabelle. You're smarter than this. Are you going to let your pet cowboy ruin your life like that?"

Mitch stood so fast he almost knocked the table over. Jacob's coffee sloshed, and, panicked, he lunged to jerk his precious plastic tube out of harm's way.

That was when Belle's last shred of doubt—or hope, perhaps—died. No point dreaming about a bluff. Everything he said was true.

He really did have something in that tube that he believed was worth a tremendous amount of money. And it undoubtedly was a nude of a very young Belle, a painting that would destroy the reputation of Ava Andersen Irving forever.

But at the same instant, Belle also realized, with a sudden freedom that felt like chains falling away, she didn't care.

She really, truly didn't give a damn.

"Mitch, sit down. He's right—your deal isn't the one I should be offering Jacob right now." She spoke in a gently scolding tone, a tone she never really took with anyone.

Luckily, Mitch recognized it as fake and reluctantly dropped back onto his seat.

As he did, so did about four other men in the room. Dallas, Max, Gray and Barton James.

"All right, Jacob," she said, folding her hands on the table in front of her. "I've listened patiently to both of you. Now you listen to me. Here's the deal *I'm* offering."

He nodded comfortably. He was so sure of himself. So sure of her.

*And so wrong.*

"My deal is this. I give you *nothing*. You take your pictures, the respectable one and the disgusting one, and you peddle them wherever you like. Put them on the internet. Buy time on national TV. I honestly couldn't care less what you do with them."

Mitch was very still, his head turned toward her. He was almost as still as Jacob.

"You're bluffing," Jacob said. "You'd die if anyone saw this."

She shook her head. "No. I wouldn't. Here's what you never understood about me. I don't give a darn what the world thinks. There's only one person in the world whose opinion I care about. And he already knows."

Jacob's glance at Mitch was dismissive. *"Him?"*

"Yeah. Him."

Jacob cupped his palm over the end of the tube, his fingers twitching, as if he might at any moment twist the cap off and lift the canvas out.

"Well, yes. He *knows* about it," he repeated slowly, a smile starting to form. "But he's never *seen* it."

Mitch shrugged. "I don't have to settle for pictures, Jake. I've got the real thing."

Jacob made a sound that was almost like a hiss, and his eyes narrowed to slits.

"All right, then, Annabelle," he ground out through clenched teeth. "If that's what you really want. Enjoy your next spin on the celebrity merry-go-round. I have a feeling it's going to be even more amusing than the first ride."

He stood, pulling the tube with him. But as he stood, so did Mitch. And Mitch was faster. He blocked Jacob's exit from the booth.

Once again, when Mitch stood, so did the Bell River men. Jacob had a better view this time, and his face stilled oddly. "Is this where your thug brother and his friends beat me up?"

"Oh, absolutely. It absolutely would be," Mitch agreed equably, "if Belle would let us. But for some reason we don't fully comprehend, she's asked us not to." He smiled. "Of course, I can't speak for my friends. They don't hang on Belle's every word like I do."

At that moment, as if the cue had been orchestrated, Dallas sauntered over. His black polo, khaki pants and gold star were official enough to impress but casual enough to get physical, if the need arose.

He looked only at his brother, as if Jacob weren't at the table. "Is there a problem, Mitch?"

"Yeah. This scumbag just tried to blackmail Belle. He's got something in that tube that is highly illegal and probably stolen. And he's trying to use it to extort money. A lot of money. I offered him a dollar for it, but he says it's not enough."

Dallas turned, smiling pleasantly at Jacob. "Actually, I think it's *too much*. How about this, Mr. Burns? You'll give us that thing you've got, and *we'll* give *you*..."

He drawled the last syllable, dragging it out just as Jacob had. He tapped the table, thinking, thinking. "And we'll give *you*..."

He stopped suddenly, beaming. "I know!"

Mitch stepped aside, and Dallas moved in, standing so close to Jacob their noses almost touched. Belle watched her cousin's profile. She saw his eyes dart from Mitch to Dallas and then out into the room.

Everyone was standing. Not just the four Bell River men, but everyone. Rowena, Penny, Bree, Marianne Donovan, old man Harper...

Even Crimson Slash.

Every single person in this restaurant was up on his or her feet, ready to defend Annabelle Irving.

As she watched Jacob, a pulse started to throb in his throat. She could almost hear him replaying Mitch's cutting speech.

*You'd be an instant pariah...*

She knew his face. And so she knew, knew absolutely, the very moment he decided to cut his losses and run.

Dallas saw it, too.

"So…as I was saying. You'll give us that thing you've got, and we'll give you…" He smiled and stepped aside, offering Jacob a clear path to the door.

"We'll give you a head start."

"GAWD, I WISH you'd seen her, Jude." Dallas had his cell phone at his ear and a beer in the other hand. "She looks the creep straight in the eye, and she's like…tell you what, jackass, why don't you take that tube and shove it up your—"

Belle smiled. Suddenly remembering his audience, Dallas broke off his sentence just in time. He threw her an apologetic smile, then moved into the hallway of Mitch's cabin, a vain attempt to gain some privacy.

"Okay, she didn't say it quite like that, but she was pretty fantastic. I'm not kidding. She's a *monster*. She reminded me of Ro. You know how Ro can get on a tear and—"

"We can still *hear* you," Rowena sang out irritably. But she wasn't really mad. The whole family had been saying the same thing, with more or less colorful language, for the past hour.

Belle had become an instant hero.

When they'd left the café after Jacob's departure, everyone had been too excited to settle down, so they had decided to celebrate in Mitch's cabin.

The place could hardly hold them all. People sat

on the floor and on the arms of chairs. Rowena was perched on the kitchen island, feet swinging as she nibbled bits of the nachos, pizza and burgers Marianne Donovan had sent home with them, on the house.

At first, Belle had been self-conscious, and she'd wondered whether she could bear to talk about Jacob with this many people. But soon, because everyone else was so relaxed, she felt her own anxiety begin to fade away.

Most of them, with the exception of Dallas and Rowena, didn't know details, of course. Mitch had merely told them Jacob was trying to blackmail her, hoping to get some of his grandmother's money. Even so, being blackmailed suggested some dark secret, and she had thought she might feel exposed.

But…amazingly…she didn't. Even Dallas and Rowena didn't treat Belle differently. They didn't speak in hushed tones, as if she had been injured, her image damaged…her virtue spoiled. They acted toward her exactly as they had yesterday or the day before.

The calm acceptance soothed her. She wasn't alien here. These people knew tragedy. They knew it visited people who had done nothing to deserve it. They knew all about humiliation and shame, and they knew it didn't have to break you.

Quite the opposite, in fact. Their very lives

proved how much strength could be forged in the fires of tragedy and shame.

And, in a way, remembering what Rowena, Bree, Penny and Tess had suffered helped put her troubles in a better perspective. In the big picture, against murder and natural disaster, against disease and mental illness and war, was Belle's ordeal really so unendurable?

Sure, what had been done to her had been traumatic. Yes, it had been a terrible injustice. But Moira Wright had *died,* her skull crushed when her own husband pushed her down the Bell River staircase.

Whatever else had happened, at least, in the end, Belle had lived.

There might be tougher days ahead, of course. She'd probably look for some professional help, just to be sure she processed these discoveries in a healthy way.

If Jacob spread her secrets around, that would, inevitably, be uncomfortable. And if she were ever to consciously remember that night—or nights....

She'd just have to cross that bridge when she came to it. *If* she came to it. Right now, she still remembered nothing worse than itchy costumes and boring hours trying to hold uncomfortable poses.

Again, the bottom line, no matter what struggles lay ahead, was that she'd lived. She was healthy.

And, now that Jacob had helped her answer those tormenting questions, she was *free*.

She had every reason to believe the rest of her days would be full of love and joy and purpose.

Best of all, she'd clearly been taken into the heart of this big, boisterous, eternally loyal family. She could be one of them, if she wanted. Another sister. A friend. A partner in the ranch.

*And what about Mitch?*

What could she be to him?

She simply didn't know the answer to that. They hadn't had a single moment of privacy to talk about the future—or whether they even had a future together.

Though over the past hour she'd chatted with everyone, she knew her gaze was always following Mitch. He was in the kitchen now, trying to wrest the nachos from Rowena before she ate the entire plate.

She appreciated the family's support, more than she could express. But she ached to be alone with Mitch. She wanted to know what today had meant to him. They'd both said things, in front of Jacob…

Had his words been merely for show? Had they been, like the hand-holding, just a piece of presenting "a united front"?

"I've got the real thing," he'd said. And then, later, he'd said, "They don't hang on Belle's every word like I do."

Two little phrases; that was all. It wasn't much, but it was enough. Her hopes were already building castles on that sand.

Finally, Rowena hopped off the counter and returned to the living room, where Belle sat on the sofa, flanked by Penny and Max. Popping the final nacho in her mouth, Rowena bent down and looked carefully at Belle's face.

"Okay, everybody out!" Rowena rose, waving her hands as if she were shooing geese. "Can't you see Belle's tired? Everybody out! The lady needs some rest."

Grumbling because their festive interlude was over, the others lazily gathered their things. There was the usual fuss over who would take the leftovers and of course plenty of discussion about who was on duty for various activities at the ranch that evening.

But, finally, the last of them went through the door, and the little cabin was quiet once again.

Too quiet. Perversely, though she'd longed to have him alone, now that she did, she was terrified. If he still wanted her to leave Bell River... If nothing had changed between them, after the almost unimaginable intimacy they'd shared today...

She wasn't ready to hear it.

The clouds had finally passed, and the sun had emerged just in time to go down. Above the mountaintops, the western sky was a mosaic of pearl, pink and gold. Belle stood at the window and watched the colors shift and blend, like a slowly turning kaleidoscope.

Behind her, she heard Mitch tossing bags and cups in the trash and opening the refrigerator repeatedly, trying to accommodate all the food.

He didn't speak for several minutes. She wanted to say something, but she kept trying on lines and nothing seemed to fit. She'd said "thank you" so many times already. It seemed absurd to fall back on that again.

Finally, the kitchen was quiet. And she knew, from a subtle shift in the shadowy reflections on the glass, he had come into the living room and was standing behind her now.

*Say something,* she commanded herself. Where had all her feisty courage gone? She'd had plenty to say to Jacob, whom she hated. Why was her tongue frozen when the time came to talk about love?

"Do you want to take a nap?" Judging from his voice, he was still several feet behind her. A respectful distance. A safe distance. "Ro said you were tired, and you're welcome to—"

"No. Thank you, but honestly I'm fine." She hugged herself, crossing her arms over her chest and grabbing her arms tightly. "I'd rather talk, if that's all right with you."

"It's fine," he said. "Unless you're going to start thanking me again."

She knew he was smiling, though she couldn't see it. She knew his voice that well.

"You didn't need me today, Belle. You had him on the ropes. You could have finished him off with one hand tied behind your back."

"Maybe. But I'm grateful you were there, anyhow."

This was ridiculous, making him talk to her back. She stiffened her resolve and forced herself to turn around. "And I'm very, very grateful you were able to make him leave the painting."

"That wasn't negotiable." Mitch's mouth hardened. "Unfortunately, we have no way of knowing whether he kept photos of it. I guess we'll just have to wait and see."

She nodded, wondering whether he used "we" deliberately or whether it was merely habit. That question seemed far more urgent than any question of what Jacob would or wouldn't do.

"What do you plan for the picture now?" Mitch glanced at the hearth, where the blue tube rested against the wall, half-obscured by the stone surround. "Do you have any intention of opening it?"

She stood, without answering, for several long seconds. "I don't know." She stared at the container, imagining the rolled canvases within. "The pictures are like ghosts, in a way, aren't they? The ghost of that unhappy, meek little victim I used to be."

He smiled. "Maybe. But you aren't a victim anymore. Just ask what's left of Jacob."

She didn't answer. The courage had been short-lived, and she wasn't inclined to brag about it now.

"You know, I've been thinking about what your options are." He sounded hesitant, as if he didn't want to overstep. "And I want you to know, if you decide to keep it, there's a safe at Bell River. We can lock it up there. That way, if you ever need to bring evidence against anyone, you'd have it."

*Bring evidence?* Her spirit recoiled. *No, never.* The picture had been painted a decade ago. Her grandmother was long gone, and Belle felt no urge to punish anyone else.

What would be the point? The protégés had been under no particular obligation to protect Belle, and so their betrayal was not personal. They had been young and cocky. They were coddled and told they were geniuses and offered the run of the house. In the end, they did what callous young eccentrics were famous for doing.

They did whatever they could.

Belle was no longer being eaten alive by hazy fears—and so she no longer felt the same generalized indiscriminate anger. She now knew what had happened to her at Greenwood, and she knew, finally, whose head should carry the guilt.

Her grandmother's. Perhaps Ava hadn't meant to hurt Belle, but ultimately she'd traded Belle's innocence for the empty flattery and fawning of strangers. And then, in her clumsy, eleventh-hour effort to make amends, she'd put a target on Belle's back.

A target shaped like thirty million dollar signs.

Belle shook her head. "No. I don't want to keep it. That picture—all those pictures—are just reflections of the past, and I'm tired of looking back. My job now is to build a future. And that's intimidating enough without always having the paintings lurking in the back of my mind."

"I understand." He moved to where the tube rested. He picked it up, balancing it across both hands. It clearly weighed almost nothing.

Such a little thing to do so much damage.

"Have you decided whether you want to see it before you destroy it?" He watched her face carefully. "Do you think it would help if you knew what was there, so your imagination couldn't make it even worse than it actually is?"

Again, she considered. And, again, she shook her head. "No. I don't need to see it. I don't *want* to see it. I want to burn it, to eliminate it the way I've eliminated Greenwood and so much of the money. It's funny. I feel driven to dispose of everything I can. It's as if I'm trying to clear a path, so I can move forward."

"Good for you, Belle." His voice was husky. "Good for you."

He started to set the tube down, but she stopped

him. "No, wait.... What about you? If you'd rather know what's really in the picture, go ahead and open it. I don't mind, truly. You certainly have the right, after everything you did today."

He smiled, letting the container drop with a light thud. "Are you *kidding?*"

"No. Of course I'm not. What do you mean?"

"I mean...why on earth would I want to look at a naked picture of some fourteen-year-old girl I've never met?"

"Never met..." She frowned. "But it's—"

"No. It isn't." He spoke over her words. "That picture is *not* you, Belle. You were nowhere near that room. Not the real you. Not the part of you I love best."

Her heart fluttered, as if some small winged thing had been trapped within her chest.

"The part you...love?" She was sure she'd heard him right. He hadn't said "loved," in the past tense. He'd said "love."

Present tense. Right here, right now. *Love.*

"Yes." He took three steps, and then he was next to her. He put his hand on her cheek. "Don't you know what part that is?"

She shook her head, just an inch in either direction, but it made his fingers drag across her skin, and the bliss of it weakened her knees.

Moving closer, he put his other arm around her waist—lightly, not a touch that demanded anything…and not a touch that promised anything, either. Just a tiny physical connection.

"It's your heart, of course. And your soul. Your laughter. Your courage. None of those things were present when Jacob's disgusting friend painted that picture."

She looked up at him, half-drunk on his touch, however light. She couldn't speak. She wanted to point out that he'd listed more than one part, but then she realized it didn't matter. The more parts he loved "best," the happier she would be.

He smiled, as if he knew what she was feeling. He bent his head and put his lips so close to hers she could feel the shape of every word he formed.

"So no, Belle, I don't want to look at it." He nipped at the edge of her mouth. "I'd far, far rather look at you."

"Yes," she said, as if he'd asked her a question. Her arms rose and circled his neck. Her lips waited, tingling, to be claimed. "Yes."

Finally, he kissed her. The room melted, and all the clocks stopped; all the bells rang. This was where she belonged. How, she thought, dizzy with joy, had she ever lived without his arms around her, without his mouth against hers?

Minutes—or hours—later, she pulled back her head, fighting for enough air to say what must be said.

"Mitch." Her lips were swollen, deliciously

burning, and her cheeks blazed like fever. "Mitch, shouldn't we talk first?"

Deprived of her lips, he dropped his head to her neck. "No. No talking. We make a hash of everything when we use words."

"But…" She put her hands under his chin and brought his face up until it was level with hers. "We *have* to, Mitch. I can't do that again. I can't be your lover just for today, without any hope of a future. It hurts too much. This time, I have to know—"

"You have to know what?" His mouth hovered over hers, and she dimly sensed his lips were curved in a fraction of a smile.

"What do you need to know that you don't already know, Belle? Don't you already know everything that matters? You know I love you, that I can't live without you, that I want to marry you and cherish you and have three children with you. I want to buy a dog and train horses and build a two-story log house on the Putmans' land."

"But I *don't.*" She struggled to make sense of his tone. He sounded so sure. So confident. So much like the old Mitch. "I don't know any of that. How could I? Those are the old dreams, our old future. I thought those dreams had died."

He looked deep into her eyes, his smile gone. "Did you? Did you *really* believe that, Belle?"

He touched her temple, where her stitches had

been. "Not here, in your brain." Then he lowered his lips to her breast. "But here, in your heart."

She moaned, low and urgent. His lips working softly against her, he tilted up a hot, questioning glance. His eyes burned golden in the last of the sunlight, liquid under the thick, dark lashes. "Did you really believe it *here?*"

"No," she said, because suddenly she knew it was true. Her brain was the place where all the anger, confusion and doubt lived. Her heart knew only that Mitch was her life, and she was his.

"Good." He straightened, so he could gaze deeply into her eyes. "But there is one thing I ought to say out loud, in words, because you need to hear it. It was all my fault. All of it. I'm a fool. I'm a first-class fool, and I should be taken out and shot for being so self-centered and full of misdirected anger. How I could have added to your pain, when you were already hurting so much—"

She laid her fingers against his lips to silence him.

"I don't care about any of that," she said. "That's just more dwelling in the past, and the past is gone. It's irrelevant now. All that matters to me is the future." She caught her breath. "Do we have one, Mitch? Do we have a future together?"

"If you'll let me, I'll give you forever." He ran his hands through her hair hungrily and stole another quick, unrepentant kiss. "I don't deserve you, Belle. I know that. But if you'll put your future in my hands, I promise I'll fill it with more happiness than you ever thought possible. I'll never hurt you again. Somehow, I'll become a better man."

She smiled, because she knew it wasn't true. And because she knew it *was* true, all at the same time. He would always be Mitch, but he would always be changing, becoming wiser, stronger, sweeter and more achingly desirable to her, every day for the rest of their lives.

"I don't want a better man. I want *you*. I have always, always wanted you."

He laughed softly. With those gentle fingers she knew so well, he took her by the hand.

"Then come with me, my brave, beautiful Belle." He tugged her softly toward the bedroom. "The future we're looking for begins right behind that door."

*Three months later*

Sunset on Sterling Peak was as sweet as melted candy. The bright orange aspens and the crimson maples swirled together down the mountainside, and sometimes the sky streamed with the same colors, until you couldn't really tell where earth ended and heaven began.

Or so it seemed to Mitch that early September day as he paced off the space where their bedroom would be. His new wife sat under the silver-blue spruce, sometimes yawning, sometimes sketching, sometimes just gazing down at Silverdell, a half smile on her lips.

*Oops.* His feet were still pacing, but his brain had lost count, distracted, as always, by how beautiful she was and how her very presence made his world feel touched by magic. Even the air he breathed seemed cleaner, the oxygen sparkling in his lungs, as long as Belle was near.

They'd bought the Putman land the same day they'd run off to the courthouse to get married. Since then, they came up here almost every evening. She loved to watch the lights twinkle to life. And he loved watching her.

So really, for him, heaven and earth were the same place, anyhow.

Tomorrow, construction started on their dream house. They hadn't changed a single timber from those first plans they'd made, so the house would be far from grand. It wouldn't impress anyone who had ever seen Greenwood or even Bell River.

But it would be theirs. They would be the first ever to live in it. They would laugh and cry, fight and make love in this house. They would fill it to overflowing with memories. They'd put such a mark on it that no matter how many generations passed, or how many owners held the deed, the Dellians below would still call it "the Garwood place."

It felt like a new beginning, free from the shadows of her past.

Jacob must not have recorded his "find," or else he'd thought better of broadcasting the story to his friends in the art world, because no breath of the secret Annabelle Oil ever reached as far as Silverdell. Jacob had married an heiress last month, Mitch had read online somewhere. So it didn't seem likely he'd need to sell Belle's secrets to make ends meet anymore.

Mitch and Belle had burned the secret painting in the moonlight that first night, when they had finally had enough of each other that they could bear to leave the bed. Still unrolled, the canvas had caught fire easily. It burned down to the last fiber, and when the ugly, acrid smell of melting oils and black smoke finally dissipated with the dawn, the world felt clean and new.

They didn't try to pretend it hadn't ever happened. They talked about it often, at first. They discussed what might be wrong with Jacob and whether he would keep trying to destroy her. She told him whenever she remembered something new from her past, which wasn't often. She even speculated about which protégé might have drugged her and painted the secret oil. Sometimes, in rare moments of true healing, they even could joke about it.

Eventually, though, the subject came up less and less frequently. These days it was rarely mentioned. Belle was busy, almost too busy, with charities and Bell River and their garden and the house. He was slammed, too, getting the Garwood Chore Jacket manufactured—it would, they'd decided, be called the Bell River Chore Jacket. And Garwood Stables would open next spring.

But best of all, Belle was drawing again. He watched her graceful hand sweep across the sketch pad now and wished he could peek over her shoulder. But it was too new, too fledgling and fragile. He'd let her build confidence before he butted in.

So he went back to counting. Their bedroom would be the largest room, with a wonderful view through a picture window and a porch that would lead out onto the vegetable garden she was already planning.

"Hey, mister!" Belle craned her neck, trying to see him without getting up.

He came around the aspen that blocked her view and grinned. "You rang, lazybones?"

She smiled back, indifferent to his teasing, and tossed her hair over her shoulder. It cascaded down her back, reminding him of the golden autumn leaves falling all around her.

"Hey, mister," she repeated. "Wanna see a pretty picture?"

"Sure," he answered lightly. He tried to remain nonchalant. But this was a first. Mostly, she kept her sketchbook in her nightstand, always shuttered. She never left it lying around, and he could only wonder if it was still filled with half-finished faces and scratched-out, ruined ghosts.

He ambled over, loving the sound the leaves made as he walked. As he got close, she held out the sketch pad, stiff-armed, as if she wanted him to just take it and look at the picture somewhere else.

He smiled, but inwardly he felt like such a heel. The last sketch of a face she'd ever completed, to his knowledge, was his own. He'd been such a jerk about it, complaining that she'd made him look too young, too callow, too ineffectual and weak. It had seemed to reflect back to him his deepest fears about himself.

He took the pad, aware even from a distance that the picture exploded with color. Orange, red, gold. Obviously, she'd been drawing the scene around them right now.

But to his surprise, a man dominated the picture. The man stood at the edge of the meadow, looking down on the sparkling white lights below.

It was him.

He still looked young, he saw. He still stood with just a touch of boyish cockiness, and the smile on his face was unguarded and free. But in spite of all that, this figure didn't look like a boy. This was, indisputably, a man.

The worst you could say was he looked a tiny

bit smug, perhaps too wholeheartedly content with his land and his life.

But hey. The picture didn't lie. He saw that same bliss every time he looked in the mirror. Sometimes it almost scared him, how smugly contented he was.

He said a quick prayer right that moment, his head bent over the sketch. He didn't ask for anything but her happiness and safety. And he added a line or two extra, just to make it clear he understood he was the luckiest stiff in the world and didn't deserve half the joy that had already been heaped on his plate.

"Do you like it?" She had risen to her feet and joined him. Something on his face must have calmed her fears already, because she was smiling.

"Yes," he said simply. He studied the strong, happy man and hoped he would always look like that in her eyes. "Yes," he said again. "I do."

"Good." She laid her head on his shoulder. "Do you know what it's called?"

He laughed. "King of the Hill?"

She shook her head, smiling still. "Close." She took one of his hands and rested it softly against her stomach. "Guess again," she said.

His fingers began to move, almost by instinct. Every time he touched her, even if it was just an accidental brushing of shoulders as they shared the sink in the mornings, he wanted to make love to her.

She stilled his fingers, putting her palm over his and pressing gently. "Guess again," she repeated.

"I don't know," he said. He ducked his head to try to read her expression. "You're going to have to help me here."

She looked up at him, and the radiance on her cheeks almost took his breath away. "It's called *A Father's World,*" she said.

He was such a moron. He still needed another three seconds to understand. He tilted his head quizzically, and she began to laugh. She looked down at where their hands twined over her belly.

And then…well, then his legs turned to jelly, his head went dizzy and his useless mouth suddenly forgot how to form real words.

He babbled something incoherent, staring into her blue eyes, her beautiful blue eyes…. *Would their baby have her eyes?*

"A…Fa…we…you…can't…no…real…"

He slammed his mouth shut, horrified. What the hell was wrong with him? What was that awful noise? Somewhere below this muttering baboon was a man on fire with joy. He hoped that, somehow, she could see that.

She twinkled up at him with those wonderful eyes. "Couldn't have said it better myself," she declared, laughing.

Then she lifted his hands from her stomach and brought them to her lips. Her kiss against his knuckles was sweeter than anything had ever been in this whole magnificent, miraculous world.

He tried again. "We're…you're…you're saying we're going to—"

She put one finger across his stumbling lips. "I'm saying no more dawdling on the house, mister. Because by the time spring comes again to Sterling Peak, you are going to be a daddy."

\* \* \* \* \*

*Be sure to look for the next book by*
*Kathleen O'Brien!*
*Coming in 2015 from*
*Harlequin Superromance.*

# LARGER-PRINT BOOKS!

**HARLEQUIN** *Presents*

*PASSION GUARANTEED SEDUCTION*

## GET 2 FREE LARGER-PRINT NOVELS PLUS 2 FREE GIFTS!

**YES!** Please send me 2 FREE LARGER-PRINT Harlequin Presents® novels and my 2 FREE gifts (gifts are worth about $10). After receiving them, if I don't wish to receive any more books, I can return the shipping statement marked "cancel." If I don't cancel, I will receive 6 brand-new novels every month and be billed just $5.05 per book in the U.S. or $5.49 per book in Canada. That's a saving of at least 16% off the cover price! It's quite a bargain! Shipping and handling is just 50¢ per book in the U.S. and 75¢ per book in Canada.* I understand that accepting the 2 free books and gifts places me under no obligation to buy anything. I can always return a shipment and cancel at any time. Even if I never buy another book, the two free books and gifts are mine to keep forever.

176/376 HDN F43N

| | | |
|---|---|---|
| Name | (PLEASE PRINT) | |
| Address | | Apt. # |
| City | State/Prov. | Zip/Postal Code |

Signature (if under 18, a parent or guardian must sign)

### Mail to the **Harlequin® Reader Service:**
**IN U.S.A.:** P.O. Box 1867, Buffalo, NY 14240-1867
**IN CANADA:** P.O. Box 609, Fort Erie, Ontario L2A 5X3

**Are you a subscriber to Harlequin Presents books
and want to receive the larger-print edition?
Call 1-800-873-8635 today or visit us at www.ReaderService.com.**

* Terms and prices subject to change without notice. Prices do not include applicable taxes. Sales tax applicable in N.Y. Canadian residents will be charged applicable taxes. Offer not valid in Quebec. This offer is limited to one order per household. Not valid for current subscribers to Harlequin Presents Larger-Print books. All orders subject to credit approval. Credit or debit balances in a customer's account(s) may be offset by any other outstanding balance owed by or to the customer. Please allow 4 to 6 weeks for delivery. Offer available while quantities last.

**Your Privacy**—The Harlequin® Reader Service is committed to protecting your privacy. Our Privacy Policy is available online at www.ReaderService.com or upon request from the Harlequin Reader Service.

We make a portion of our mailing list available to reputable third parties that offer products we believe may interest you. If you prefer that we not exchange your name with third parties, or if you wish to clarify or modify your communication preferences, please visit us at www.ReaderService.com/consumerchoice or write to us at Harlequin Reader Service Preference Service, P.O. Box 9062, Buffalo, NY 14269. Include your complete name and address.

HPLP13R

# LARGER-PRINT BOOKS!

## GET 2 FREE LARGER-PRINT NOVELS PLUS
## 2 FREE GIFTS!

HARLEQUIN®

*Romance*

### From the Heart, For the Heart

**YES!** Please send me 2 FREE LARGER-PRINT Harlequin® Romance novels and my 2 FREE gifts (gifts are worth about $10). After receiving them, if I don't wish to receive any more books, I can return the shipping statement marked "cancel." If I don't cancel, I will receive 4 brand-new novels every month and be billed just $4.84 per book in the U.S. or $5.24 per book in Canada. That's a savings of at least 19% off the cover price! It's quite a bargain! Shipping and handling is just 50¢ per book in the U.S. and 75¢ per book in Canada.* I understand that accepting the 2 free books and gifts places me under no obligation to buy anything. I can always return a shipment and cancel at any time. Even if I never buy another book, the two free books and gifts are mine to keep forever.

119/319 HDN F43Y

| | |
|---|---|
| Name | (PLEASE PRINT) |

| | |
|---|---|
| Address | Apt. # |

| | | |
|---|---|---|
| City | State/Prov. | Zip/Postal Code |

Signature (if under 18, a parent or guardian must sign)

### Mail to the Harlequin® Reader Service:
**IN U.S.A.:** P.O. Box 1867, Buffalo, NY 14240-1867
**IN CANADA:** P.O. Box 609, Fort Erie, Ontario L2A 5X3
**Want to try two free books from another line?**
**Call 1-800-873-8635 or visit www.ReaderService.com.**

* Terms and prices subject to change without notice. Prices do not include applicable taxes. Sales tax applicable in N.Y. Canadian residents will be charged applicable taxes. Offer not valid in Quebec. This offer is limited to one order per household. Not valid for current subscribers to Harlequin Romance Larger-Print books. All orders subject to credit approval. Credit or debit balances in a customer's account(s) may be offset by any other outstanding balance owed by or to the customer. Please allow 4 to 6 weeks for delivery. Offer available while quantities last.

**Your Privacy**—The Harlequin® Reader Service is committed to protecting your privacy. Our Privacy Policy is available online at www.ReaderService.com or upon request from the Harlequin Reader Service.

We make a portion of our mailing list available to reputable third parties that offer products we believe may interest you. If you prefer that we not exchange your name with third parties, or if you wish to clarify or modify your communication preferences, please visit us at www.ReaderService.com/consumerschoice or write to us at Harlequin Reader Service Preference Service, P.O. Box 9062, Buffalo, NY 14269. Include your complete name and address.

HRLP13R